Grace closed her eyes briefly, remembering that night. She shuddered. "I'm going to have some bad dreams for a while."

"Understandable." Mitch had brought the inevitable cup of coffee in with him and reached for it now, taking a couple of swigs. "It feels like beating my head on an invisible brick wall. I want answers. Seems like I'm not going to get any soon."

"I hate that," she admitted.

"You ain't the only one." He paused. "I've got all my men keeping an eye out for anything suspicious. I'm not ready to move on as if this is nothing but chance."

"I don't think I can."

His gray eyes met hers. "Grace, understand that I'll do anything to protect you."

Mitch's kindness reached beyond an ordinary friendship. He was offering something more. Something a whole lot bigger.

"Thank you," she answered, her voice thick.

"Hey," he said quietly. "I didn't mean to make you sad."

"You didn't." She turned her face back to him. "You... just made me feel special."

He smiled slightly. "Go

a special woman. Stub

D0979764

Dear Reader,

Writing this book took me down some uncomfortable paths. Grief has no timetable, and a stubborn widow is plagued by it two years after her husband died. We have all known grief, and for some of us it doesn't ease for a long time. Especially when death strikes suddenly and there is no time to prepare.

Grace Hall has nothing left but the dream she had cherished with her late husband. She clings to it as best she can, but it is getting harder.

Dreams can vanish, sometimes slowly, always painfully. In the end, this story is uplifting because inevitably grief gives way to renewed life.

Rachel Lee

CONARD COUNTY CONSPIRACY

Rachel Lee

HARLEQUIN
ROMANTIC
SUSPENSE

HARLEQUIN

ROMANTIC SUSPENSE™

Recycling programs
for this product may
not exist in your area.

ISBN-13: 978-1-335-75958-0

Conard County Conspiracy

Copyright © 2022 by Susan Civil-Brown

This edition published by arrangement with Harlequin Books S.A.

For questions and comments about the quality of this book, please contact us at CustomerService@Harlequin.com.

Harlequin Enterprises ULC
22 Adelaide St. West, 40th Floor
Toronto, Ontario M5H 4E3, Canada
www.Harlequin.com

Printed in U.S.A.

Rachel Lee was hooked on writing by the age of twelve and practiced her craft as she moved from place to place all over the United States. This *New York Times* bestselling author now resides in Florida and has the joy of writing full-time.

Books by Rachel Lee

Harlequin Romantic Suspense

Conard County: The Next Generation

Killer's Prey
Deadly Hunter
Snowstorm Confessions
Undercover Hunter
Playing with Fire
Conard County Witness
A Secret in Conard County
A Conard County Spy
Conard County Marine
Undercover in Conard County
Conard County Revenge
Conard County Watch
Stalked in Conard County
Hunted in Conard County

Conard County Conspiracy

Visit the Author Profile page at Harlequin.com for more titles.

For all the people who helped me along this amazing path, especially my incredibly patient family.

Chapter 1

Grace Hall awoke to gunshots in the middle of the night. The sound startled her, causing her to sit up abruptly and twist toward the window. She wouldn't be able to see anything unless she pulled the curtains open.

Her heart hammered. She wondered in her sleep-fogged state if someone was attacking her house. Two more shots. This time she could tell they were farther away. Not right here.

She flopped back down on her pillow, staring up into the inkiness that filled her bedroom at night. She had some security lights outside, bright spotlights on poles, but seldom switched them on because they used electricity she could ill afford.

Tonight she wished she had turned them on. But would she have pulled back her curtains anyway? Not likely.

She lay there, reasoning more clearly as sleep seeped

away. Some drunks, she decided. Who else would be shooting into the night? They'd found a wide-open area and had taken advantage of it. That had to be the reason. Too early for hunting season, and anyway, there was no night hunting allowed.

This was one of the few times she felt acutely aware of her isolation. There had been times after her husband's death when she'd felt it to her core, but she had moved past that. While the huge expanse of ranch land surrounding her sometimes seemed to swallow her, it no longer consumed her. Being alone had brought its own solace.

Her heart slowed down and sleep crept close again. She'd check in the morning for damage, but for now she'd sleep.

There was a little bit of chicken inside her, Grace thought with mild amusement. She didn't want to go out there even though the Wyoming day was bright.

She dawdled over a breakfast of coffee and scrambled eggs. A piece of toast from a loaf of rye bread reminded her she needed to go to the store again.

Another trip to the store daunted her, but not as much as before. People had realized she didn't like to be asked how she was doing. *Fine* was a lie and they didn't really want to know the truth. Just an empty, meaningless gesture. They asked, she answered and they moved on with their own lives.

She'd let her friends slip away, not that a ranch wife had room for many, because time was at a premium. She'd worked as much as her husband had, caring for their sheep.

She sometimes wished they'd been able to get the

goats she'd always wanted. Their antics would be so much more entertaining than the placid sheep.

She and John had never been able to see their way to the kind of fencing needed to keep goats from going walkabout. Those animals could jump almost anything. Plus, they needed special dietary supplements since the grazing here wouldn't provide enough. It was one of those *someday* things they'd never gotten around to.

There'd been a lot of those, she thought as she washed dishes. Too many, like the children they'd dreamed of having. Waiting, always waiting for the right time.

Was there ever a right time?

Eventually the nibbling worry drove her out the door to stand reluctantly on the wide, covered porch. A little more than a mile. A mile where those rowdies could have damaged her fences last night. A walk that would do her good, allow her to check her mail and probably reassure her.

Those guys might have found a great open space to do their manly shooting into the night, joking about firepower and probably full to the gills of the beer they'd been swallowing for hours.

They shouldn't have even been on the roads, but who was going to stop them? While sheriff's deputies drove along here, they couldn't come frequently. Too much area, too few deputies. The department needed more funding.

Random thoughts filled her as she went out the front door. The night's chill lingered but would be gone in a few hours. For now she needed the sweater she wore.

The blue sweater John had given her their last Christmas together. Soft and warm, like a hug.

The morning was bright, the sky a cloudless blue. A range of Wyoming mountains filled the western horizon, not far away. A truly beautiful summer day on the way. She headed for the mailbox.

In the distance she caught sight of the sheep, near the top of a rise. Mitch Cantrell, her neighbor and friend, now owned the sheep and leased her grazing land. Salvation for her, because otherwise she'd have had to entirely let go of the dream she and John had been building. Profitable for Mitch, she gathered. He'd even been able to hire two shepherds, a luxury she'd long ago given up.

The morning began to cheer her up despite everything else. Maybe she should push herself to get back into the mainstream of life. John wouldn't have wanted her to grieve indefinitely.

When she was within sight of her mailbox, about a half mile away, she saw a sheep lying on the ground. They never did that. Was the ewe ill?

She walked closer to the fence. What she saw sickened her.

There was blood all over the animal.

Those drunks last night must have used her as target practice.

She stood frozen for a few minutes, then ran back to the house as fast as she could. No cell connection out here, so she needed the landline. Rage had begun to replace horror. A fury so big she wasn't sure she could contain it.

First she called Mitch. His voice sounded a bit crackly, probably because he was using his satellite phone.

She dropped the news without preamble. "Mitch, a ewe has been shot in the pasture near my driveway."

A moment of silence, perhaps because of the satellite delay. "I'm on my way. Stay inside, Grace."

"I'm calling the sheriff."

"Good. I'm out on the range, but not too far away. Hang in there, stay inside. Thirty minutes max."

Grace called the sheriff. She heard immediate concern from the dispatcher who took her call. To judge by the roughened voice, it was probably Velma.

"We'll get someone out there as fast as we can, Grace. The nearest patrol is about thirty minutes away. Stay inside."

Stay inside? That was what everyone wanted, despite her not having an urge to go out to the sheep again. She did stand on her porch, keeping an eye out down her driveway to the county road. Just in case.

Those idiot drunks might come back to admire their mayhem. She hoped they would. She had a rifle and a shotgun inside and wasn't afraid to use them.

Mitch was the first to arrive. He came in his four-wheel-drive pickup. She guessed he had driven overland instead of taking the road. He did, however, come tearing up her drive, spewing dust and loose gravel, wasting no time.

He passed the sheep, coming to her immediately. He practically jumped out of the truck and trotted up the steps to her.

A hardworking figure of a man, broad-shouldered and browned by wind and sun. Wearing the inevitable jeans and shotgun chaps. He must have been on his horse before jumping into his vehicle.

"You okay?" he demanded.

"I'm fine, but I'm angry enough to explode."

"I don't blame you. Will you be okay if I go out to take a look? I barely saw it as I raced by."

"They're more important than I am." Livestock mattered. They were life and livelihood.

He paused, his gray eyes narrowing. "Don't ever let me hear you say that again."

She'd say it as often as she wanted, she thought defiantly. Because it was true. Even though Mitch owned them now, she and John had worked hard to build that flock. Long summers and cold, dangerous winters. Yeah, the sheep mattered more.

Part of that dream was now in tatters, but it was a part that meant the world to her.

She watched as Mitch reached the sheep and climbed out to look. He'd barely begun his examination when a sheriff's SUV rolled up, five-pointed gold star on its sides. She recognized Guy Redwing as he climbed out to join Mitch. The man had a distinctive stride. Well, so did Mitch, from years in the saddle. Guy was one of the deputies who, when patrolling out here, always came to her door to ask how she was doing. Somehow she didn't mind it when *he* asked.

The men stood looking and pointing, then Guy went back to his vehicle and stood beside it. Probably calling for assistance.

Grace couldn't stand it another minute. Hurrying, she closed the distance and joined the two of them.

"You notice anything?" Mitch asked her.

"Gunshots in the middle of the night. I thought some drunks were out here firing into the air." She hesitated, battling down fury and hating her perceived cowardice. "I didn't dare come out to look."

"Good," Mitch said. "Good. Wise move. Who can predict what a bunch of drunk men might do?"

She hadn't thought of that, but she knew what he was

suggesting. Gang rape. All of them ginning each other up. Anger turned into a shudder.

"The techs are coming out," Guy said as he returned from his car. "Don't touch anything."

Flies were buzzing around now, emerging from drowsiness as the temperature rose. The odor began to grow, too. Feeling her gorge rise, Grace turned away.

"You don't have to stay for this," Mitch said almost gently. "My sheep, my problem."

"My land, near my house. My problem."

Let him argue with that. She didn't want to think too much about what had happened, or about what *could* have happened, but she meant to stand her ground. She had been dismissed too often over the last couple of years since John had died.

Nobody of importance. A widowed ranch wife. Sympathy that had quickly blown away like autumn leaves.

Except for Mitch. He'd been her friend and John's after they bought this place He always checked in with her since the funeral. Friendly over a cup of coffee, occasionally bringing a dish over that his housekeeper had made. Always asking if there was any way he could help out.

A genuinely nice guy who had often kept her from feeling totally alone. Letting her know she had a friend no matter what.

But she wouldn't allow him to dismiss her as others had. Too many others. While he never had before, she refused to let him start now.

"Have it your way, Grace."

She thought the corners of his eyes crinkled, suggesting a smile.

She spoke again. "Yes, I will."

"I always thought you were as tough as barn nails."

She didn't know if she liked that analogy, but it would do. She *was* tough. She'd *had* to be tough, except in the middle of the night when she sometimes cried herself to sleep.

But she was still here, still standing, refusing to yield ground in her own driveway.

When the crime scene techs arrived, she faced the fact that she couldn't do anything else. Not that they'd find something useful.

She didn't need a police report to tell her that this crime wouldn't be solved. Shots fired on a deserted road from a vehicle nobody had seen? No evidence.

A sheep was dead. Mitch was going to take the loss. He'd survive it, but loss of livestock was a ding on any rancher's bottom line.

In fact, killing livestock was about the worst thing you could do in these parts. She wouldn't be the only angry person when word got around.

She turned and walked back to her house. It didn't look as much like a refuge as it had yesterday.

Mitch watched her walk away. He was more concerned about her than about the ewe. Yeah, it was ugly. Even horrifying. Clearly those men last night hadn't been content with a single shot. They'd used that poor animal for target practice. Anger simmered inside him.

But Grace was another matter. All alone out here. Gunshots in the night and no one around to make her feel safe, or help her deal with it. Then this morning, to find this atrocity so close. Not out on a distant pasture, but right near her driveway.

She might stride away with purpose with back straight and shoulders squared, but she wasn't always the brave woman she appeared to be.

No, she was as stubborn as an army mule. Only stubbornness could have kept her out here by herself. Never give an inch. That was Grace's motto.

He admired it, but it worried him, too. She was unlikely to ask for help even when she needed it. She probably never would have mentioned the gunshots last night except for the sheep. Or maybe if her fence had been damaged.

Otherwise, she would have rolled with the blow, as she almost always did.

Hell no. She wouldn't have told him about a broken fence at all. Instead she'd have tried to figure out how to pay someone. Given that he knew she was squeaking by, it would have annoyed him no end to learn she'd done that.

Damn, he had hired help he could send over.

His thoughts needed to be corralled. He'd have to quit imagining things that hadn't happened, and deal with what was.

A dead ewe. Some drunks, most likely, thinking they were having fun. Still, the ewe was dead.

He could absorb the loss financially, but the act itself incensed him. What kind of person got his kicks from shooting up a defenseless animal? Hell, a steer was more of a threat than a sheep.

Guy Redwing wrapped up the investigation, as little as it was. Techs in Tyvek suits bagged and took the remains for examination. Mitch doubted they'd learn much.

"So," he said to Guy as the techs took the ewe, "what's your impression?"

Guy hesitated. "Drunks shooting up the county."

That wasn't all, Mitch sensed. "Got any other cases like this?"

Guy shook his head. "One and only. Maybe others will turn up in the next few weeks."

Mitch studied the man, thinking he was being close-mouthed, but about what?

Was it the savagery? Or something more?

Guy spoke again. "Grace ain't around enough to have made anyone angry. So drunks it is."

Most likely, Mitch thought. Grace couldn't have an enemy on this entire planet.

The techs had had to cut the barbed wire to get to the animal. He pulled out his satellite phone and called one of his hired hands. "I need you and Jack at the Hall place to patch some barbed wire. Today."

When he got the response he wanted, he disconnected and watched the police vehicles drive away.

Then he headed up toward the house.

Grace saw Mitch coming. Unable to help herself, she'd stood at her front window watching the distant activity. She wasn't surprised when Mitch drove his pickup her way.

A tan-colored vehicle with high suspension to get over rough ground, and enough dings to testify to its working life, the truck seemed to suit the man who, despite all, had remained her friend even though she wasn't much of a friend to have.

Sighing, she went to open the door for him, accepting the fact he wanted to help her in some way, but also accepting the fact she didn't want to be alone right now.

This event had jarred her, and not much shook her anymore. The senseless killing of that sheep bothered her at a deep level. Remorseless. Cruel. Those guys probably still laughing about it.

What had a friend once called it so many years

ago? Oh, yeah. Testosterone poisoning. She'd found the phrase cute, but over the years hadn't had much call to think of it. Out here, she had met a lot of hardworking no-nonsense men. Men like Mitch.

That didn't mean there weren't any jackasses, but none of them had evoked that phrase in her. Maybe it only applied to *young* jackasses. The idea brought a faint smile to her mouth, a smile still there when Mitch climbed the steps.

"Hey, ranch lady," he said. "Can I beg for a cup of coffee?"

She waved him in. "Always. Let me make a fresh pot."

"Whatever's burning in there will do for me."

She laughed at last. "Sure. Bitter, concentrated. Blech."

She led him to her farmhouse kitchen, a big room from past times, too big for one person. Mitch seemed to half fill it, though.

While the coffee brewed, she leaned back against the counter and folded her arms over her sweater. "They won't catch 'em."

Mitch relaxed against the wall on the far side of the room. He seldom encroached by getting too close to her. She'd begun to notice that.

"Of course they won't catch the guys. Unless they brag about it."

"We can hope they're that stupid."

He passed his hand over his face. "A couple of my men are coming over to mend your fence. Cops had to cut it to get to the remains. Speaking of stupidity, there's that ewe. What was she doing so far away from the flock?"

Her brows rose. "That's a good question."

* * *

Mitch watched Grace as the coffee brewed. She'd always been a lovely woman, but now she was awfully thin. Once she'd been "pleasingly plump" as people would call it, a plumpness that gave a fullness to her curves. All that had vanished since John's death. Well, he could understand it. Her hair was still inky black, her eyes still the bright blue of a summer sky. Her smile was wide and infectious beneath a small, straight nose.

He'd just like to see her smile more. He remembered her before John's death and didn't think John would be happy about the way she was now. In fact, he was sure of it.

He stifled a sigh, knowing he couldn't do a damn thing about it. He turned his attention to a matter that was at least somewhat under his control.

"I need to question my shepherds," he told her. "I hired them to protect the flock, obviously. I'd like to know if they have any idea why that ewe was so far away."

She nodded. The coffeepot finished quickly. She'd evidently only brewed enough to offer him some. She filled a large mug and passed it to him. "Why wouldn't the whole flock have followed her? That's what they usually do, follow each other."

"I don't know. I'll ask Zeke and Rod if they have any ideas." Those were not their real names, coming from Portugal as they did, but those were the names they preferred to be known by. Given how the Portuguese pronunciation was so easily massacred, Mitch understood it. God knew, he'd tried unsuccessfully.

"I suspect she must have been ill." Even sheep could refuse to associate with one of their number who was seriously sick. Protective mechanisms operated at a basic level. He needed to be as sure as possible, though. Strange things were afoot no matter how he looked at them.

Yet he didn't want to make too much of this. He'd been dealing with livestock his entire life, and weird things happened. Like cows practically dancing with glee when he let them out of their winter pasture, where they lived on hay, alfalfa and some supplements, into a freshly greening spring pasture. All of a sudden those supposedly "bovine" creatures began to run around as if they were spring lambs themselves.

It always tickled him to watch that.

This was definitely not tickling him, however. And worse, tough as she wanted to be, Grace was looking a trifle drawn. Still disturbed. Unwilling to admit to even a bit of weakness.

Damn stubborn woman.

How many erstwhile primary school teachers would take on the dream of a man like John Hall? He'd worked ranches. He'd married the teacher and Grace had quit her job. Then a year later, the two of them had jumped to buy this ranch at a court-ordered auction. John's dream of raising sheep had become Grace's and she'd worked beside him every minute to build this place.

He sometimes wondered if she'd had dreams of her own that she'd relinquished for John. Or if in him she had found the answer to those dreams. That was a question he'd never be able to ask.

He sipped his coffee, seeking another subject to discuss, something that didn't have to do with that slaughtered ewe. Something to turn her away from grim thoughts.

"Thank you," she said presently. "I appreciate you having your men come fix my fence."

That drew a hollow laugh from him. "Your fence, my fence, who cares? It's helping to contain the sheep. I'm hardly going to give them an excuse to wander into a road, and where one goes they all go."

Except last night.

Then a thought occurred to him. "You need to go into town anytime soon? I ought to make a run for provisions. I'm feeding myself, my housekeeper, three hired hands and two shepherds who are pretty good at feeding themselves out in the pasture, but they still need staples."

She knew all this, of course. The problem with the years was that you got to know someone, at least on the surface, and conversation became sporadic. The details had already been shared.

Plus, you knew where all the Do Not Trespass signs were planted. Grace had quite a few, and he guessed he did, too.

Grace's smile was wan, but still a smile. "I was thinking about it when I was making breakfast this morning. I need to stock up."

"Well, then, let's go do it today. Plenty of room in that pickup to carry supplies for a whole bunch of people."

"Thank you for the offer. I'll take you up on that."

A short while later, he departed with the feeling she wanted to be alone for a bit. The princess, returning to her isolation in her tower.

Well, the large landowner, not princess. Fact was, they'd both been recently approached by an industrial farming group that had made an offer for their acreage. Neither of them had had the least trouble in turning down the offer.

It was some damn good land, better than most, with

streams that ran sweet well into the summer with mountain runoff, ponds that stayed full unless there was a drought, and some good trees.

Although the cows had nibbled the bottoms of the tree branches until they looked as if someone had come along and pruned them all off at the same height.

His own topiary.

He was glad to see his hired hands Bill and Jack already at work on the fence. Bill touched the brim of his cowboy hat as Mitch drove by.

As he reached the end of Grace's drive, he saw a black sedan turn in. Betty Pollard, Grace's only girlfriend, the only one who came to visit occasionally. He gave a friendly wave, glad to know that Grace wouldn't be alone after all.

Then he returned to his own place, full of questions, with only a few hours to seek answers before he came to get Grace for the trip to town.

Grace heard a car pulling up and looked out her front window to see Betty Pollard. A close friend over the last couple of years since they'd met. Betty had pushed past Grace's reserve, and Grace always enjoyed seeing her.

Except this morning. She'd have preferred a phone call first, because she really didn't want to entertain anyone, not Mitch, not Betty.

The beginning of a cheerful mood in the morning had been dashed when she came across that ewe. She was still shocked that anyone could have done such a thing. Shocked that it had happened so close to her home.

She was getting bluer by the minute. Counting her blessings hadn't worked well since John's death. That particular shock didn't ever seem to quit. It still seemed impossible that a heart defect had killed a young and healthy man like him instantly.

She watched Betty climb out of the black sedan that looked so out of place. Grace had often wondered how Betty kept it clean, what with all the dust around here. Even now a layer was already starting to build on that shiny black surface.

Betty waved, obviously seeing her through the window.

Grace half-heartedly waved back and went to open the door.

Betty breezed in as she always did, this time without a smile. "I heard," she said.

Heard? Already? That seemed quick.

Betty must have noticed the question in her eyes. "You should get a police band radio, Grace. Never miss out on any of the so-called excitement in Conard County. Tickets. Rowdies at a roadhouse. A drunk staggering around who needs to be led home. Why in the world would you want to miss all that?"

Despite herself, a laugh escaped Grace. "I guess it was more exciting this morning?"

"Believe it. Do I smell coffee?"

"The pot's empty, I'm afraid."

Betty smiled. "Then I'll just make more." She marched into the kitchen. "My God, I can't imagine how you must have felt when you found that. I'd be feeling attacked if that was my sheep."

Grace didn't bother to tell her it was now Mitch's sheep. He hadn't wanted their arrangement broadcast for some reason, so she kept quiet.

"I don't feel personally attacked," Grace answered. "Just some drunk idiots having what they think was a good time."

Betty shook her head as she measured out coffee and filled the machine with water. "I'd be scared to death to live out here if I were in your shoes. Really, you need to think about selling. You need a life."

That wasn't the first time Betty had suggested selling. Every time she did, she set Grace's back up. But Grace was unwilling to get into an argument over it, and she knew perfectly well that Betty would argue when she believed she was right.

"Just think about it," Betty said.

"I will," Grace answered, to end the topic .

"Anyway," Betty said, plopping herself at the table, "let me tell you my good news."

That perked Grace up. "Good news? Do tell."

"I fully intend to. I met a guy."

Grace felt a smile spread across her face. "Just a guy?"

"Well, more than a guy," Betty said impishly. "I mean, it's all brand-new and could disappear by next week, but at the moment he has me over the moon."

Grace had often been surprised that Betty didn't have a trail of men following her everywhere. Blonde and beautiful in every respect, nice to be around. Except she gathered Betty was very picky. A good thing to be when it came to romance.

Inevitably, she thought of John. They had fit together like peas in a pod. A great match, though it had surprised her when it began.

"Anyway," Betty continued, "he's sexy enough to catch my eye. And so far he's been considerate and fun to be around."

"A great combination. Do I know him?"

"I don't think so. He's not from around here. I only ran into him because we were both in Casper at the same time. At the same bar with dancing. We meshed so well I don't think either of us saw another person there."

Grace smiled again. "I'm happy for you, Betty."

"Too soon to be happy. But for the moment I'll enjoy it. Now about you. You need to get out there more, Grace. There are some really nice people in the world."

"You're right. I'm just not ready."

"You will be," Betty said with certainty. "Anyway, I've got to run. Dan and I are meeting midway for lunch at one of the roadhouses. The way it's been going we may close the place tonight."

Betty left after giving her a hug and another suggestion to sell the ranch, leaving Grace with yet another pot of coffee. She turned it off. She felt caffeinated enough to want to crawl out of her skin.

Instead she set about cleaning a bathroom and dusting. Dusting was a perpetual task out here, except during the winter. And it was getting time to pull out her windows and clean the frames. If she didn't do that, they'd get to the point where they wouldn't open or close properly.

Endless household chores. Maybe she did too many. Or maybe she didn't do enough.

Either way, they kept her busy.

Betty drove away, thinking about Grace and her situation. The woman ought to be ready to leave that ranch. She should have been ready a long time ago.

Betty had the feeling that it would take more to convince Grace to move on with her life. If a butchered ewe couldn't persuade her, then what would?

Sighing, Betty pondered the problem. She needed to get Grace to sell.

Chapter 2

Mitch picked up Grace around noon. A trip into Conard City seemed like just the ticket after her morning.
He was going to insist on one thing, however. This time
she was going to accept his offer of a satellite phone, the
only thing that worked out here other than a landline.

It had bothered him for some time that she was all
alone, except on those occasions when he could find
time to check in with her. Brave and stubborn or not,
she needed to take better care of herself.

The first item on his agenda was feeding her. He
claimed to be ravenous, so she didn't object when he
suggested eating at either the truck stop diner or at
Maude's. He gave her the choice, but she was indifferent.

"I'm fine either way, Mitch."

He decided on the truck stop. At least it wouldn't
be full of locals, which might inadvertently make her
uncomfortable.

Her discomfort with meeting people had become apparent to him. Sometimes he wanted to point out John wouldn't have liked her feeling this way, but he figured it was a lost cause. Everyone grieved in their own way, on their own timeline. It wasn't something that could be marked on a calendar.

The diner wasn't very busy. He supposed a lot of drivers snoozed outside in their growling big rigs. The waitress who came over to take their orders was middle-aged, full-breasted and kindly. Her graying hair was confined in a net, something not often seen anymore.

Grace's order seemed too little, so he ordered extra toast and ham, hoping to tempt her to join him. Damn, this woman needed to eat before she vanished.

"Did you talk to your shepherds?" she asked.

So much for distracting her from the morning's ugliness. "I got a hold of Zeke. He said the flock scattered during the night and they suspected coyotes had scared them but thought it was strange they didn't just knot together for protection. Anyway, after they scattered, he and Rod started rounding them up. He didn't notice a ewe missing until this morning. He also suggested I spring for some herding dogs, and he's right. But they don't come cheap."

"A lot of training?"

"Zeke said most herd by instinct but still need to learn commands so they do what *we* want them to. Apparently one trained dog can train others, even puppies."

"Maybe Cadell Marcus," she offered, mentioning a local dog trainer.

"Maybe. I'll check with him, but I thought he mainly trained police K-9s and service dogs."

"Since he can do that, he might be able to branch out. Then there's Ransom Laird. He's been raising sheep forever. He helped John and me out when we first started. In fact, we bought the beginnings of our flock from him."

"That's a good idea," he allowed.

Breakfast was served and he watched her pick at hers. He wished he could find a way to increase her appetite, although after this morning that might be difficult.

"How is Betty?" he asked, diverting the conversation.

"She's doing well. Has a new man in her life and seems really happy. And she pushed me about selling again."

"She doesn't give up, does she?"

Grace smiled. "I guess not."

Mitch agreed with Betty. He understood Grace's attachment to the land and the house but also spent a lot of time worrying about her solitary existence. She was practically in the middle of nowhere by herself. What if she got hurt?

That was why he wanted to push the sat phone on her. What if she couldn't reach him, her nearest neighbor, on her landline?

Mostly she needed the phone so she'd have communication wherever she went, like down there to find the ewe this morning. He imagined her running back to the house to call him and the cops.

Nope. He wasn't going to let that continue, but he had to find a way around her stubbornness, and a way to get her to eat. She didn't seem any more interested in conversation than eating. Nothing he could do about that either.

"Let's go, Grace. I need to go to the feed store."

She nodded. " Livestock must be fed."

He headed for the feed store first because he needed horse feed. Several hundred pounds of it, in fact. He wasn't the only person riding horseback around his ranch. After the feed, there was still enough room in the truck bed for some heavy-duty provisioning. He had to care for his employees.

He needed a flat cart to load all the provisions on, and this grocery provided those carts for the people who came in from outlying ranches with big shopping lists.

Grace needed only a standard-size cart and went her own way in the store. She walked with her eyes straight ahead, as if she didn't want anyone to speak with her.

This was getting out of hand, but he didn't know what to do.

He was glad to see her pausing to speak with the minister. It had kind of shaken the Conard County when a woman was sent to head up Good Shepherd Church, but they'd gotten used to Molly Canton over the last couple of years. A pleasant middle-aged woman who wore black dresses or slacks, with a white collar around her neck. She usually presented a cheery or sympathetic face, and right now she was engaging Grace in a conversation Grace probably didn't want to have.

Molly was stubborn, though, maybe as stubborn as Grace. It was the only way she had survived her initial introduction to this county, which was still trying to live the way it had a century ago. Change didn't come easily.

He moved closer and heard Reverend Molly telling Grace about some social opportunities at the church. Trying to draw Grace back into life. Everything from a quilting group to a Bible study group, with a few things thrown in between.

Grace's answers were polite but noncommittal.

Finally Molly shook her head, saying bluntly, "You know, Grace, building a shell around yourself isn't helpful. Shells can be cracked, and the results can be dangerous. At least think about joining us, even if only for Sunday services. Whether you believe it or not, there are plenty of people around here who still care about you and haven't forgotten you."

Then Molly moved away and began to pick out some produce for her handbasket.

Mitch came up beside Grace. "She's right, you know. Baby steps, Grace. Just baby steps. Betty and I aren't enough."

She looked at him, her blue eyes swimming a bit. "I know," she said hoarsely. "But I still can't."

If she kept telling herself that, she never would. He resisted shaking his head even a little bit and put on a smile. "I think I've got almost enough for my small army."

She looked at his cart. "Where do you put it all?"

"Well, I've got an unheated porch that does pretty well as a refrigerator for dry goods, and a couple of refrigerators and large-chest freezers. You need to come over some time and see how we manage to put it all together."

"Maybe I should."

If so, it would be the first time since John's death. Maybe it was a first baby step.

On the way home, before he could press her about taking the satellite phone, she spoke, saying something that chilled him a bit.

"Mitch, what if it wasn't just some thrill seekers last night?"

It wasn't a possibility he wanted to consider, but it had been stalking the edges of his mind anyway.

Such a brutal, unnecessarily brutal, thing to do. Maybe some drunks or it might be something much more.

When they reached Grace's home, he insisted on carrying her reusable bags inside for her. He suspected she had purchased more than she had originally intended, maybe to postpone another trip.

Unfortunately, because he had cold and frozen items in his own truck bed, insulated bags or not, he couldn't stay long.

But he *could* address the issue of the satellite phone.

"Grace?"

"Mmm?"

"I need you to do me a favor."

She smiled. "I think I owe you more than one."

"I don't count them, but I'd like this one anyway." He'd brought a spare phone in with her groceries and handed her the brick and charger. "Take this, please. I have a few extra at home, so you won't be depriving me, but you'll give me peace of mind."

She looked at the heavy phone. "Mitch…"

"I know, you want to be independent. I get it. But this morning you could have saved yourself a run to the house to call me and the cops. It's more than that, though. I worry about the rest of the time."

"Meaning? My life is uncomplicated."

Far from it, Mitch thought, but he persisted. "You like to go for walks out there. What if you fall and get hurt, and can't get back to the house? If you think I want to be hunting you three days later, you're sadly mistaken."

She'd been avoiding his gaze, as if she hated to be

pressed about anything, but now she looked at him. "I'll be fine."

"Most of the time that's true. It's the one time I'm seriously worried about. Take the damn thing and don't be a fool."

He was always so careful about what he said to her that she appeared taken aback. He'd called her a fool. Well, it was time she stopped being one about something so simple.

But she still didn't take the phone, and irritation surged in him. "Damn it, woman, you don't have to be so stubborn about everything. Most of the time I understand it, but not this time. All I ask is that you keep it charged and take it whenever you go out. Even to the mailbox, judging by this morning."

She looked down and he figured she was thinking about it. Well, that was a step forward, well past the few times she'd flat-out refused. Maybe this morning had shaken her enough to at least consider it.

Then, to his great relief, she reached out and took it. "You'll have to show me how to use it."

"These modern ones are simple. Hell, if I can use it, anyone can. But I'll be happy to show you."

Grace doubted he'd have found it difficult to use the phone, even a more complex one. Over the years she'd seen how handy he could be with darn near everything. He'd taught her and John a whole lot when they'd been neophyte sheep ranchers trying to get their operation up and going.

An endless font of knowledge about the land, the weather, the running of a large operation. Heck, even when they'd been small, with a tiny flock, he'd showed them a great deal that had made life easier. Come lambing season, he'd been on hand, or had sent someone over.

He especially had helped to protect against coyotes who constantly prowled and in larger numbers during lambing. She and John had spent a lot of chilly spring nights out there with shotguns. Not that that was the only time they needed to worry. Eventually when they could afford it, like Mitch, they'd hired some help. With John's passing the work had become more than she could manage without hiring an additional person, and the flock had begun shrinking until she had to let the help go.

Doing it alone proved impossible. Mitch had solved the problem, explaining that he wanted to diversify because cattle were showing less of a profit as the years went by. Like her and John, he wanted the wool, which was still in high demand.

Seemed fair enough to her. She knew the value of that flock, but they had to be cared for. It was impossible for her to do it alone and kept her from having to sell the vestige of big dreams.

She was sure Betty had her best interests at heart, but so did Mitch, and he'd never once pressed her to sell. Instead he'd made it possible for her to stay.

Stifling one of her endless sighs, she began to put her groceries away. She'd bought too much, she supposed, but now she wouldn't need to go to the market for weeks.

That was okay by her.

Mitch had plenty to do once he arrived back at his ranch. Jeff, another of his hired hands, came to help unload. They trucked the feed over to the barn after dropping off the groceries with Mitch's housekeeper, Lila, leaving her eyeing a pork roast with pleasure.

Mitch nearly chuckled. Usually Lila did the shopping herself, but she tended to be too careful with his money. He appreciated that, but he also understood the appetites of six hardworking men better than she did. For a while she had kept trying to serve normal-size portions and complex recipes. No more.

Jeff had taken care of the horses who appeared to be content to munch on their feed after spending most of the day on the range or in the corral. Mitch owned six good mares, durable and well-behaved. Believing that none of them should have to work every day, he kept at least two corralled at any given time, rotating them.

Before heading back into the house, he paused to pat each of them and murmur pleasant words. Ears pricked forward, listening, a couple of them gave him a horse hug, pressing their necks to his head.

He decided he'd try again to invite Grace to go riding. Maybe this time she'd accept the invitation. He worried about her, maybe more than he should. At some point the desire to live had to kick in. Didn't it?

Bill picked up the two large dinner buckets Lila had made for the shepherds and jumped onto the ATV to deliver them. Lila at last seemed to understand that two men living on the range couldn't pop in for a snack or raid the fridge. She was always generous.

Greeted by the aroma of roasting pork, Mitch walked through his log home. When he'd inherited it from his dad, it had been little more than a small cabin. The cabin had expanded a bit at a time, always keeping the rustic logs, and now he had a few extra bedrooms and an office for his business affairs, while the mud porch had been enlarged for food storage.

Not a bad accomplishment over fifteen years.

Neither was his herd, which he'd managed to grow considerably despite selling off steers. And the sheep. He was discovering that not only were they profitable, but they appealed to him in a different way than his cattle.

But the house, despite Lila's presence, and the comings and goings of his hired hands, felt empty.

As he stood in his bedroom that night in front of an open window, he looked out over his life's work. The bunkhouse out back glistened with light pouring from its windows.

Not too many windows, just a few. Just enough of them to give a view of the outside world so this wouldn't feel like a cave. Windows were an expensive luxury in a place with long and cold winters. Maybe someday he'd have more, when he could afford triple-paned glass.

In the meantime he relied on woodstoves and fireplaces when necessary.

Oh, cut it out, he told himself. Taking inventory of his house was a diversion to keep him from thinking about Grace.

His growing attraction to Grace made him question his loyalty to John. An attraction that surprised him considering how thin she'd become and how prickly she could be.

And stubborn. My God, the stubbornness. Part of him admired it but it frustrated another part of him.

Grace. Over there alone tonight. Again. But tonight held new fears, fears she was probably determined to dismiss.

Someone had shot up that ewe. In a very visible place. And while Guy Redwing had appeared to treat it like some hijinks gone bad, Mitch suspected Guy wondered, too.

The more Mitch thought about it, the more it struck him like a message rather than a drunken spree.

Who was trying to say what?

His worry for Grace increased.

Chapter 3

Grace had always enjoyed the longer late-spring evenings, especially when she was able to sit on a wooden rocker on her porch.

But this evening felt a little creepy. She had to force herself to go outside, with a blue Sherpa wrap around her shoulders, and rock gently, watching as night slowly stole the last color from the day.

In the late spring there was still plenty of greenery, especially in front of the house, which had never been heavily grazed. It faded slowly into gray as the sky relinquished all but starlight. No moon because of the new moon.

A very odd time for anyone, drunk or not, to be out shooting. The ewe, being fairly white in color, might have been easy enough to see, but what was she doing there in the first place?

That was what worried her. Out of place. An unnecessarily grim event. How could anyone have any purpose in doing that?

She wished John could be here, to share her thoughts, to discuss all this with. To reassure her and calm her increasingly agitated feelings.

He'd been good at that. She'd sometimes told him that he'd smile into the teeth of a tornado. Hardworking and blessed with a cheerful nature. Nothing got John down.

Well, except when she started wanting to plant flowers and bushes out front. Like they could afford it. Like the dang plants wouldn't probably wither and die when August moved in with its hot, dry breath.

John could read her like an open book and absolutely hated telling her she couldn't have her wish.

"I know it was ridiculous," she said into a night springing alive with a breeze that blew down from the cold mountain heights to displace the warm air over the ranch land.

A lot of things became ridiculous when you were trying to build a future out of nearly nothing. Her desire had been sheer self-indulgence and she wished she hadn't made John feel bad. It had seemed like such a minor thing at the time, though.

Too many things had, and it did no good to think about them now.

Reverend Molly was correct. Grace needed to get out more, to step back into the world.

Except she felt frozen in time, like a fly in amber.

She turned her head and looked over toward Mitch's place. She couldn't see it from here, but she wondered what was happening over there. He might not have a family, but he was surrounded by people anyway.

Maybe he'd gone to bed already. A rancher's day

started early. Maybe he sat in front of one of his fireplaces, his feet on a hassock, sipping the bourbon he occasionally liked.

She still had a bottle in her cupboard from when his visits had been more frequent. He and John had liked to shoot the breeze in the front room during icy winter nights. She should remember to offer him some, the next time he came over.

She wished he'd come again soon. She'd been pushing him away, trying to keep her grief to herself.

Nurturing it, she supposed. Indulging. Cherishing.

"Damn it," she said aloud.

There had to be a point when grief was no longer John's due, and a point that life became hers.

She just wished she could find it.

The morning brought another crisp, sunny day. Having so much help meant Mitch could sometimes take time when he wanted it. After a hearty breakfast, prepared by Lila, he stood, ready to go out.

Lila spoke. "You ought to ask that widow lady over for dinner. Seems like she could use some company."

He smiled. "I've tried. I'll try again."

"You do that."

Indeed, he headed straight for Grace's place. Used to be he'd ride over, weather permitting, but this time he took his truck again. He needed to look some things over.

And this time he didn't drive overland. Instead he followed the road, giving himself a different view of ground he knew as well as the back of his hand.

The image of the sheep was clear in his mind's eye and he wanted to think about the perspective from the road, what would have been the best place for the rowdies to park.

He knew Guy had searched around for some tire tracks but hadn't found anything. Why would he? The county road was paved, however full of potholes. Grace's drive was not.

Why would it be? Miles of paving would cost dearly, a luxury neither of them could afford. Every spring they had a grader come out to level his and hers off, followed by trucks full of gravel.

He never let Grace know he was paying for part of her costs. She'd have killed him.

Would have had every right, too, he thought. She'd been refusing any kind of charity for a long time now. Woman had her pride.

Each time he thought he might have a decent view of the spot where the ewe had been discovered, he pulled over and climbed into the bed of his truck to take a look.

He'd even brought his rifle with its scope, because, to him, the sheep had appeared to be shot by a rifle, not by a shotgun. That would make sense, too, if you wanted to take more than one shot. Drunks fooling around. A shotgun would have been no fun at all.

Better targeting ability with a night scope. It would allow the shot to be taken from a greater distance, requiring more skill.

He pressed the rifle against his shoulder and targeted the area the ewe had died. Once he'd decided whether it was a good location, he moved on. By the time he had surveyed all the likely positions from the road, he'd covered about five hundred meters in either direction and had found more than a dozen places from which the shots could have been taken.

Would any of them have had the skill to shoot over such distances? Or the desire to?

Frustrated that he couldn't pinpoint a good spot but satisfied he'd checked everything, he stowed his rifle and headed up to Grace's house, hoping she wouldn't think he was being overprotective.

One thing now seemed clear: the shooters hadn't been *that* drunk. A stable hand was necessary to sight through a scope.

Hell. What did that mean?

Grace was glad to see Mitch. Her night had been restless, stalked by danger she could never see. So weird.

"I haven't had a nightmare in years," she told Mitch as she offered him coffee and a wedge of pecan ring. "You see this? I was up at three kneading dough to let it rise and hunting in my cupboard for a bag of pecans I was sure I had."

She put her hands on her hips. "Think about that. Then I had to warm the oven a bit to get the dough to rise because it was too chilly in here and it might have risen sometime this afternoon. Who does that?"

"A baker maybe. Damn, it's good, though. I'm glad I dropped by." He studied her across the plate and the mug. "Restless with nightmares, huh? Not surprising after yesterday morning."

"Maybe not." She dropped in the chair facing him, propped her elbow on the table and rested her chin in her hand. "Feels like I'm spending most of my time in this room. I've got a perfectly good front room, but here I am again."

Her gaze drifted downward, and he waited, enjoying the pecan ring. He only wished she'd have some, also. She needed it.

"It's John," she said finally, still looking down. Her voice quavered a bit.

"John?"

"We used to spend a lot of evenings in that room, mostly in the winter. I can't sit in there, Mitch. I see him. Hear him. It's… I just sit in there and feel so sad. So sad."

He wanted to reach across the table and take her hand but wondered if he'd cross a line. With Grace he was never sure.

"I don't feel it as much in the bedroom," she said, surprising him. "Probably because about a year ago I threw out the linens and painted. It's a different room now. But the front room?" She shook her head. "If I got rid of every reminder, it would be empty. I don't know if that would be any better."

She sighed and lifted her face. "An empty room might only make it worse."

He hadn't thought about that, but she could be right. A gaping hole where once there had been a life.

"I wish I had answers, Grace."

She smiled wanly. "Me, too. This is all new to me. Still."

He tried to imagine her level of grief and loss but couldn't. Some things had to be experienced and thank God he'd never had to live through this. Losing his parents had been different, maybe because it was expected. They hadn't filled every part of his life the way John had filled Grace's. The two of them had been a tight, compact unit, wrapped up in each other and the ranch. Yes, there had been friends and acquaintances, but nothing like the two of them had been to each other.

He finished the cake, still wishing she'd have some. "How about this," he suggested. "I know the furniture in there is heavy. Most of it was built in the days when a chair or sofa was meant to last generations. But I could help you move things around. Change it up a little. Just think about it."

"That might help. I'll definitely think about it."

He hoped so since he lacked other ideas.

She shook herself a little. "I saw you out there on the road. You kept stopping. At least I thought it was you. It's quite a distance."

"Oh, it was me. Just trying something out."

"Which was?"

He shrugged one shoulder, wanting to make light of it, unwilling to lie, and very much afraid that he might give her another reason to be upset.

"Well, I was trying out vantage points from which to shoot at that ewe."

"Oh." Her face shadowed. "Why?"

Did he want to tell her? If he didn't, she'd probably guess he was withholding. Grace was reasonably intuitive about people, maybe from reading all those kids when she was teaching.

"Just that…well, I don't think it was a shotgun."

She shook her head. "I heard it. A rifle." Then understanding dawned on her face. "A rifle," she murmured. "They couldn't have been that drunk, could they?"

Exactly what he thought, but no need to confirm it for her.

"Then why the hell?" She jumped up from the table and started to pace. The room was big enough to allow it. "This all seems so crazy!"

"It does." He wasn't going to deny it. "Anyway, they could have shot from a bit of a distance out there. I was just looking for the places where they might have done it, but I bet it was from a truck bed, for that extra elevation. You'd have to be *really* drunk or stupid to fire from within the cab. Or to carry a loaded gun inside."

He wanted to let it go at that. Even though Grace might have a new reason for nightmares, he wasn't prepared to ever lie to her.

Once you lost a person's trust, it was damn hard to regain it.

She still paced, although more slowly. "Why would anyone do this?" she asked. "Except as a sick joke."

She turned toward him suddenly. "What about that company that wanted to buy our land?"

She'd tried to tell herself that couldn't possibly be, but the suspicion wouldn't go away. This entire incident was almost surreal.

She couldn't imagine that anyone had done this with an eye to hurting her or scaring her. She'd limited her social life to almost nothing, so who could she have offended?

No one knew that Mitch now owned the sheep, so it was unlikely the perpetrator had been angry with him for some reason.

"I need this to make some kind of sense," she told Mitch. "Any kind of sense."

"Me, too. It's not easy to just shrug off."

Grace immediately realized that saying such a thing was pointless. Everyone wanted events to make sense, and sometimes they just didn't and never would. Like when one of her students developed cancer. How the hell could anyone make sense of that?

She returned to the table at last, glad she had Mitch to share her concerns with. Concerns she hadn't wanted to share with Betty, friend or not. Once again Betty had pressed her to sell the place. Grace wouldn't even consider it, no matter how many times someone told her it was pointless for her to remain out here alone. Dangerous, even.

She looked at the satellite phone in its charger, its red light blinking, grateful Mitch had insisted she take it.

He was correct about the phone. Especially when she walked the land, enjoying time in the fresh breeze and sunlight, hearing the distant baas of sheep, which had been a comforting sound for years. She could almost believe the world was right again.

The world would never be right again. Maybe it was time to start rebuilding. But how and where? Diving into a social life at church daunted her. She doubted she could take any groups yet.

At heart she'd always been an introvert living in an extrovert's world. She had managed, but she'd never regretted exchanging her life for a quieter one with John.

She looked at Mitch. "I love it out here. Always have."

"I honestly wondered how much you gave up when you married John."

She half smiled. "Absolutely nothing. I think I was built for this life."

Some of which was gone now, but she had to stop thinking that way. It was holding her down, holding her back.

"I'm not ready to give John up," she blurted, astonishing herself with the bald statement.

Mitch nodded, his work-hardened face softening. "I know. I miss him, too."

"Part of me is beginning to think I've let this go on long enough. That I really need to let go and move on."

"Grief has its own timetable, Grace."

"You're right." But now she felt exposed just for having said the truth out loud. It sounded…over the top, now that she'd heard the words hanging on the air. Nothing, however, changed the facts. She wasn't ready to let go of John. Maybe it was time to put something around that hole in her heart and life.

On the other hand, getting busy might only be a distraction, or a flight from the grief itself. Maybe it needed to burn out in its own time. Although it would never be entirely gone. Ever.

"Want another piece of pecan ring?" she asked, turning the conversation to something less threatening. A brief break from her gloomy thoughts.

"Only if you'll have one."

Again she smiled faintly. "Pressure?"

"Hell no. This is so good you need to taste it. You must have lost twenty or so pounds and are starting to look like someone in severe need of nourishment."

Even as irritation rose in her, it collapsed before becoming fully born. "You're right," she admitted. "Although a pecan ring is hardly nourishment."

"It's calories. Enjoy them."

She retrieved a plate for herself and brought the it over to the table. "Help yourself, Mitch. I'm not going to eat the whole thing. It'll wind up in the compost when it dries out."

"We can't have that." Using the knife, he cut himself a generous piece, then foisted an equally big one on her.

"I never eat that much," she protested.

"Try. Compost, remember?"

A stillborn bubble of laughter tickled her stomach. Laughter was so rare to her these days that she welcomed it. "Taskmaster."

He held up a hand. "Hey, you're talking to the guy who runs a cattle ranch. I never take no for an answer."

"Are you sure the ranch doesn't run *you*?" Man, was she teasing? She'd almost forgotten she could do that.

"It probably *does* run me," he admitted, forking off another bite. "But I like to pretend I'm the boss."

"It's a good illusion."

"That's exactly what it is. But it gives me one advantage."

"Which is?"

He half shrugged. "I was able to tell Bill he's the boss for a couple of hours."

Finally, at long last, the bubble of laughter rose and emerged quietly.

Mitch smiled at her. "I like that sound."

She did, too. It felt good. Maybe it was time to pull out those comedy DVDs that she and John used to laugh at so easily. Time to reclaim something.

The loneliness might come again, but laughter would help.

Then she made a huge decision. "When you have the chance, I'd like to rearrange the living room. But only when you have time."

He nodded. "That's what I have help for. Two of us will come over tomorrow or the next day and make quick work of it. I'll call to let you know. In the meantime, if you can, think about how you'd like to reorder the room."

That wouldn't be easy, but she had to do it. She couldn't keep living in two rooms.

"I will," she answered, as much of a promise to herself as to him.

Then he startled her.

Mitch asked, "Want to come riding with me some morning?"

* * *

Mitch thought she was making remarkable progress all of a sudden. He hoped to help keep her going in this direction. He feared her response, and that she would shy away from any more change.

She used to love riding the range on horseback. She'd often mentioned how peaceful it was, how beautiful to be out in the pasture with the sheep. But it might re-awaken the very sorrow she was trying to edge past.

Then she astonished him. "I'd really like that. I hated giving up the horses."

And everything else, he thought. The dream, the sheep, the hired hands. The horses.

He'd watched as the financial burdens had become too much for her and had been glad that he was able to take over the flock of sheep. He'd always wanted to try his hand at sheep. Now he had a good excuse to go ahead.

He was grateful he didn't have to watch her struggle to try to do the job alone. It was truly a bigger job than one person could handle. He'd figured she wouldn't be receptive to the idea of him sending help over.

Two birds with one stone. He'd gained something he wanted and she'd been relieved of a huge burden. The latter seemed the most important to him, but he never wanted her to guess that.

Just like he didn't want anyone in the county to know he'd bought her flock. He didn't want people to think he'd taken advantage of the widow. Or worse, that he'd saved her. Yeah, he'd had mixed feelings about doing it. She deserved her pride. Let them all think she was making it, that the shepherds were hers.

He'd encouraged her enough about moving forward

for one day. He wondered what she'd change her mind about it.

Well, he couldn't do a damn thing about that, except keep trying gently.

He cared about this woman. A great deal.

Rising, he promised he'd come over in the morning with a couple of mounts, then left quickly so as not to give her time to make excuses.

He just hoped she'd sleep better tonight.

As ugly as the killing of the ewe had been, he couldn't think of a reason why anyone would do it maliciously.

Well, except for using a ewe for target practice.

That was pretty bad, but not likely threatening.

Chapter 4

Fog blanketed the world in the early morning. The fog was surprising in a place where dryness lowered the humidity until it was next to nothing.

Maybe an unexpected cloud was moving in.

Mitch sat on his porch, his booted feet up on the rail, and waited for Bill to arrive. Lila had provided him with an insulated carafe of coffee and a plate full of homemade blueberry muffins. That woman loved to bake and if he wasn't careful she'd add a few unwanted pounds to his frame. Even with hard physical labor, that was always possible.

She mothered him. He smiled faintly into his coffee mug and decided that mothering was a sign she liked working here. She could have made his life hell by reducing her cooking to basics, claiming she had enough to do keeping up with a bachelor's house.

Not Lila. Never a complaint. Well, he *did* try not to

ask too much but still. The woman was a workhorse, not only taking care of him but making sure his hired hands and his shepherds were fed.

Those lunch pails were always welcome out on the range, and if his men were closer, all they had to do was run by the kitchen. His shepherds had a specific list of staples they preferred. Things that wouldn't spoil. Those men were pretty much self-reliant.

As he waited for the fog to burn off, he enjoyed watching wisps of it moving slightly on stirring air. Eventually a morning breeze would sweep it away if the sun didn't dry it out.

Despite his plans to ride with Grace that morning, he wouldn't have minded a bit of rain. Rain was *always* welcome out here, greening the pastures and rangeland. Helping to fill ponds and keep creeks running. Most of his neighbors were getting to the point of needing it desperately.

He was blessed in his land and he knew it. John and Grace were similarly blessed, so he understood why that industrial stock company had wanted to buy them out.

He wondered if Grace had begun to think that might be a good idea after the ewe's killing. But no, Grace had a stiff backbone and she'd lost enough already. He'd be floored if such a thought even crossed her mind.

He poured more hot coffee and succumbed to a second muffin. Lila appeared, wiping her hands on her apron, to ask if he needed anything else before she started the eggs and bacon.

"Dang it, Lila, you'll kill me with kindness."

She chuckled, her large bosom shaking slightly. "A hardworking man needs good food. And them muffins ain't that bad for you. No sugar."

He looked at the plate. "Really?"

"I've been cheating on that the whole time and you never noticed." She winked at him. "Tomorrow maybe banana bread."

He groaned and she laughed as she returned indoors.

Grace had dealt with some of her stress by baking, but it sounded like a slightly irritating task for her. The dough wouldn't rise because the house was too chilly?

The things he didn't know.

Bill should arrive soon, Lila would most likely give him muffins and cook him breakfast, as well. He'd wondered lately if Bill and Lila were taking a shine to each other. They were both in their early forties and seemed to like hard work. A starting point. Lila's cooking could only help.

He grinned, trying not to open a muffin-filled mouth.

The ewe kept bursting into his thoughts, however. He wanted to talk with Zeke and Rod again, get them to be more specific about what had been happening just before the shooting. It still struck him as odd that the sheep had scattered that way. Zeke hadn't looked very happy about it.

Yeah, he needed to get a herding dog. Maybe he'd ask Grace to go with him to find one with enough instinct for Zeke and Rod to finish the training.

Ransom Laird, a guy with a mega flock of sheep, might be able to point him in the right direction. Or Cadell Marcus, the K-9 trainer. Or even the vet, Mike Windwalker.

He and Mike got along pretty well, which was good, because cattle often needed attention, as did sheep. Non-ranchers seemed to think you could just put them out on the land and they'd take care of themselves.

Nope. They needed vaccinations, various kinds of treatments, and his cows sometimes had female problems. Not just a "sow them then reap them" kind of business at all. Most animals needed a bit of TLC occasionally.

He often felt he had a bit of connection with his cattle, particularly the cows. The steers, on the other hand, he tried not to get too close to, because they'd be off to market. A reality of his life and not one that especially pleased him. Necessity drove him.

The sheep, however, could be shorn every spring and go back to grazing and making lambs. Well, except for the rams. They could get difficult during breeding season and he needed to keep an eye on them because they'd get into some amazing fights. They needed to be separated from the ewes after they bred, and care had to be taken that they weren't alone. Sheep, like humans, didn't handle isolation very well.

When the lambs were weaned, the ewes could be milked, a surprising source of income.

Sometimes he thought he'd be better off just selling off his cattle and going full-time to raising sheep.

When he considered how sheep needed the company of other sheep, his thoughts turned to Grace. She couldn't indefinitely live alone and avoid social contact. He sometimes was surprised that she'd made it this long.

Before he could delve into his feelings about Grace, Lila called him to breakfast. When he stepped inside, delicious aromas reached him. Nothing like the scent of frying bacon.

He was halfway through his breakfast when Bill showed up. Lila had evidently been anticipating his arrival, because she had his bacon cooked and the eggs already beaten.

Mitch smothered another smile.

"What do you need today, boss?" Bill asked as he tucked in.

"Help me get the horse trailer hooked up, and two horses saddled. I'm going to take Grace Hall riding."

Bill nodded. "Good for her."

"I hope so."

Bill looked up from his plate. "I keep thinking about that ewe. Something ain't right."

"I agree. But what?"

"Danged if I know. I'm thinking Miz Grace shouldn't be all alone out there. I could send Jack or Jeff to keep an eye out from time to time."

"Just make sure she's not aware of it."

Bill grinned. "That one's as prickly as a pear cactus."

Mitch answered drily. "You've noticed."

"Hard not to. After her man died, she chased me off when I hung around a bit to keep an eye out on matters. Furious that I might believe she needed help."

"That's Grace all right."

After breakfast, he and Bill headed out to the barn. The horses had been groomed just last night and were showing signs of restiveness. They needed to be out.

"Maybe corral a little later," Mitch suggested. "A run in the sun would do them good."

"That it would," Bill agreed.

When they'd hooked up the horse trailer, they saddled two mares and led them aboard. Mitch preferred mares for their endurance.

Once the mares were secure, Mitch set out for Grace's house. The last of the fog had begun to burn off, although the sky was getting clouded. Rain, Mitch hoped. Just a little.

Or a lot. But not when he and Grace were riding. He

wondered if she'd go out to the flock to meet up with Zeke and Rod. It was worth a try.

When he pulled up in front of her house, the sky started to darken a bit. Not good for riding.

A gust of wind buffeted him, bringing stinging dust with it. The temperature had dropped just since he'd set out.

Grace came out onto the porch to greet him. She even smiled. "Bad day for a ride?"

"Maybe. I suggest we ride a little anyway. If something starts blowing up, we'll head back, but I've got two mares who are saddled and won't be very happy if they don't get out to stretch their legs."

That caused a laugh to escape her, a delightful sound. He'd been missing it.

She was dressed for the ride, wearing cowboy boots, jeans and a light jacket, her black hair caught back in some kind of elastic thing. What he didn't know about women's clothing would probably fill a book.

The horses never liked backing out of the trailer. They performed the act on pure trust, like jumping a fence they couldn't see when they got too close. They knew Mitch and backed down the ramp one at a time, seeming to know he wouldn't let them stumble.

He gave the reins to Grace to hold while he closed the trailer.

"Mount up," he said and paused a minute to watch her swing upward into the saddle easily. He didn't mind the view of her bottom, either. He wondered if that was disloyal to John, then decided not. Grace was a free woman now.

Daisy sidled a bit with her signature prance as she felt Grace's weight and the promise of a ride to come.

Dolly responded almost the same way when Mitch mounted.

The weather was still okay, and from Grace's response on the porch, Mitch believed she was looking forward to this as much as the horses.

Or as much as him.

Two men watched through binoculars as Grace and Mitch passed through a gate and struck out for the range.

"Well, hell," Larry said to Carl. Both men looked scruffy, their clothes a bit dirty because they didn't have enough to change very often. Their beards were also a few days past the two-day unshaven look that was so popular. Larry still had a few biscuit crumbs stuck to his chin.

"What do you think it means?" Carl asked.

"What do *you* think?" Larry said sarcastically.

Carl shook his head. "That Mitch guy hasn't been spending that much time with the woman. This might be just neighborly."

"We should be so lucky," muttered Larry. "This was supposed to be easy."

"If shooting that ewe didn't scare the woman, we need to come up with something better."

"She's not going to be as easy to scare if that guy is living in her pocket now."

They took another look through their binoculars. Magnification made the riders appear much closer than they were. There were too many glances from the guy to the gal to please Larry, who tended to be pessimistic about most things.

"Hell's bells," he said, more emphatically.

"Oh, take it easy," Carl retorted. "One horseback

ride doesn't mean he's moving in with her. We can still frighten her, regardless."

"Yeah? How?"

Carl rolled onto his back, hating the way the brush poked at him. "Well, there's fire. Since killing a sheep didn't upset her very much, we maybe need to get stronger."

"We've got limits on us," Larry responded. "The boss doesn't want us to go too far."

"No murder. Well, there's a lot we can do short of that. Let me think."

Carl didn't think fast. He knew that. Thinking wasn't his strength. His strength had been herding cattle. Repairing fences. Riding a fence line to check for breaks. Long nights under the stars, listening to the restless stirrings of hooved feet, gentle lows as the cattle spoke to each other in their indecipherable language. Yeah, he thought of them as talking.

He'd loved that life. The current situation with the beef market had cost him the only thing he loved: being a cowboy.

"You know them shepherds?" he asked presently.

"What about them?"

"Furriners. Taking our jobs. Come all the way from Portugal instead of people hiring hardworking Americans."

"Yeah," Larry answered. It ticked him off, too. "But we ain't shepherds, Carl."

"What difference does that make? It's herding animals, right?"

"Yeah," Larry agreed after a bit. "Looks easier than herding damn cattle, too."

"So what's she need them damn Port-a-gees for?"

Larry thought about that. Good question. "No killing," he said.

"I know, I know. But we can make them look so damn stupid they get fired."

"How's that going to scare the woman into leaving?"

"Cuz she can't run the place alone."

Larry thought about that, too. "It'd make me happy, but don't mean the woman will up and leave."

"I don't see why we can't work this deal for us."

Larry nodded, turning over to stare up at the graying sky. "We're gonna get wet. I wanna think anyway."

Together they rose and trudged back to their camp, an army surplus tent and a couple of sleeping bags that had seen better days. Bedrolls. They'd just about worn them out over the years.

As much as the boss wanted that ranch, the two of them wanted to have jobs sleeping under the stars again.

It was enough motivation for them, and the cash they'd been promised only made it better.

Yeah. Now they had to figure out how to get it done.

Grace had expected to be saddened by the ride, had expected to recall the many times she'd ridden like this with John. That didn't happen.

Riding beside Mitch had shifted everything somehow. The sun, the breeze, the movements of the horse beneath her, the creak of saddle leather... Perfection. A fine day, with great companionship.

They surmounted a rise and saw the flock in the dip beneath them. Grace reined in and watched. She and John had worked so hard on that flock, but without a hired hand, without John, she simply hadn't been able to do it by herself. She'd begun to lose sheep.

She'd run into the wall of her own limitations. Perhaps she needed to find something that expanded her limits, to remind her that she was capable, not a failure.

Mitch, too, seemed to be enjoying the ride. "I miss the time I used to spend on the range herding."

"Why would you do it less?"

He looked at her with a rueful smile. "Because some things have to give way to being reasonably successful in this business. In any business, I suppose. I'm making decisions that I didn't use to have to, for one thing. Have to organize more for so much livestock. Tend to more medical problems. Round and round. Hell, everything is taking more time."

"I hadn't thought about that."

"Your flock is growing. You and John used to spend nights out here protecting lambs from coyotes. Now it takes four of us. Not a lot of time for riding."

She nodded, knowing he was right. Wouldn't John have been pleased to see how the flock had grown? Mitch's flock now.

She sighed, and Daisy sidled beneath her.

"What?" Mitch asked.

"Just thinking of what might have been. Pointless now. You're doing a great job taking care of the sheep."

"I've had to learn a lot. Intensive course."

She looked away from the flock toward him. "John and I learned the hard way."

Mitch shook his head. "You guys were doing pretty well."

"How are your shepherds doing? And why from Portugal?"

He shrugged. "Talking to other people who raise sheep, I was told that a lot of Portuguese shepherds are well practiced with tending flocks. Better than someone we'd have to train here. I took the advice, and so far I've been really pleased. I mean these guys rarely leave the flock, and if they do it's one at a time. I had cowhands who were less conscientious."

She'd had some experience with that.

"Wanna go down and meet them?"

She did. Together they rode down from the rise toward the flock who had gathered close, although not in a knot. She loved seeing them, their mostly gentle ways, the beauty of their now shorn wool, although that would be growing back soon enough.

Mitch spoke. "I had some little kids out here last spring. One girl, about three, pointed and said, *'Blankies!'* I believe she meant blankets, and I still think of it."

"That's adorable!"

"I thought so. Through the eyes of a child the world becomes a magical place. Have you ever wished you could regain that sense of wonder?"

"Sometimes. Adulthood kind of squashes it."

"Maybe, but it doesn't have to kill it."

Didn't it? Responsibilities took over, ugly things happened, the wonder and magic vanished, left to youngsters who could still feel it. That was one of the things she'd enjoyed about teaching, how the younger kids could get so excited about little things. That mostly disappeared with the assumed worldliness of middle school, but until then, life was bright, shiny and new.

She doubted she'd ever experience that again. Life had carved it out of her.

But she could still enjoy approaching the flock, watching the two shepherds who still used crooks. She'd never expected to see that.

The flock parted to let their horses through, and the two men approached with smiles.

"Something up, boss?" asked one of them, a swarthy man with shaggy hair. The other man looked like his brother.

"Nothing, Zeke. I just wanted to show Miss Grace the flock."

Zeke smiled her way. "They're doing well," he said with an accent, but not so much Grace couldn't understand him.

Mitch said, "I've been thinking about that sheep dog you want."

The other man drew closer. "Yes," Zeke said excitedly. "Good protection against the coyotes. Good way to keep the sheep moving where we want them."

"When do you want it?" Mitch asked. "It might take some time. And what exactly are you looking for?"

The two men spoke to each other in Portuguese.

Zeke faced them finally. "We use Komondors at home, but there are good breeds more easy to find here. Australian shepherds. Border collie. Many more, I think."

"Probably. About the training…"

Rod bobbed his head and spoke in Portuguese again. Zeke translated. "One dog part-trained. We can make better. Then puppies."

"Puppies?" Grace asked, surprised.

"Puppies learn from older dogs. Easy."

Grace hadn't considered that. An interesting idea.

Mitch spoke. "So once you get an older dog trained to your liking, puppies can just learn. How many puppies?"

"One or two," Zeke said. "Two are better. Two dogs herd better."

"I'll definitely see what I can do. After that ewe was killed… You still don't know why she left the flock?"

Zeke shook his head. "Sheep run all over. Don't do that 'cept wolf or coyote gets in flock. No wolf, no coyote."

Mitch lowered his head, pondering. "It's so strange. Please keep thinking about it. Something had to make those sheep run like that."

Grace spoke again. "Snake?" she suggested.

"Nighttime," Mitch answered. "Snakes don't move fast at all when it's cold. Zeke and Rod would have found it."

Zeke nodded emphatically. "No snake."

After a few more minutes of casual conversation, she and Mitch turned their mounts away, heading back up the rise. "So you're going to get herding dogs?"

"That ewe made me nervous. I guess I really need to think about it, expense be damned. The flock is getting so big now that I doubt Zeke and Rod could round them up easily if they scatter."

"True," she answered, "but it's still a mystery."

"Yup. And maybe we're both worrying too much. Shouldn't happen again, but if it does, then we can worry."

That made sense to Grace, much as she'd like an answer. It wasn't easy to say, *Oh, well*, about something like that, but right now it would be wise to let go. Worrying never got a person any closer to answers. It just used up time and energy.

"It won't happen again," Mitch said.

"You sound more determined than convinced."

He laughed.

Grace gave herself over to the pleasure of swaying in the saddle. She'd missed this. The sun had risen high enough that she felt its touch prickling her back despite the slowly darkening cloud that still moved in. She unzipped her jacket, planning to remove it but quickly felt the remaining nighttime chill in the air. Later, then.

Mitch spoke as they approached a small copse of trees that grew beside a creek. "How's a picnic sound?"

She looked at him. "Wouldn't that take a lot of time?"

He shook his head. "Whatever makes you think Lila would let me head out without a full saddlebag of food? I don't have to make it, just eat it."

It was her turn to laugh, this time more easily. "Sure," she said.

"I know she didn't give me peanut butter sandwiches."

"Hey, what makes you think I'm opposed to peanut butter?"

He flashed a grin. "You don't know Lila."

They dismounted under the trees. The breeze was freshening, and the brief visit from the sun was over. Clouds were thickening, more than earlier, and hanging low.

"We might have just enough time," Mitch remarked. "It's beginning to look like we're in for more than a light rain."

She agreed, turning to look out over the range toward the mountains. Those clouds seemed to be sinking as they crested the high altitude, possibly heavy with their burden.

She wondered if it would hold off until they got back, then realized she didn't care. It had been a long time since she'd been out in the rain, growing wet and cold. Right then it seemed like a great prospect.

She turned around again and saw that Mitch had spread a blanket and was putting out plastic containers and paper plates secured by real silverware.

"What did Lila do? Send an entire restaurant?"

"Well, she knew I was going to have company." He winked. "I'm sure there's something for every taste."

"I'm not picky," she protested.

"Maybe it's high time you were. Anyway, sit down and let's enjoy as much of this feast as Mother Nature will allow."

It certainly was a feast, Grace thought as she watched him open containers. Fresh-made potato salad. Sandwiches thick with roast beef and cheese. More sandwiches with ham. A container of carrot sticks. A dessert that looked yummy enough to eat by itself. A thermos of coffee and several bottles of water.

"This could feed an army!" she exclaimed.

"Never too little from Lila, not anymore. What would you like?"

She settled on a ham sandwich and a small spoonful of potato salad along with carrot sticks.

"Don't be afraid to ask for more," Mitch said. "The less I bring home with me, the less trouble I'll be in."

She had a hard time imagining Mitch in trouble with anyone.

After Grace had eaten a bit, she said, "Everything's so fresh!"

"That's Lila. She believes in keeping a roast in the fridge and baked ham. And don't talk to her about store-bought potato salad."

"I'm surprised she doesn't make her own salami."

Mitch held up a hand. "Don't give her any ideas."

Grace smiled. She was enjoying this morning. She'd feared it might awaken memories of John, but it hadn't. Not really. They'd spent a lot of time out here on horseback, but this was somehow different. She leaned back on an elbow as she finished her sandwich.

Looking up, she saw the clouds had swallowed the whole sky. "We don't have much time," she remarked.

He followed her gaze and nodded. "Nope. I'll start packing up while you finish your sandwich."

She watched him seal the containers and slip them with practiced ease into his saddlebags. She felt the first icy drops of rain as she stood while he folded the blanket.

"Let's go," he said. "With any luck we'll make it to your place before the deluge."

A deluge sounded good. A dark, rainy day, a perfect day to be indoors. Wrapped in warmth and snuggly clothes. Yeah, she could enjoy that.

They didn't follow an easy pace as they made their way toward her house. The horses seemed glad to cut loose and break into a full gallop. The wind blowing through Grace's hair felt refreshing, even as it grew damper.

The day had begun to turn wild, and so did she. Soon she wanted to grin into the teeth of the storm. It had been so very long since she'd allowed herself to be this free.

The skies opened up just after they passed through the fence to her driveway. Another couple of hundred feet took them to her barn. Mitch jumped down to open the door and Grace rode through. He followed behind with his mount.

Luckily, Grace hadn't thrown away much when she gave up her own horses. The girls, as Mitch called them, stomped and snorted, possibly because they could still smell the previous occupants. Or maybe they were getting cold.

She helped Mitch remove the saddles—she could still do that!—and place them on the padded sawhorses.

Then came the comb and towels to dry them as much as possible, followed by blankets.

Daisy and Dolly settled quickly in the stalls.

"I've got some hay in the loft," Grace said. "I don't know if it's still good for them. And a bag of oats in the back."

"I'll check."

Mitch ascended the ladder at a quick pace, and soon forkfuls of hay began to fall.

"So it's still good?" she called up.

"I wouldn't be pitching it down if it wasn't."

She knew exactly what to do with it. She pitched hay into the stalls and more into their feeding troughs. Daisy and Dolly appeared quite happy with their improved circumstances. Using her muscles this way brought a sense of contentment to Grace. She might be stiff later, but that was okay.

She'd missed so much over the last two years.

The time arrived to dash into the house even though Noah's flood continued to pour. Mitch dug out an old tarp she'd nearly forgotten and threw it over them. They ran huddled together to the front porch and shed the tarp to stare at a gray curtain of rain.

"Can't see a thing," she remarked. The warmth from caring for the horses was rapidly diminishing.

"Let's go inside," she said. "I don't know about you, but I'm starting to freeze. How are you going to dry off?"

He shrugged. "If you don't mind, a towel or two will be enough. I'm used to this."

Once she'd been used to it, too. Not anymore.

She dashed to her bedroom, reluctant to keep him waiting out there cold and wet. It would be inhospitable, even more so after the morning he'd spent with her.

She returned wearing dry jeans, a heavy shirt and socks. In her arms she carried the towels he'd asked for, as well as a spare comforter. "You're not going anywhere soon," she remarked.

"I could call one of the guys to come get me. Leave the horses here for a bit."

Astonishingly, her stomach plunged. "In a hurry to go?"

He shook his head as he used the towels to get rid of the worst soaking, then wrapped the comforter around his shoulder. "No rush," he answered. "But I left the bottle of coffee out in the barn with my saddlebags."

"Well, heck," she said, placing her hand on her hip. "I've been known to make a pot. I may even know how to do it."

"That's not what I meant. I don't want to impose."

"Damn it, Mitch, stop worrying about that. You just showed me a wonderful morning. How could I feel imposed on? You need to warm up." She tilted her head a bit. "Come to think of it, so do I."

That pulled a smile from him as she waved him to a chair and he sat, still wrapped in the comforter, a Southwest pattern she'd always liked.

The minutes ticked between them in silence, as if they couldn't find a safe thing to say, as if casual conversation seemed pointless.

Finally Mitch said, "I'd like to leave Dolly and Daisy with you for a few days, if you don't mind."

She brought the carafe and two mugs to the table. "Why?" she asked simply.

"I think they'd like a few days of TLC rather than being workhorses most of the time. You could let them out in your corral when the mud dries a bit. Now, I *know* they'd like that, running around without a saddle."

She nodded, smiling faintly. "I guess they would."

"I'll come over to help care for them. Clean hooves, pitch hay, muck out stalls. That kind of thing."

She waited, hoping there'd be more but unsure what that might be. Then it occurred to her that he was offering her something to do besides mope around this house and think about all she'd lost.

She loved horses. She loved everything about them. It would be nice to have them around again, for however little or long Mitch wanted. He couldn't do without them indefinitely, but a few days maybe? She liked that idea.

"I'd be happy to keep them here. As long as you want. I miss horses."

He nodded. "Most of us would. Anyway, I'd appreciate the help."

Perhaps he was seeking an additional reason to come over. The thought danced through her pleasurably. Mitch had always been there for her. Mostly he'd given her space. He didn't tread on her healing and grief.

Fat lot of healing she'd done. Plus it would definitely be nice to see more of Mitch.

"It's a sealed deal," she told him. Now all she had to wonder was just how much she'd agreed to, then decided there was no point in worrying about it.

Mitch would be coming over every day. She could deal with it.

An hour later, Mitch asked Bill to have someone to come get him. He wanted to leave his truck and horse trailer here for ease of a return journey with his mares. Or in case Grace needed to take the horses somewhere for some reason. He didn't want to leave her high and dry.

Rain still poured in sheets, making the driveways a bit hazardous even with the gravel. "Do me a favor," he said to Bill. "Don't get stuck."

Bill laughed. "You still got them two horses. They can pull."

"Not if I can help it. Mind yourself."

Bill laughed again.

Typical of Bill to laugh, Mitch thought as he disconnected. Bill wasn't just a handyman and range boss. This country was bred into his blood.

"The creeks are going to be running high after this," he remarked to Grace. "Not too high, I hope."

"Me, too."

Mitch handed her the towels and comforter. "Sorry for the laundry. When Bill gets here I'll grab my saddlebags. Lila will be wanting her precious containers back."

"Precious?" Grace asked.

"Don't let one of them disappear. The wrath of a dragon."

He left Grace smiling and went out to the porch to wait for Bill.

It had been a good day. Not only had Grace seemed to have enjoyed their ride and picnic, but she appeared delighted by having horses around again.

The way to a man's heart might be through his stomach, but the way to a woman's was through a horse.

The thought still had him grinning when Bill pulled up. In the four-wheel. Of course. They drove over to the barn so Mitch could get the all-important containers, then headed back to his ranch.

He never felt the eyes trained on him. Never thought the sheep hadn't been the end of what was going on.

It was all so senseless he had no real reason to suspect anything else.

Except part of him didn't quite believe that.

From the far side of the road and protection of brush, Carl and Larry watched.

"Well, hot damn," said Carl to Larry. "The guy's leaving."

"It's effing wet out here. And still daylight. Who cares the man is leaving? No use to us."

"Later, after dark, it might be."

"Not if it's raining like this. All we'd do is leave footprints."

Carl couldn't argue. He sighed and pulled his poncho hood tighter around his face. "We'll think of something."

"We have to. The boss ain't happy."

Carl shook his head. "No kidding. You'da thought the sheep would be enough to scare a widow off. Nobody around to help her."

"That rancher ain't too far away."

"Far enough. Eff it. I want a fire, something hot to eat and coffee."

"How you gonna build a fire?" Larry pointed to the rivulets running down the slope beneath them.

"Time to break out the tent. I brought a surprise in the back of that side-by-side."

"Yeah?" Larry looked interested. "What's that?"

"A propane camp stove, idiot."

Larry sat up. "Guide me to it."

"I figure our brains will work better when we ain't starving."

"And when we warm up a bit. Let's go."

Pitching a tent wasn't unusual for either of them.

Line shacks were practically a thing of the past, so they had that basic army surplus tent, heavier than they would have liked, but sufficient. Damn, the thing was so old it still had wooden pegs.

However, inside it was dry and, with the front flaps open, safe to turn on the stove. They set it up on its short stand, then turned on the blue flame. The heat was a draw all by itself. The dried food they'd brought would heat up in a little of that rainwater. They set a couple of tin pans outside to collect it, along with their aluminum coffeepot.

Neither of them had any difficulty with the old-fashioned utensils. The coffeepot might be banged and dented but could still perk the coffee.

"One advantage to this damn rain," Larry remarked. "We don't have to carry water from a stream."

That pulled a chuckle out of Carl. "Got that right, man."

When they'd at last drunk plenty of coffee and filled their guts with reconstituted beef and potatoes, they leaned back to smoke a cigarette. A bit of a challenge given how damp everything was, but the stove helped. They left one burner lighted for the heat it provided.

"Got no ideas," Larry eventually said.

"Keep thinking, man. After this rain stops, some things'll be easier."

"Mebbe."

Wisps of smoke rose to the top of the tent. Some even twisted their way out the open flap.

Carl spoke. "Shouldn't be too hard to scare that widow woman off."

"Seems like that's what we thought when we took this job. Now shut up and think."

Both reached for the pack of cigarettes at the same time. For once they laughed.

Yeah, they weren't stupid, Carl thought. They'd come up with something.

Strangely, the rain gave Grace a sense of security in a different way. Sheets of falling water blocked the world out completely.

In her bedroom there was an old-fashioned chaise that she'd inherited from her mother. Curled up on it with a blanket across her legs, she opened the newest novel she'd ordered online. She still liked printed books, most especially hardcovers.

Only one page in, she realized she wasn't focused on it. Her thoughts kept trailing back to Mitch, to the wonderful morning he'd shown her. He'd given her back good memories of riding on the range. And the picnic. She and John had sometimes done that, but nothing quite so nice and relaxed. Those picnics had always been a bit rushed because of all the work they needed to do.

She liked that this had been different. Mitch's attention had been entirely focused on her, not on some next task that awaited. The pressure wasn't there.

Of course, Mitch's life couldn't be like that all the time, considering what a huge ranch he ran, but he'd spared her the time anyway.

He'd made her feel special.

What was more, he'd reminded her that there could be hours without unending pressure. Without a weight on the shoulders. As her and John's flock had grown, so had the workload. Success carried its own price. She suddenly was glad to be free of it. In the early days it had been a romantic adventure, building their lives, making plans, visualizing the future.

At some point responsibility had edged most of the romantic dreams out and had left reality. She didn't regret it, but, well, today had been a nice change. More like the early days.

Tucking her knees up under her chin, her book forgotten, Grace ran back through her memory. She wouldn't have traded it, not any of it, if that would have meant giving up John.

But was it so wrong to realize the degree of freedom she had now?

Her thoughts turned back to Mitch, as if tethered to him by a spring.

A good-looking man. A capable man. A very kind man. One who'd been willing to devote a chunk of his day to making her smile and feel happy.

Hugging her knees, she smiled again. Mitch was breaking through the cocoon that had swallowed her for so long. That was a positive thing, right?

Mitch recalled his morning with Grace pleasurably. It had been enjoyable, if nothing fancy. He hoped he was right to think that he'd drawn her out a bit. Damn, he'd been worrying about that woman since John had died.

John had been a close friend, but so had Grace. Those winter evenings stretched out before the fire, shooting the breeze, playing cards, talking about similar problems that arose from raising stock. They'd shared a lot.

But Mitch's secret, one he'd almost buried successfully, was his attraction to Grace. She had a way of smiling that could light up her face, a laugh that rang on the air almost like a bell. A serious face that caused her brow to knit. An anger that occasionally sparked in her blue eyes.

What had caused him to bury his response to her as a woman had been the glow on her face almost every time she looked at John.

He wondered if John had truly realized how fortunate he was. He hoped so. Grace had deserved his appreciation and love.

For all she said otherwise, Mitch still suspected she'd given up a lot for John. For love.

Grace had no background in farming or ranching. The daughter of a small-town family in Maryland, she'd had no connection with life out here on the rangeland of Wyoming. Then, upon graduating with her degrees, she'd been employed to teach at the reservation for two years. Next thing, she'd taken a job here in Conard City.

He'd never asked about her time teaching on the reservation, and she'd never volunteered much. He suspected she'd run into a lot of pain there.

Why wouldn't she? It was not as if he hadn't had the opportunity visit the rez. Some tribes had done well over the last couple of decades, but they had to be on a road to draw traffic, at a good destination. Reachable. Up north, here on the prairies, everything seemed to be out of the way to everyone except long-haul truckers.

The forgotten people on the forgotten lands. Gutted by European invasion, then gutted by the way they'd been treated for so long. Trying to put themselves back together after they'd been stripped of almost their entire way of life.

Yeah, he knew, and could only imagine some of the sorrow that had followed Grace from that job.

Two years had probably been enough for her. Surrounded by so much sorrow…a whirlpool that sucked you in.

He wondered if her parents were still alive. Probably not, given that she never spoke of them, they never came to visit her even in the time since John's death. All alone in every respect.

Cripes, he had cousins within a couple of days' travel time. Not the closest family, but close enough they kept in touch, mostly by email. His mother's alcoholism had somehow stunted the family unity that others had. Then her liver had killed her and his father hadn't been far behind. Grief? Or had his father worked himself to death? This operation certainly hadn't been prosperous until after Mitch took over.

He wondered if he could get Grace to talk about herself more. Maybe let her question him beyond the casual talk that had filled most of their conversations over the years. They needed to establish a connection somehow.

Or was that just his own need?

Hell. Standing on his porch he watched the continuing deluge and wondered how to occupy himself with something besides bookkeeping.

Delightful smells had begun to seep through the screen door behind him. He guessed Lila was dealing with the dreary day by cooking up a storm.

The image made him laugh. *Cooking up a storm?* Hah!

He wondered how Zeke and Rod were doing out there amid this, then decided it was a waste of his time. Those two seemed utterly self-sufficient even in the dead of winter.

Unlike most ranch hands they didn't take a Friday night to go get into some trouble at a roadhouse. Every month he took their pay to a large bank. Maybe to save it for a rainy day. Maybe to send it back to their families. None of his business.

There was so much he didn't know about the people in his life. Like Lila. She'd taken this job after leaving a ranch over near Boise. After a divorce that he suspected had been bitter. Maybe the guy had been abusive. She'd sure come a long way to escape.

He sighed. He could go pitch out some stalls. Check the condition of tack. Look for some repairs to do.

His problem was that Bill and the others had probably dealt with all that. They were making him a superfluity in his own life. He'd better watch it or he'd become one of those guys who sat behind a desk for the rest of his days.

The thought amused him. He'd never be that guy. Nope, when this weather cleared, he'd be back out on the range. Not even three hired hands could take care of everything now that his herd had grown so much.

Reluctantly, he went inside to his office. Paperwork always waited. He hated the never-ending task but it had to be done.

Grace trailed along with him. As did the dead ewe. He absolutely preferred thinking about Grace.

The rare smile he'd seen on her face.

The rain let up during the late afternoon. Bill, Jack and Jeff trailed in, leaving sodden ponchos and boots on the porch.

"Hey, Miz Lila," Jack said. "Thanks for the dinner invitation."

Lila shook her head. "Seems stupid the three of you eating out in the bunkhouse on a day like this. I was in a cooking mood anyway."

Mitch watched with a faint smile as Lila fussed over

all three of them, seating them at the big farm table, insisting on serving them herself.

Yep, Mitch thought, there was a special spark between Lila and Bill. Next thing he knew, she'd be cooking in the bunkhouse instead of in here.

Not that he thought she'd willingly part with all the fancy cooking gear she'd accumulated. Never had Mitch thought he'd become familiar with catalog stores that catered to chefs, but he had. If she mentioned she wanted something, Mitch went hunting for the best. Copper clad pots hung from a rack overhead. A wooden block was filled with every expensive knife made. Only the best. Now, lately, Lila had been talking about a magnetic rack for those knives. He guessed he'd better look for that soon.

He suspected she watched cooking shows on the TV in her room.

The conversation didn't remain lighthearted for long.

"That ewe?" Bill said. "We been talking."

Mitch looked up from his chicken piccata. "Yeah?"

"Yeah," said Bill. "Funny thing, that."

Mitch didn't think he meant funny as in humorous. "Any ideas?"

The three men exchanged looks.

Jeff answered. "Feels like a message."

Mitch stiffened. "Why?"

"Because it don't make no sense," Jack answered. "None. Middle of nowhere. No other such things anywhere."

Jeff nodded. "Feels directed."

Mitch put his fork down, and Lila began fussing.

"You three! Let the man eat his meal before you go getting him all upset."

Mitch shook his head. "It's okay, Lila. I'm ready

to hear anything about that ewe because it's bothering me, too."

"Like anybody could know," she sniffed but went back to checking something in the oven.

"Nothing else makes any sense," Bill said. "Question is who's sending a message and who they're sending it to. Awful close to Miz Grace's place."

Yeah, it was. That wouldn't stop nagging him even though he couldn't think of a passable excuse why anyone would want to frighten Grace. A more inoffensive woman had never lived, and she'd barely been off that ranch in two years. Had she bumped someone at the grocery with a shopping cart? He couldn't imagine she'd done anything worse.

"Give me a reason," Mitch said. "One good reason why anyone would want to upset Grace."

The three other men exchanged looks. Bill, his range boss, answered. "Because they think she hired them two Portuguese shepherds?"

Mitch sat up straighter, his dinner forgotten. Could someone really be so disturbed by that? Just two men, not an invasion of foreign workers. Far from it.

Equally disturbing was the possibility that his insistence on keeping the sale of her sheep private could have opened her to so much anger.

"Just spitballing," Bill said after a bit. "Sounds crazy even to me."

Mitch nodded. Aware of Lila's disapproving gaze, he resumed eating. After another couple of mouthfuls, he said, "You guys are keeping an eye out her way, right?"

"Much as we can," Jeff answered. "Don't seem like much going on over there."

"I hope not. I left Daisy and Dolly over there with her, along with my truck and trailer. Just in case. I'm planning to ride over and clean out stalls for her. Maintenance."

"We can do that, boss," Jeff replied.

"Let me do it at least the first few times. She doesn't really know you guys and I want her to feel comfortable. I'll introduce you more over the next couple of days."

The men seemed content with that and dinner continued without any more unpleasantness discussed. They talked about the cattle, mostly, how well they were fattening. Soon enough some steers would be off to market.

Which reminded him to check the prices at the stockyards. That could have a big impact on whether he chose to ship.

Business must go on, or there'd be five other people looking for work.

Chapter 5

Grace woke in the morning to sunshine. After breakfast, she decided to go out to the barn to check on the horses. The idea filled her with pleasure.

She'd missed having horses. Even missed their scents and the way they made the barn smell. Their neighs and their whinnies, their hooves clomping on wood and hay. Everything about them, including the work of caring for them.

Unfortunately, the ground was still muddy. Not an ideal time to let them out into the paddock. She didn't want their hooves to soften up. In the meantime, she could curry them after cleaning their stalls and laying fresh hay.

She wore her rubber Wellingtons rather than her work boots and was soon glad as the mud grabbed at her feet and splattered her lower legs. Practically time for hip waders, she thought with amusement.

Inside the dark barn, she turned on the work lights, glad to see none had burned out from neglect or age. The horses nickered as soon as she stepped inside, then Daisy neighed and tossed her head.

Ah yes, horses. Loving and magnificent. Didn't ask for much. Pats on their necks, good feed, a dry place when the weather was bad and plenty of exercise. Take care of them, win their loyalty and they'd run themselves to death for you. Not that she ever wanted to see that.

Made her think about the mustangs she and John had considered adopting. No guarantee they'd ever make quality mounts, but they'd be safe. Too many people thought they were nuisances, swearing they ruined prime grazing land.

Grace and John had never seen them that way. They were gorgeous, running free in their herds, somehow symbolic. As for their hooves, they turned the ground, true, but grasses grew in their wake. Their grazing didn't take too much since they moved so often and quickly.

Maybe she ought to get a couple of those mustangs. She'd have to clear it with Mitch, though, since he leased the land.

Daisy found some hay and chewed placidly while Grace brought out Dolly. Then she returned and began pitching everything out of their stalls. That manure and dirty straw could go on the compost heap out back of the barn. Speaking of which, it probably needed to be turned soon.

One thing at a time. Her back and shoulders had just started to ache when a sound drew her attention to the wide-open barn doors. Her heart skipped a beat.

A shadowy figure, astride a horse and beneath a

cowboy hat, sat there. As well as he could sit, however, on a mount that would rarely hold entirely still. Full of vigor, the horse sidled, tossed its head and stomped a foot with impatience.

Grace caught her breath, thinking he could be an image right off a book cover or out of a movie.

"I said I'd help with that," Mitch remarked.

"I need the exercise and I like being around the horses."

He laughed. "I figured. Well, let me help anyway."

He swung down from the saddle with practiced ease and tied his horse to a stanchion. "This is Princess," he said. "Mainly because she thinks she's one. Hey, where are your work gloves?"

She looked down at her hands and realized she was going to have some blisters. Why hadn't she thought of that? "Too eager, I guess."

"You're going to need bandages by nightfall if you keep this up. Where are the gloves?"

"I think on a peg by the tack room."

He strode back there, then cussed. "What am I going to do with you, Grace?"

She stiffened. "What the hell are you talking about?"

"They shouldn't have been left out here. They're open at the cuff. Do you know what could be in there? Like a poisonous spider?"

Oh, heck, he was right. She lost her resentment.

"You're off duty until these get replaced. Don't think I'm criticizing you. A lot on your mind."

True. After she sold her horses, she'd never thought again about work gloves. No reason to blame herself, but she felt vaguely ashamed anyway. Too much around here had gone to hell.

Mitch set to work without another word. He moved

with practiced skill and plenty of strength while she perched on an old sawhorse.

When he was almost done, and ready to open the back door, he asked, "Wanna keep the girls for a few more days? I doubt they've had a run in the paddock yet."

"Too much mud."

He nodded. "Another day for that, mebbe."

He carried out a few forkfuls of hay and manure before saying, "That compost pile is getting a little too hot. I'm going to have two of my men come over to turn it."

She wanted to argue, but given the state of her hands, she decided against it. She had a lot to relearn. A whole lot. "Thanks, Mitch."

"Glad to do it. You need to take care of those hands, anyway. You got some spare work gloves?"

"Somewhere in the house. Maybe."

"Then find 'em but wait a few days. If you got blisters...well, I don't need to tell you about that."

No, he didn't. Infection could set in fast. "I wanted to ask you a question."

"Sure. Just let me get this last bit out of here."

When he finished and had used a big broom to sweep the remains out the back door, he pulled off his gloves and came to stand facing her.

Dolly and Daisy stirred restlessly, nickering quietly as if to say, *When do I get my breakfast?*

Grace nearly laughed at them.

"So, what's the question?" Mitch asked.

"What would you say if I got a few mustangs?"

He tilted his head, thinking. "You know most of them are impossible to break."

"I don't want to break them. I just want to give them a place where they won't be considered nuisances. But that's up to you."

He nodded, still clearly thinking. "I'm not opposed," he finally said. "But let me think about logistics. They sure are magical running across the range. But I don't want them to be giving my mounts any ideas."

Now she *did* laugh. "You think they could?"

"I need to check into that. I don't think there'd be a problem but I'd rather know before we have to make a hard decision."

"I have to agree with that." She hugged the possibility to her heart. It would feel like a new lease on life. Something to look forward to.

Mitch saw the expression on her face and ardently hoped he could make this happen for her. Grace so badly needed to plan again, to have hopes and pleasures laid out before her.

The Bureau of Land Management would probably be glad to turn over two or three horses. The mustang issue was becoming big, and so many horses had been rescued by the BLM that culling was under discussion. He hated to even think of it.

To him horses were one of God's gifts to the world and should be treasured. Not raced, not overused as beasts of burden, but treated with gratitude. They were helpmeets more than they were tools.

Probably an unusual attitude for many people, but that was the kind of man he was. To him, animals were not simply stock on a store shelf.

At Grace's suggestion, after they curried the horses he joined her for a brief cup of joe and a piece of that pecan ring, a lot of which was still left. She should have eaten more of it.

He knew better than to mention it. He'd already

pressed her enough about the gloves. He wished he could get past her prickliness so she'd let him help more.

"I'll send over one of the guys to turn that manure pile either this afternoon or tomorrow."

She bit her lower lip. He knew what was coming. "You all must be so busy. I don't want to take your time."

"Screw that," he said bluntly. "Trust me, I won't harm my operation by having one of my boys do a few hours of work. In fact, knowing them, they'll be glad of the chance to do something helpful. I know they love riding the range, but not all the time."

He leaned forward, as if sharing a confidence, which he guessed he was. "If you ask me, Bill would like to spend some more time with Lila. So if I give him a few hours of work that'll bring him home at the end of the day, he'll be grateful. Right now, riding herd keeps him away for days at a time."

She smiled. "He's getting sweet on her, huh?"

"That's how it looks to me. One of these days she's going to be cooking in the bunkhouse and bringing me my dinner in a can."

That pulled a small laugh from her. "She wouldn't."

"Probably not. She'd hate to leave all those expensive kitchen tools behind." He grinned. "You'd never guess, but I've become an expert shopper for chef's equipment."

"Now, that's fascinating. Lila did that to you?"

"Believe it. She loves to cook, she's great at it, and every time she mentions how nice it would be if… Well, I get around to finding it for her. I don't know how much more she can put in that kitchen, but I'm sure she'll let me know."

He left Grace with a smile on her face.

Very big step, he thought. Now he'd better look into those mustangs.

* * *

Betty Pollard dropped in to see Grace around mid-afternoon. Grace was glad to see her, and offered her some of that everlasting pecan ring.

"Mmm, this is good," Betty said as she sat at the table and ate. "Could I move into the living room with this? It's so much more comfortable."

Grace nearly froze. She avoided that room like the plague. She couldn't step in there without remembering John, without seeing him there.

"Betty..." She paused. Maybe it was time to stiffen her spine and just face it. No single room could contain John anymore. She liked to think he was everywhere.

"Sure," she said after her moment of reluctance. "Help yourself to any chair. Want me to bring the last of this cake?"

"I think my waistline can stand it."

Betty carried the plates and mugs while Grace followed with the coffee cake and the nearly full pot of coffee.

She was relieved to see when she entered the room that Betty had chosen the couch, not John's chair. For her part, she avoided her own and joined Betty on the couch with the cake and carafe on the coffee table.

"Now, isn't that much nicer?" Betty asked with a smile.

Depended on your perspective, Grace thought. After a minute or so she didn't feel the sorrow quite as strongly. Sitting on that couch with Betty felt different.

Grace spoke. "How's it going with the yummy mystery man?"

Betty's smile widened. "He's gone past yummy to scrumptious."

"That's great. I'm happy for you."

"We'll see how it goes. I haven't had the best luck with men. Anyway, he works on a ranch farther out, toward the north edge of the county. Can you imagine me with a cowboy?"

"Maybe that's the change you needed."

Betty laughed. "You might be right. I can hardly wait to see him on a horse."

Inevitably Grace thought about the image of Mitch in the barn door that morning. She understood what Betty meant but didn't want to say anything. Mitch wasn't interested in her that way.

She couldn't help feeling a little tingle in her heart, then almost immediately felt guilty.

"You need to find someone," Betty said. "It's been two years, Grace."

"Maybe someday," Grace said stubbornly. She'd know when the time was right, if it ever was.

"I'll drop it," Betty answered promptly. "I've just been worried about you."

Grace blinked. "Why? I've been doing okay for a long time now."

"Depends. I'm especially worried about that sheep."

Grace's mood darkened. "It was just some drunks," she lied. She didn't want to discuss the possibilities.

"You may be right, weird as it sounds. But I keep thinking about it, and you know I've been wishing for a long time that you'd just sell this place and move into town where you wouldn't have to be alone so much. God, it'd take twenty minutes for the cops to respond out here. At least that long for EMS. You need to think about those things, damn it."

Well, that was the strongest statement she'd heard from Betty on this subject. Did she really think the ewe was that important? Maybe some kind of warning?

A chill passed along Grace's spine, but she caught herself. If it was a warning, it had failed. Totally.

"I'll be fine," she insisted, "but I'd promised I'd think about it and I will." A promise she didn't intend to keep. She was so tired of this discussion. She knew Betty cared for her, but the pressure was irritating. Especially since she was far from ready to give up this dream of hers and John's. She'd already lost too much.

Betty moved on to talking about her new man. "Would you believe he likes to dance? How many men like that? Not many, I can tell you. He not only likes it, he's good at it. He's taught me a bunch of new steps. I was kind of meh about it. I like the closeness of having a man's arm around my waist, moving back and forth and hoping he doesn't step on my toes."

Another laugh escaped Grace. Was she changing somehow? Regardless, Betty's description was a riot. "That's a man for you."

"Sho' nuff," Betty answered and grinned. "Most of the time I'm happy to sit on the side, but not with Dan. He likes it and I'm learning to like it, too. Country-style dancing. I didn't know it could be so much fun."

Betty stayed about an hour, then excused herself, saying, "I've got to get ready for tonight. I'm not sure which roadhouse we're going to, but I'm sure it's a good one."

She paused on the way out. "Grace, don't forget what I said."

"I won't." Although she intended to forget immediately. Leave the house she'd shared with John? The wide-open country she'd come to love?

The implication in Betty's mention of cops and EMS still bothered her. Was something going on? No way to know, and very unlikely anyway.

A little while later, Deputy Guy Redwing arrived. Grace invited him in and offered him coffee, an essential invitation on the ranches. When someone came this far out of the way, you offered hospitality however limited.

"Thanks for the coffee, Miz Hall."

He had a nice smile, Grace thought. Amazing that he still racketed around as a bachelor.

"I come with bad news," he said as he sipped. "Well, not bad but disappointing."

He added the last quickly as if he realized he'd opened the conversation with exactly the wrong words.

Before Grace could ramp up her feelings, she settled down. "Disappointing how?"

"No solution to what happened to your ewe. There hasn't been a similar case in the county, not anywhere. There also wasn't any evidence that might help us track the perpetrators."

"I kind of expected that," she replied. "Mitch suspects it was done with a rifle, maybe with a scope, from the road."

Guy nodded. "I agree, much as I'd prefer to give you some useful information. Seems like a weird time of year for a hunter to be practicing, but you never know."

"That's probably all it was," she said after a moment or two. "Maybe a kid with a new fancy rifle."

"That would make sense. Couldn't wait for autumn. Anyway, we're going to keep up a more frequent patrol for a week or so."

Grace felt almost guilty. That was using a lot of county resources. On the other hand, it *would* make her feel safer.

Not that she wasn't safe, she reminded herself as she watched Guy drive away. A kid with a shiny new rifle or scope or both. Yeah, that was the likeliest explanation.

It was time to make dinner. God, she hated cooking only for herself. With John it had been fun. Most nights they'd cooked together, with a lot of laughter.

But it did her no good at all to think about that.

"The boss ain't happy," Carl said to Larry as they lay on their backs and looked up at the stars.

"Surprise," said Larry.

"Yeah."

They fell silent for a while, maybe pretending they were back on the range. It couldn't work, though. The sounds were all wrong. The smells were wrong, too.

"So what's the boss want now?" Larry asked.

"Something scarier."

"Oh, that's easy."

"We're kind of limited."

"By *her*," Larry pointed out. "Scarier, huh? I'd sure like to know why she's so determined to frighten the widow lady."

"That ain't gonna make our job any easier."

Considering that, they continued to look up at the stars.

"We'll think of something," Carl said finally. "We ain't stupid."

That was something they both agreed about. They just had to put their brains to it.

Because there must be more frightening things they could do.

Chapter 6

During the night a week later, Grace awoke from a nightmare so jumbled it had terrified her. Her heart hammered wildly and she couldn't catch her breath.

What the heck? Life had returned to its bland normalcy, nothing had happened...

Then she saw a red glow at her window, reflected dimly by her ceiling. Fire.

Oh my God. There'd be no help. No help at all because the fire department was so far away. Leaping out of bed, she jumped into her jeans and a sweatshirt, hoping it wasn't the house. *Please, God, not the house.* That would kill her.

When she reached the kitchen, she knew it wasn't the house. The barn was in flames.

There were horses out there.

With no other thought than to save those animals, she stuffed her feet into boots and ran out, straight toward the fire. Give her time to save those horses. Please.

* * *

Mitch was wakened by his sat phone ringing insistently. Jack and Jeff were out on the range with the cattle. What had gone wrong?

He sat up and grabbed the phone, pressing the button. "Yeah?" he said, his voice still rough with sleep.

"There's a fire over at the Hall place," Jeff replied.

Mitch hit high gear immediately. "Bad?" he asked as he pulled on clothes with one hand.

"Big," Jeff answered. "Jack and I are riding over as fast as we can."

It was dark out there, Mitch thought. They had to take care with their horses. "I'm getting the four-by-four," he told Jeff.

Not fast enough for a fire. Not even the fire department. Ranchers out here were pretty much on their own.

They at least had some firefighting equipment of their own. Big hoses attached to pumps that fed from the ponds or a well, depending.

His heart slammed repeatedly as he raced toward Grace's. What if it was her house? What if she hadn't wakened in time to get out?

Waking nightmares followed him through every mile.

Grace reached the barn. It was burning from the sides. Old dry wood was acting like tinder but at least it hadn't reached the roof yet.

Ignoring the heat of the barn door handles, she pulled them open, feeling her hands burn. She heard the horses screaming from inside as terror shook them, cries loud enough to be heard over the roaring, crackling flames. The doors were heavy, seeming to move in slow motion.

Her overriding purpose was to open the stalls and

drive the horses toward the barn door if they didn't run on their own. They might not realize that safety lay out in the dark night because they were so panicked.

The fire created a hellish light inside the barn. Smoke made the air almost too thick to breathe and see through.

Luckily, she knew every inch of that barn and could have walked it blind. She knew exactly where the stalls were; she just had to get to them as she pulled the neck of her sweatshirt up to cover her mouth and nose. It helped a little.

She reached Dolly's stall, feeling almost breathless, weakened by the smoke-filled air. She fought to open the heavy gate with its steel bars on the top, glad the horses weren't tethered inside the stalls.

Dolly continued to scream and buck, unaware of her freedom.

Grace couldn't take one horse out at a time, for fear the roof would catch and collapse on them all. She hurried as fast as she could to Daisy, who was rearing repeatedly. Ignoring the hooves that might kill her, trying to stand behind the stall door, she called the horses.

"Daisy. Dolly. Outside."

Whatever the horses had previously understood, they didn't understand it now. With no choice, Grace chanced those rearing hooves and stepped in to grab Daisy's halter. It was impossible with the horse bucking in terror.

Giving up, she risked the rear hooves and slapped Daisy hard on the hindquarter. The whites of Daisy's eyes were showing, but the slap caught her attention. Grace slapped her again, harder.

At last Daisy galloped toward the door. A few seconds later, a panicked Dolly followed the run for freedom.

Thank God, Grace thought as she staggered after

them. Smoke had robbed her of coordination. The barn had grown so hot she could feel her skin beginning to shrivel.

Mitch arrived to find the barn going up in flames. He saw the horses dashing out and running far away. Only one way they could have gotten out: Grace.

His heart stopped when he didn't see her immediately. Jumping from his vehicle, he ran toward the barn. The roof had begun to burn and he feared she was unconscious from smoke. Could he drag her out before that roof caved in?

It was as if he moved in mud. A small distance had just become miles. Before he quite reached the barn, his face already burning, he saw Grace come stumbling out.

At last his speed returned. He raced toward her, dragging her away from the raging death. No telling how far that fire would spread when the roof came down.

He picked her up like she was as light as eiderdown and began running again, getting her as far as he could from the conflagration.

Just as he neared her house, Jeff and Jack came riding up at nearly a full gallop.

"Everyone's out," he shouted. "Get the fire!"

It didn't take long for the two men to find the rolled-up fire hoses and the pump. Mitch was less concerned about the barn than he was about Grace.

Her eyes fluttered as he carried her inside the house and put her on the bed. Her face was seriously reddened and when her hands flopped at her sides he saw the beginnings of blisters.

God in heaven. She'd risked her neck to save the horses and now she was a mess. He pulled the satellite phone off his belt and called for firefighters and medics. She needed care. Bandages. Oxygen. He felt so damn helpless.

Then she groaned. "Mitch?"

"I'm here."

"The horses?"

"Damn it, woman, they ran for the hills faster than you did."

"Good. Barn?"

"My boys are fighting the fire. Medics are on the way. Can you breathe okay?"

She drew a shaky breath. "Yeah. The air tastes bad."

"I'm not surprised."

"The fire, Mitch. Go help."

He hated to leave her, but she was right. A prairie fire might take more than her barn. "I won't be long," he promised.

"I'm not going anywhere."

Humor in the midst of this. He'd always known Grace was tough, but that beat everything.

Jamming his hat on his head, he went out to help.

By the time he got out to the barn, Bill had arrived and the three men were spraying the fire hoses on the ground around the barn, and at its sides.

They weren't going to be able to save a damn thing. Except Grace's house. They had to prevent it from spreading toward her house and igniting the prairie. Nothing would stop those flames once they escaped.

Mitch joined his men, helping to hold the hose that Bill struggled to manage alone. While they didn't have the full pressure of a fire truck's pump, the flow of water was still enough to make controlling the hose difficult.

Round the building they moved, spraying every bit of ground for six to eight feet around. The entire barn roof now shot roaring flames to the sky.

Mitch prayed that the building would collapse downward into itself and not to the side, where it could kill two of them and spread the fire farther.

When he heard a loud groan from timber, louder than the surging flames, he shouted for his men to get back. "It's falling!"

They all heeded him, hurrying backward with hoses that still spewed toward the barn. Barely audible over the beast they were fighting, he thought he heard sirens.

Thank God.

As the fire trucks screamed up, the barn roof collapsed. Other than the groaning of wood, like a howling beast, it was surprisingly quiet. As if the roof had already lost most of its weight to fire.

The firemen unwound the hoses from the tank trucks, like the well-trained team they were, and began drenching the barn and the area around it. Four others took the hoses from Mitch and his men, relieving them and their aching muscles.

Then all Mitch could do was stand back and watch as the fire unit worked to drown the fire.

At last two ambulances arrived and he turned from the fire, hurrying over to them, to take them to Grace.

"You don't look so good yourself," one remarked.

"Don't worry about me," Mitch said as he led them into the house. "I'm a little scorched. Grace is burned."

He stood near as the EMTs bent over Grace and began assessing her. First came an oxygen mask. Before long, they wound gauze bandages around her hands and forearms and spread some kind of gel all over her face.

"I want to see the barn," she said weakly, her voice muffled by the mask.

"You don't," Mitch said.

One EMT was on a radio, talking to someone. Maybe a doctor?

Then the man turned to Mitch. "We're taking her to the hospital. Now. You should come along, too."

"Later," Mitch said impatiently.

"Mitch?" Grace's voice was still weak.

"Don't worry about anything, Grace. Just let these guys take you to the hospital. I'll handle everything else."

Then they brought in the stretcher.

After he saw her aboard the ambulance, he spared a few seconds to watch it race down the drive toward the road, sirens screaming. They didn't think a slow ride was going to be good enough.

That sight enhanced his fear for Grace. Then, because he'd said he would, he turned back toward the barn.

He didn't believe for one minute that this had been an accident.

The fire was mostly extinguished before the sun had climbed much above the horizon. Two more tanker trucks had arrived to help.

The barn was now a smoldering skeleton of ruin, black ribs reaching toward the sky. Smoke still rose from the blackened heap and the few standing stanchions. Water still gushed from fire hoses. The job would not be done until the fire team was sure there was nothing left that was hot enough to nurse another flame into conflagration.

Burned earth surrounded the barn but at least it hadn't spread.

He couldn't stop worrying about Grace, wishing he could be with her. He wondered if this would be one blow too many for her.

He wondered how bad her burns were.

He'd have liked to race to the hospital, but he'd promised her he'd take care of this. Taking care meant assuring the fire was truly out, that her house was safe.

Another couple of hours passed before the firefighters entered the gutted building. Using axes and industrial thermometers, they worked their way through the mess, trying to be certain that no remaining chunks of wood might harbor significant heat that could later burst into new flames. Evidently the crew didn't trust that thousands of gallons of water had quelled everything.

Then one of his smaller trucks pulled up. Lila emerged with huge insulated bottles of coffee, the kind of bottles she often sent out to his workers when they were out herding or checking the fence. She also brought big steel containers of food, freshly made bread, enough sliced ham for an army, mustard and mayonnaise. He even caught sight of her homemade donuts.

She marched over to him with his own bucket and coffee, ordering him to eat something "for God's sake."

Then she pulled a folding table out of the back of the small truck, set it up, and encouraged the fire team to come eat. They came in shifts, grabbing paper plates and loading them. Coffee went into more tin cups than Mitch had realized he owned.

Lila evidently thought ahead. She had probably started cooking as soon as she heard about the fire. Amazing woman. He hoped he'd never lose her.

Now that the fire had been nearly contained, he thought constantly about Grace. He imagined her in the emergency room, being assessed and given any treatment she needed immediately. Then she'd be moved to a room by herself. Medicated for pain, he hoped. Because at some point she'd start to feel her burns. All of them. He had no idea how badly injured she was.

He needed to know. Impatience began stalking him. Waiting for the firefighters to finish up this last part majorly frustrated him. He should be driving to the hospital.

But Lila was standing over him. He accepted the fact that he wasn't going anywhere until he'd eaten as least some of the bounty she'd brought.

"I'm not hungry," he said.

"I made them sandwiches just the way you like them. Now eat one before you leave for the hospital. When you get there, have them check you over, too. That looks like more than a sunburn on your face Last I heard nobody gets sunburned in the middle of the night."

Hell. He didn't want to eat. He could have pushed past Lila and left for town, but he didn't want to suffer her wrath, especially when it might include Lila quitting her job.

So he ate the ham sandwich fast, barely tasting it or the Swiss cheese he normally loved. Heck, he couldn't even taste the spicy mustard.

The fire crew had begun to roll up their hoses, signaling an end to their part. He was about to be free.

He finished choking the sandwich down and drank a cup of the piping hot coffee. Then rose. "I gotta go, Lila."

"I know you do, but they ain't no reason not to take more food and coffee. Waits can be long at a hospital."

He couldn't argue with that. He paused long enough to tell his three men where he was going, and to turn the reins over to them. "I've got my phone. Call me if anything important happens."

Then he set out for the Memorial Community Hospital, driving much faster than the speed limit. He couldn't wait to get to Grace.

He kept remembering those moments when he feared she'd been overcome in the barn, that the roof might cave before he could find her and drag her out.

The instant when he'd seen her staggering out of there alive still hadn't been quite enough to puncture his fear.

That fire was no accident. He was sure of it.

So who had it in for Grace?

Mitch left the extra sandwich in his truck, taking only the coffee bottle. The hospital machine coffee was good only in a moment of desperation.

Not that he cared about that. All he wanted to do was check on Grace, and in a relatively short time he learned that he couldn't. Not family. No authorization. He couldn't even find out how bad she was.

He was on the verge of punching a hole in the wall when Mary, one of the previous sheriff's daughters, approached him.

"Mitch?"

He'd met her many times over the years and tried to smile as he turned toward her. A social nicety when he didn't at all feel like smiling or being nice. Not when he wanted to chew steel and spit out nails. "Hey, Mary."

"You're here for Grace Hall, right?"

"Yeah, but they won't let me see her."

Mary nodded understandingly. "Rules, you know. To protect a patient's privacy. Anyway, doctor said she can't have regular visitors until tomorrow."

"She's got no one else. I'm her neighbor, I lease her land. We've been friends for years."

Mary looked around and drew him into an unpopulated alcove that appeared to have been set up as a small adjunct to the waiting room. Quite an empty waiting room, but he didn't have a thought to spare about how unusual that was.

"I can't take you to see her," Mary said. "She's heavily sedated and can't tell us to give you privileges."

"But how is she?" A word, just a few words before he lost his mind.

Mary touched his upper arm. "She's got burns on her hands that require some treatment. Otherwise it's all minor. She's going to feel a lot of pain for a while, though, so I can't tell you how soon she might wake up and want to give you access to medical information."

He nodded, accepting it. At least now he'd learned *something*. "I'm going to sit right here," he announced. "I need to know."

"You do that. I'll keep on it. But, Mitch, you really need to get something to eat. It's going to be a long haul." She started to turn away, then looked at him. "You really need to see a doctor, too. You might not realize it, but to my eyes it looks like you might have some noncontact first-degree burns on your face. If you haven't felt it yet, I can promise you're going to when the adrenaline wears off."

She left him to his own devices.

First-degree burns? He'd had them before and figured he could sit it out. It'd hurt, she was right about that, but nothing he couldn't tolerate. Last thing he needed was some doctor filling *him* full of painkillers or sedatives. What use would he be to Grace then?

He sat with his coffee, not hungry. Hell, for once in his life he didn't even want coffee.

Instead he thought about Grace, and how intertwined their lives had become over the years. All the time since she'd married John he'd felt attracted to her. An attraction he'd buried deeply because it was wrong. She was another man's wife. The wife of a good friend. He'd known John before he met Grace.

John had been a ranch manager before Grace, before they bought the this place. It hadn't seemed strange to Mitch that John had wanted his own ranch. What still seemed strange was that Grace had so quickly abandoned her teaching job for a life as a rancher's wife.

He knew how good Grace was at ranching, how hard she had worked right beside John. He got the attraction to the life, he understood the joys of it, but it still surprised him how well she had settled in. Town didn't often blend well with country, but in their case it had.

They had been deeply in love. No one could miss it. It was there in every glance, every smile, every light touch. He'd envied them because that kind of love had never visited his life.

Much as he perhaps understood her prolonged grief, he understood something else as well. Grace needed a life for herself. She needed to stretch, to find new activities, to make more friends. He and Betty Pollard couldn't possibly be enough in the long run.

Thinking about Grace inevitably led him back to the same question: Was someone out to hurt Grace? Was the barn fire deliberate?

He believed it was, but he couldn't know for certain until the arson investigator had a chance to look it all over. It might be days until the investigator could conclude the cause.

In the meantime, he had to put all those thoughts in the back of his mind, because Grace needed someone to care for her right now.

He was damn well going to do it, whether she liked it or not. He admired her determination, but it just wasn't safe for anyone to be as alone as she was, not out there in the wide-open spaces. Too many bad things could happen, and help was far away.

Like with her barn. If his men hadn't seen it, God knew what might have happened.

Sometimes he wished he could shake some sense into her.

Out among the trees, two men with binoculars scanned the burned-out barn.

"The boss is going to like this one," Carl said with satisfaction.

"If not," Larry answered, "I don't know what the hell else we can do."

"If she don't like it, she's crazy."

Larry snorted. "She's already halfway there. But yeah, if that don't send that Hall woman running, she's as crazy as the boss."

They'd already decided the boss was nuts. What the hell was so important about moving that Hall woman out of there? They guessed they'd never know. Not that they really needed to.

It was a job. Just get it done.

It was evening before Mary showed up again. Mitch was stiff from the lousy waiting room chairs. After telling the desk where he could be found, he'd paced the parking lot. The rest of the time he'd watched patients come and go. Nothing serious.

Mary smiled. "Grace wants to see you and she verbally gave us permission to talk with you."

He jumped up. "Thank God."

"I'll warn you she's still groggy on morphine, but she's talking and somewhat alert. She may fall asleep on you, so don't worry."

Mary led him to the door of Grace's room. She opened it and called in cheerfully, "Look who's been waiting all day to see you."

Mary nodded, leaving him along with Grace. He crossed to her bed, not wanting to startle her, and saw her blue eyes blinking at him. She looked half-asleep and he was grateful for that. He couldn't imagine the pain she'd feel from her hands if she'd been fully conscious.

"Mitch," she whispered.

"I'm here, darlin'," he said, slipping up. He tensed, then decided she wouldn't remember. Morphine was like that, he'd seen a few times.

"How bad?"

"The horses are fine. Jeff and Jack are out looking for them but are pretty sure they ran for home. Only a fence would keep them from making it."

"Good." She sighed, her eyelids drooping. "The barn?"

"Gone."

She swore faintly, something he'd rarely heard her do.

"Barns can be rebuilt. You and horses not so much."

The faintest of smiles reached her lips. "My face hurts."

"Not surprising. They've got you pretty well gooped up. Anyway, you don't need to worry about your pretty face. It'll be there when you leave here."

"Yeah." She inhaled deeply, as if she still needed to draw more air.

He'd have to ask Mary about that when he had the chance, away from Grace's hearing. He didn't want her to worry about anything else.

"My hands are bad. Lots of bandages. I don't feel them yet."

Maybe the morphine? "That's probably a good thing."

Her eyes were almost closed now. He wondered if she wanted him hanging around in her room, or if he should wait outside. He didn't want to ask her, not when she was clearly having a hard time talking.

Then a nurse came into the room. "Time for more morphine," he said cheerily. "Dreamland for you, Ms. Hall."

"I'll be waiting when you wake up," Mitch said. "You just go to sleep now."

The morphine was already running into her IV line. She started to speak but fell into the arms of Morpheus before she could do more than make a sound.

Thank God. When she *could* feel her hands again, it would be awful. He'd seen them. Not quite raw meat, but close.

He stepped outside and looked around for Mary. Five minutes later she found him.

"I need to know" was all he said to her.

"Of course. Let's step into the waiting room."

Once again it was empty. "Quiet night?"

"We all need one sometimes."

They sat side by side, and he asked impatiently, "Well?"

"Second-degree burns on her palms. A lot of skin is lost but not enough to require any kind of graft. It was blistering, nothing deeper. They'll be fine, but it's going to take a while. Face has first-degree—no problem there except discomfort. She was in shock when she got here, typical of burn cases."

"That's it?"

Mary shook her head. "Not quite. She had a lot of smoke inhalation, which we treated with bicarbonate. It's going to take a few days to get her blood acids back to normal."

He nodded, taking it all in.

Mary reached out and touched his arm again. "Mitch, she's going to be fine. Completely fine. She just needs some recovery time."

A coiled spring deep inside him began to let go. "Completely?" he repeated.

"You have my word on it. You can come down off the ceiling now."

She smiled. This time he returned it and blew a long breath as tension released its hold. "Thank you, Mary."

She rose. "Take my advice and get back to your ranch. Eat something, rest a little if you can. She's going to sleep most of the night. Come back earlier if you can't catch eight hours. I'll tell the desk you have Grace's permission to visit and get her medical info. You won't be locked out."

That was another relief. He couldn't have tolerated coming back here to find someone guarding the gate. "Thanks," he said again.

Then as she walked away he put his head in his hands, ignoring the tenderness of his own skin. God, how close it had been. Too close.

He had to find out who was behind this before they struck at Grace again. Determination filled him, making him sit up straighter. Someone was going to pay.

Feeling marginally better, he took Mary's advice. He'd be no good to anyone if he were sleep deprived. He also needed to talk to his men, check out the entire situation. Then maybe he could snag a few hours in the sack.

Back at the ranch, he found a couple of worried people, Bill and Lila. They were all over him almost before he got in the door.

"How is she?" Lila demanded even as she dragged him toward the kitchen for food and a drink.

"I need a shower first."

"We need news first," Bill said. "Plus, damn it, you need to eat. You look like hell, boss."

"Thanks a bunch."

Mitch quit arguing and soon had a meal fit for a king spread in front of him. Lila and Bill joined him at the trestle table with cups of coffee. Lila shoved two fingers of whiskey in front of him.

After a bite or two, Mitch discovered he was ravenous. That seemed to please Lila, who sometimes appeared determined to fatten him up like a steer headed for auction.

"Okay," he said presently. Never had he possessed a more attentive audience. "She's going to be all right. Hands are a mess, but they'll heal. She had smoke inhalation. They're going to keep her for a few days. I talked to her briefly and she was concerned about the horses and the barn. Of course, she wouldn't be in this mess if she hadn't saved those horses. You should have seen her stagger out of that barn."

"Damn, she's brave," Bill said.

"Damn straight," Mitch agreed. "Whenever they release her, she's going to need some help, though."

"Consider it done," Bill said.

Lila offered, "I'll go over and cook and clean for her. That's if you don't mind."

Mitch shook his head. "I don't mind. Like I said, she's going to need help. I doubt her hands will find it comfortable even to hold a cup of joe or a fork, but I know damn well she'll try. Well, I don't want her doing any more than that."

They both nodded.

"As for the horses," Bill volunteered. "Came this way like we thought. Couldn't pass the fence. I think they're both happy to be bedded down in their own stalls, though."

"Wouldn't you be?"

Mitch ate until he couldn't hold another bite, then reached for the highball glass holding his whiskey. "Thanks, Lila. That was a truly great meal." He then downed half the whiskey.

"Don't I always feed you this way?" Then she laughed. "I'm so glad everything is going to be okay."

"Except the barn," Mitch remarked.

"About that," Bill said. "Had a few of our neighbors stop by this afternoon. I think we might be having a barn raising almost before you know it."

Let Grace stick that in her craw, Mitch thought with amusement. She was going to get help even if she didn't want it. That was what neighbors did in these parts. "That's really great. The four of us could do it, but it'd take us a lot longer."

"Plus me, Jack and Jeff aren't the best carpenters. We'll have plenty of help. Might get it done over a weekend, if enough folks show up."

Mitch eyed Lila. "You up to cooking for an army?"

She grinned. "I kinda think we'll have a lot of wives showing up to pitch in."

Maybe, thought Mitch as he left the remaining whiskey in favor of that shower. Part of the tradition, for the wives to get together to help feed all the men at an affair like this.

He didn't care if that sounded sexist. That was the way things were in these parts. If some of the women wanted to join in the building part, they'd be welcome. And any of the guys were welcome to cook.

He was hardly interested in how folks chose to split the labor.

In the shower, the events of the last day finally, truly hit him. He placed his palms on the tile and shook, water pouring over his head. His chest squeezed so hard he could barely breathe.

He'd come so close to losing Grace. He couldn't bear the thought.

The words that came out of his mouth were more prayer than cussing.

He *had* to find the person behind this. He *had* to or Grace would never feel safe again.

Chapter 7

Mitch arrived back at the hospital in the wee hours and sat by Grace's bed while she slept. From time to time he walked to the uncovered window and looked out at the surrounding town.

It seemed not so long ago that buildings hadn't reached out this far, but during a brief time the semi-conductor plant had brought people to town and provided local jobs. There'd been a spurt of growth. Gone now, but the signs remained.

He doubted the community college provided enough jobs for all those houses. Or maybe they did. He didn't much care. His ranch was still mostly empty land, giving him an unobstructed view of rolling prairie and mountains. Just the way he liked it.

He turned back to Grace's bed and resumed his watch in the chair.

A nurse came in and drew some blood, then checked

the IV. Something was tweaked, then she left without a word.

Probably trying not to disturb Grace.

He couldn't even reach out to hold her hand, to let her know in the depths of sleep that she wasn't alone.

He turned his thoughts to something that didn't make him feel as bad. A barn raising, huh? Nothing like that had happened recently. There'd been one years ago when that tornado blew through. Most of the damage had been to roofs, but one barn had taken a lot more. Too much damage to save.

He'd helped that time, wouldn't have dreamed of not doing it. He could still remember, however, the great scar that storm had left across his own land. Fifteen feet wide, it had cleared the ground of grass and everything else. He was still grateful that none of his herd had been there. Unlike that movie, it wouldn't have been funny.

"Mitch?"

He leaned forward in his chair. "I'm here." The sound of Grace's wispy voice filled him with joy.

"Everything? The horses?"

She couldn't remember what he'd said earlier. Good. He didn't want her wondering uncomfortably about that *darlin'* that had escaped him.

He cleared his throat, to make his voice as calm and reassuring as possible. "The horses are fine. They ran home, like you'd expect."

"Good." As hard as it must be for her to talk right now, she managed to sound satisfied. "I was so worried about them. God, they were so terrified. I can't imagine being trapped in that fire."

He didn't want to imagine. "And you," he said. "I saw you stagger out of there. You could have died, Grace. The roof collapsed just a little while later."

"I'm okay," she repeated. Then her voice began to slow again. "The barn must be gone."

"Yeah. Don't worry about that now. There'll be plenty of time to deal with that when you feel better. I'm just glad it wasn't your house."

"Me, too…" Then her voice began trailing away. "Go home, Mitch. You've got work…"

Then she disappeared into drug-induced sleep. Better that way. She didn't need to be awake for most of this.

One of the nurses stopped him outside Grace's room. "She'll sleep most of the day. Come back this afternoon."

The sun had begun to rise, casting a dim, golden light outside. Yeah, he had to get back to the ranch. To see the damage in the light of day.

Nearly an hour later, he pulled up Grace's drive. Even at this distance he could see equipment waiting.

Wasn't it too soon to be starting a new barn?

He saw several front-end loaders in a line. Probably getting ready to clear the land.

Then he saw the arson investigator standing with a clipboard and a case full of chemical sniffers and other tools of her trade. She was looking at the heap of rubble, burned pillars that pointed crookedly at the sky.

It was Charity Camden, the department chief's wife. An arson investigator with a lot of experience before she'd come here on an investigation and met the chief. She'd stayed.

"Hey, Mitch," she said, smiling. "How's Grace doing?"

"She'll recover. Her hands are a bit of a mess. Also, smoke inhalation."

Charity screwed up her nose. "Been there. No damn fun."

"I wouldn't think so. Got any ideas?"

"Absolutely. An amateur's job. Kerosene on four sides of the barn. I guess they, or he, didn't much care if we could tell."

"Just kerosene, huh?"

She nodded. "Spread around. The barn was dry, right?"

"And old. No rain for a while except last week. Not enough, I guess."

"At this time of year? Nothing stays wet for long." She shook her head. "A firebug? Or just someone who's mad about something. Grace got any enemies?"

It was Mitch's turn to shake his head. "She's hardly been out of the house since her husband died."

"Well, damn. I hope we don't have another fire. I absolutely hate arsonists, and those who repeat? They all ought to be in prison for life. Lives are at risk in every fire."

He couldn't disagree with that. "There were two horses in that barn. Grace got them out before the thing collapsed."

Charity drew a sharp breath. "My God. No one told me that. Most people couldn't make themselves get that close to a raging fire."

His answer was simple. "Grace loves horses."

"I guess so." She bent and started packing her equipment. "This was easy for me. I've got everything I need for a report. You can tell your neighbors to get at it."

That was when he noticed a group of men standing farther out, smoking cigarettes. Now he knew why those loaders were sitting there.

As Charity left, he walked over to them, shaking hands with men who'd been ranching around him his entire life. They all had faces marked by years in the sun and wind and by hard physical labor. "Thanks for coming, guys."

One of them tipped a water bottle over his cigarette butt to put it out completely. "We gotta clear the land, Mitch. Can't start a new barn with all that there. That is, if we got the go-ahead."

"You got it," he said. "Grace has a few more days in the hospital."

That made the man, Edgar, frown, but then he smiled. "Might have a nice surprise for her. Folks are talking about getting started tomorrow."

"That's fantastic."

One of the other men, Orson, spoke. "Least we can do. Man, you look like you need a meal, some coffee and some sleep. Just go home. We can clear this mess between us. Hear?"

He was so grateful to his four friends he wished there were words. But they didn't need them. All of them understood.

Orson especially, since he'd lost his barn to that tornado.

When Mitch drove away, he heard the loaders rev up, then their roar as they started scraping debris out of the way, making the land level.

Lila served him a huge breakfast and most of a pot of fresh coffee. "How's Grace doing?"

"Still mostly knocked out on morphine. I'm going back later."

Lila nodded. "Jeff and Bill are heading over to her place to see what they can do to help. Jack'll keep an eye on the herd. And, of course, you got them shepherds to look after the flock."

All neatly sewn up. He might start to feel extraneous. "There are four men out there clearing up the rubble. They're talking about starting to raise the barn tomorrow."

Lila nodded her satisfaction. "Good. Who are they?"

"Edgar, Orson, Tom and Jim."

"Good men. I'll talk to their wives. They might have some idea of how many will be there tomorrow. Meantime, I can take lunch out to the ones we got."

"I'm sure that'll be welcome. Charity Camden was out there when I arrived."

Lila sat down. "What did she say it was?"

"Arson. Someone poured kerosene around the outside of the barn."

"With the horses in there? For God's sake, what is this world coming to?"

"Beats me," Mitch answered as he took more of the thick slice of ham. "Hey, this is good."

"Always is, and don't talk with your mouth full."

He'd have laughed if his mouth *hadn't* been full.

Lila was silent for a minute or so. "I'm scared what this might mean. For Grace especially."

Mitch took a long swallow of a glass of milk. "Me, too," he admitted. "Very much so. But I can't think of anyone who'd want to hurt her."

"Except maybe those folks who wanted to buy these ranches."

He started to shake his head. "Why, though? Big companies don't need to stoop to this. Anyway, they could afford a better arsonist."

Lila frowned. "That could be the point."

Mitch felt a punch in his gut that killed his appetite. "Dang, Lila, you have a devious mind."

"Comes from having a devious ex. Get your appetite back, boss. When Grace wakes up this time, she'll probably really need you."

Then she winked. "I need you to take her some of my cinnamon buns. I'll even pack a couple for you."

"Junk food," he teased.

"Not my cinnamon buns. Look, the hospital gives her the healthy stuff if she can eat it. She needs something tasty."

"I doubt she could pick up one. Her hands are bandaged."

"That's why God made you. You can feed her pieces."

He laughed for the first time since the barn caught fire.

He really *did* need some sleep. No avoiding it. After a shower he hit the bed, his mind still racing over all of it. Not for long, though. His body demanded its due, and soon he was carried away on dreams of Grace that at least weren't filled with threat. Sleep brought him a short span of peace.

It was late afternoon when he at last climbed into his truck with the promised cinnamon buns in a plastic container beside him.

He detoured over to Grace's place and was amazed. Those men with loaders had done quite a job. The ground where the old barn had been was flat now. The last bit of detritus from the fire had been carted away some distance. Out of the way, soon to be out of sight. It wouldn't be long before something grew among the rubble, turning the ugliness into a small, living hill.

Nature was a wonderful thing.

* * *

At the hospital, he found Grace considerably more alert, although not her usual self. Still groggy, but awake. She couldn't be comfortable.

She managed a small smile when she saw him. "Mary said you were here most of yesterday and this morning. Mitch, you've got better things to do with your time."

"Nothing more important than you."

"I'm probably blushing, but you can't see it. Red like a lobster already. Sweet of you to say that."

"Just the plain truth. Are you hurting much?"

"Mostly my hands but they won't let me wake up enough to start screaming. Might scare the other patients."

He grinned. "That's my Grace. Say, Lila sent me with a bunch of cinnamon buns. She thinks you need something tasty."

"I do," she admitted. "Jell-O and something like cream of wheat, ugh. Hard for me to eat, though. Spoon only." She held up her hands. "I can't eat one of those buns, Mitch. Couldn't hold one."

"That's what I said until Lila reminded me that God made me to feed you pieces of bun."

A quiet laugh escaped her. Probably didn't want to stretch her face too much.

"She's a gem," Mitch said. "Keeps me in my place."

"Can't be easy."

Mitch laughed. "Nope." He was so damn glad to see her spunk returning he could have done a jig right there. Except he didn't know how.

The door opened and in walked Betty Pollard. "My God, girl," she said without preamble. "I heard about the fire. How are you?" Only then did she say, "Hi, Mitch."

"Betty."

Grace held up her hands. "Pretty good, all things considered."

"How did you get burned?"

"Saving the horses," Mitch answered.

Betty frowned. "I didn't know you had horses."

"They were mine," Mitch answered. "She's damn brave."

"More than brave," Betty agreed. "I don't think you could have gotten me that close. I hate fire."

"Most of us do," Grace answered. "I'm going to be fine."

"I hope so," Betty said sincerely. "But when are you going to listen to me? Out there all alone, now you're burned and how long did it take for help to arrive?"

Grace shook her head slightly. "Only as long as it took Mitch and his men to arrive. I was already coming out of the barn."

A prettier picture than he would have painted, Mitch thought. He remained silent, however. This was Grace's story to tell, and since Betty was *her* friend, Grace had a right to say what she wanted .

"I'm serious, Grace. You need to be in town. Even Mitch is too far away."

"I don't think so," Grace replied. "I'm tired of talking about it, Betty. I don't want to leave my ranch."

Betty frowned but fell silent a beat or two before saying, "Your decision. I just worry about you."

Mitch leaned forward to look at Grace. "I can leave if you two ladies want to talk."

"There's nothing private," Grace said. "Stay, Mitch."

It almost sounded like a command, which surprised him. Well, maybe she wasn't in the mood for pressure from Betty.

Remembering the cinnamon buns, knowing Lila had probably packed enough for six, he said, "Anyone want a cinnamon bun?"

Betty rose. "Thanks, Mitch." Then she moved closer to Grace. "But I have to go meet my boyfriend."

"Sounds like you two are getting serious."

Betty smiled. "Time will tell. I'll come by and see you tomorrow, okay?"

"Sure. I'd like that."

Grace didn't speak for a while after Betty left. "Damn, I wish she'd stop pressuring me to move to town. I know she means well, but lately she's been ramping up. Now, after this, she'll be impossible."

"Can't blame her."

Grace frowned at him. "You, too?"

"Nope," he answered honestly. "I worry, sure. That's why I kept pressing you to take the satellite phone. But everything else is your decision."

Grace sighed. "Thank you. I'm not a baby. I can make my own decisions, even if they're not smart. It's my *right* to be stupid."

Mitch had to laugh again. "I've never heard it put that way before."

"Well, it's true. Making mistakes is how we learn, and we learn better from them than things that go right. I didn't do anything to burn my barn down, so that wasn't even stupidity on my part."

"No, it wasn't," Mitch agreed. He was determined not to tell her about the arson until she got out of here. Assuming Charity didn't show up with questions in the meantime.

He opened up the box of cinnamon buns. He'd been right. There were six huge ones in there. "Now I get to perform my God-given purpose. You ready for some pieces of bun?"

She gave him another small smile. "They *do* sound good. Very good."

"Then hush and save your mouth for eating."

The process was crumbly, spreading crumbs on the front of her gown, but she ate and even laughed once when a larger piece fell on her.

"Woman," he said, "you're going to need a broom and dustpan at this rate."

"Maybe you need to reconsider your purpose."

"Damn, you're something else."

The evening nurse appeared eventually. "How are you feeling?" she asked Grace.

"I hurt," Grace admitted frankly.

"I thought you might. Doctor cut your morphine in half, and it's time for another dose. But if you feel you need more, let me know and I'll call her." Then she injected the morphine into the IV port. "That'll make you groggy. Probably won't knock you out, but it'll probably make you care less."

"That might be good right now."

Mitch waited until the nurse finished checking everything, even brushing crumbs off Grace. He hadn't wanted to do that himself considering where they had landed.

"Mmm, that smells good," the nurse remarked.

Mitch held up the plastic container. "Help yourself."

"You're the devil's right hand, Mitch Cantrell. I'm on a diet. I'll live with just drooling over the aroma."

"Wow," Grace said when the woman had departed. "From a God-given purpose to being the devil's right hand. Quite a fall."

"That's me. Up and down all the time."

It wasn't long before Grace began to doze and told him to go home. "You can't sit here like my babysitter. Enough other people are getting paid to do that."

"I'll see you in the morning, then?"

"I wouldn't miss it."

He went home, feeling considerably better.

Chapter 8

Midmorning, after getting himself filled in on the state of the ranch, Mitch drove over to Grace's to check on the house and make sure no pipe had broken or anything else.

Houses left alone could become a serious headache if no one was there to notice little things.

Before he could go into the house, he noticed a bee-hive of people around the bare earth where the barn had been. Turning off his ignition, he headed on over and was astonished.

Piles of lumber were already stacked in several places. He guessed some of Grace's neighbors had been out getting the wood while the others had cleared the detritus.

He wouldn't have expected anything that fast. His heart swelled. Good neighbors. The best. He walked over to talk with the crowd, to thank them. None of them wanted to be thanked, however.

"Least we could do" seemed to be the common sentiment.

Maybe Olson said it best. "Neighbors gotta come together when there's trouble. We're no earthly use if we don't."

Mitch stayed with them awhile, looking over the plans, having little enough to add. The guys knew what a barn should be, and they were about to give Grace the best.

"You go on to the hospital," Sam West said. "She must be needing a friendly face."

Sam was right, but Mitch hated to leave these folks. They were being so generous, and he wanted to pitch in. He was Grace's neighbor, too.

They seemed about as determined as Lila to get him over to see Grace, and he was glad to go. His worry remained, even though it had been eased. He'd been around too long to believe that matters couldn't go awry.

He smiled, though, as he approached the hospital. Thinking about the barn raising made him feel good. It wouldn't have been surprising if no one had wanted to do it, because Grace rarely needed a barn these days.

He guessed her need didn't enter into it. A neighbor had experienced some major trouble, and they were doing the best thing they could think of to help.

Which made him damn proud to be one of them.

He stopped in the hospital gift shop and bought Grace some flowers, hoping to cheer up her sterile room. While he rode the elevator to her second-floor room, he wondered if he should tell her about the barn. Then he decided against it. It might come better as a surprise, especially since he was convinced she'd object.

He entered Grace's room with a smile and was delighted to see the head of her bed raised, and the blue eyes he liked so much looking bright again. Not as much morphine today.

He carried the flowers to her and set them on the bedside table. "How are you today?"

She smiled back at him. "Much better. The flowers are beautiful, Mitch. That's so sweet of you."

"Momma didn't raise no idiots."

The made her laugh and the sound of it tickled him. "You *are* much better. How are your hands?"

She held them up. They didn't appear to be quite as heavily bandaged. "Painful, but they could be a lot worse. They might let me go home tomorrow."

"That would be wonderful if you can. Lila says she'll come over to look after you."

"That's really not necessary," she argued.

He sighed. "Listen to me. For once in your life, let someone help you. Lila wants to. She offered. If that's too much for your cussedly independent soul, you can come stay at my place. I've got more than enough room."

"But…"

"No buts," he said sternly. "I'd be very surprised if you're out of those bandages tomorrow, and even if you are it's going to be awfully painful to cook or feed yourself. Just, for heaven's sake, let people help you. Have you ever considered that it might make *them* feel good?"

She blinked, clearly taken aback. "Really?"

"Do them a favor. Make them feel good. I doubt they'd like their caring to be rejected, either."

She closed her eyes briefly, then looked at him again. "I hadn't thought of it that way."

"A lot of people don't. They don't want charity, but they forget it's rarely offered grudgingly, and when it's accepted, others can be happy, too."

"Wow," she said quietly.

"Yeah, put that in your pipe and smoke it. Meantime, I'll just sit here and bore you to tears with talk of cows and sheep and horses. About my limit."

She shook her head. "Don't put yourself down. It's like a new mom apologizing for talking endlessly about diapers and feedings and spit-up… All of us talk about the most important things in our lives."

He shook his head. "I ought to make time to start reading books again. Or watching some TV. Then I could tell jokes about the latest reality show."

"You don't watch TV?"

"Occasionally. So occasionally that I can't remember how to operate the clicker."

She laughed.

"Books, on the other hand… I've always loved them, but for the last few years all I seem to have time for is keeping up with journals about the best way to raise cattle and sheep. A bunch of stuff from veterinary schools. That kind of thing."

"Lots of new information?"

He cocked a brow. "Seems like there's always someone with a harebrained idea about how to do something better. It might be better, but I'd like to suggest they come out here and try to apply it to a huge herd of cattle on the range."

She laughed again. "You've still got your sense of humor."

He looked around. "Wasn't aware that I lost it."

Grace was sorry when Mitch left, but she understood. He still had a ranch to oversee. He couldn't possibly sit here for hours trying to amuse her.

But she missed him. Her nurse, Mary, appeared with a pain pill. No more morphine, which was fine with Grace. She hated the way it kept her asleep, even though she had needed it. She didn't like the odd dreams it gave her, though.

Before the pain medication could take effect, she raised her bandaged hands and studied them. They really hurt, and the earlier bandage change along with the ointment they put over her skin hadn't helped. If anything, the pain had become sharper.

Closing her eyes, she hoped the pill would bring some relief.

Which gave her plenty of time to think about events. The barn. The horses. She wanted to cry. She couldn't believe it was an accident, but who would want to do that?

It seemed extreme for some juvenile mischief. Which left what? Who?

She kept coming back to that industrial farm company that had wanted to buy hers and Mitch's land last fall. Would they actually try to burn her out?

She could think of no one else who might want to do such a terrible thing. She lived such a quiet life that she couldn't imagine anyone wanting to do such a thing to her.

It wasn't that terrible things never happened in this county, but other than a few times, the worst she'd ever heard of was a couple of drunken guys getting into it at one of the roadhouses and shooting guns at each other. That was angry, all right.

But overall, folks around here didn't seem drawn to seriously violent acts. Not that they couldn't happen.

She remembered the high, leaping flames. The sound of the horses' terrified screaming. She hoped she never heard that sound again. She hoped that Dolly and Daisy would get over it. They could be as traumatized as people.

Animals didn't forget; they just moved on quicker.

Which might be a good lesson for her.

Mitch was drawing her out. After the last two years, his constant patience and understanding were beginning to pull her out of the dark well she'd fallen into with John's death.

That was something else she'd never forget. Noticing John was late to dinner. Going out to the barn to discover what had preoccupied him.

Finding him dead and already feeling cool to her touch.

The agony that twisted in her gut, the guilt because she hadn't been there. What if she could have helped him?

Even though the doctors said it had been instantaneous, that no one could have done anything, she couldn't quite believe it.

John had been healthy and strong. How could he have been carrying a genetic heart defect all his life? It defied understanding.

Questioning it didn't help one damn thing.

John was gone, and now her barn was gone, as if life were stripping everything from her.

As the pain pill began to take effect, easing her discomfort, she fell into dreams more pleasant than the ones she'd had on morphine. Mitch. Riding a horse with him.

Not everything was bleak.

Sometime during the night, she woke with tears running down her cheeks.

Weeping for the old dreams lost. Weeping for the new ones that couldn't be born.

Chapter 9

Two days later, Mitch picked up Grace from the hospital with her hands still bandaged and a bottle full of pain medication.

"I guess the new rules about pain meds don't apply when you're burned," she remarked as she studied the bottle once they climbed into his truck.

"Haven't you heard?" he asked. "The CDC revised its advisory, saying it was never meant to keep doctors from treating patients as required by good medical practice."

"I guess that means this bottle is okay."

He laughed. "I wouldn't worry about it, Grace. Your doctor prescribed it. Best medical practice in your case."

She returned his laugh with a smile. "I won't argue that it keeps me from screaming sometimes."

"There you go."

He could hardly wait for her to see the barn. He'd

helped some with it yesterday and had enjoyed how fast it was growing. They'd probably get to work on the roof today. Amazing what you could accomplish with a large group of determined people. With people who laughed, joked and even sang sometimes, turning the work into a party.

Then there was the food. The long folding tables were never allowed to become bare. Fantastic home cooking filled them. Maybe Grace would try some. The cooks would undoubtedly press her to eat. That was part of hospitality.

As they approached her ranch, he heard her draw a sharp breath.

"Pain?" he asked immediately.

"No. Mitch, what's that near my house?"

"Well, your neighbors decided you needed a new barn."

"Oh my God," she murmured, her voice barely audible over the roar of his engine and the rattle of everything else. "Oh my God," she repeated more loudly.

"Remember after that tornado years ago? Folks turned up pretty fast to build Orson a new barn."

"But I..."

"What? Your neighbors are giving you a gift."

Grace fell silent and he let her admire the construction as they drew nearer. She probably felt overwhelmed.

As he'd expected, women swarmed the truck as he parked near the barn. They didn't give him a chance to help her out, and insisted she come over to a folding chair near the tables, from where she could see the new barn.

"I can't... What can I say?"

"Nothing," Jenny Wright answered. "We all know

what it means. Now, what are you going to eat, Grace? You must be starved after that hospital food."

Mitch was relieved to hear Grace laugh. Overwhelmed or not, she'd decided to enjoy the generosity. The crew high up on the barn called greetings down to her.

"Leave some food for us," Edgar Cruz shouted. "Almost lunchtime, Grace."

She laughed again as Margie Cruz pressed a full paper plate into her lap. "Can you handle a spoon or fork?"

"I think so. Margie, I can't eat this much."

"Sure you can," Jenny answered. "Just take your time. Nibble away all afternoon. Drink? We got lemonade, iced tea, coffee and some cranberry juice someone sneaked in here."

"Coffee, please. The stuff at the hospital was worse than the food."

Soon a smaller folding table was set up in front of Grace so they could put her plate and drink on it.

"Now, you just relax," Margie said. "Need anything, wave. Enjoy the show. These guys are cutups."

Grace looked at Mitch and he saw the sheen of tears in her eyes to go along with her smile. He asked, "Mind if I go help the crew?"

For once she didn't remind him he had work back at his ranch. He kinda figured his cattle and sheep were capable of grazing without help for a few days.

Soon he climbed a ladder to help with the beginnings of the roof. The labor felt good.

Grace had trouble believing her eyes as she gazed at the new barn and struggled with a spoon to eat the best potato salad she had ever tasted.

These people were amazing. Why had she been avoiding them for so long? She hadn't before John had died, although most didn't have much time for socializing. Too much work.

Their generosity made her eyes well up again. Some of them she'd never had time to get to know much at all, but here they were. Mitch was right—this was a gift.

She didn't deserve it, but that didn't seem to matter to these folks.

And a barn raising seemed to be a party as well as work. They joked as they moved along at astonishing speed. Once they even broke into song, a simple melody that she didn't recognize. At least it made it possible for everyone to join in.

At lunchtime, they didn't all descend to the waiting food, but came in waves as the others continued sawing and pounding nails. They said "hi" or "howdy" to her as they came to the tables and filled paper plates and cups. Then they were happy to settle on the ground to eat, talking about the barn and whatever came next. From time to time smaller knots of them burst into laughter.

Jenny pulled up a chair beside Grace. "They're all having a good time," she remarked. "Not much excuse for a party like this, except for weddings and funerals. You need something else to eat? Maybe you're ready for a piece of cake or cobbler?"

Grace glanced at her plate. "There's still a lot of food."

"So I'll put it in a container for you to eat later. Now, how about that dessert?"

Something sweet sounded great to her, so she opted for the blueberry buckle with a crumb topping. It was a bit difficult for her to eat, unlike the food she'd been able to take on a spoon, but it was soft enough she made her way through it, a bit at a time. Her hands began to hurt seriously again.

Mitch climbed down from the barn. It must be his lunch shift. First he came straight over to her and squatted. "How are you doing?"

"I'm floored. Think I need a pill."

He nodded. "In your bag in the truck, right?"

"Yes. Thank you."

He trotted away. Jenny eyed Grace. "He's a good man."

"I can testify to that."

Mitch came back with her pill bottle and put it on the table.

Jenny rose. "Water or something else? Lemonade?"

"Water, please." Grace looked at Mitch. "I'm about to get a little groggy."

"That's fine. Just enjoy the show. If you get too groggy, let me know. I'll take you home with me. Lila is really impatient to look after you."

Then he left her, going to get his own lunch.

He was indeed a good man.

She swallowed her pill with some of the water Jenny gave her. She followed Mitch's instructions and enjoyed the incredible show.

"Hell," Carl said to Larry. "This ain't gonna convince the woman to move."

Larry agreed as he stared through the binoculars at the quickly rising barn. "Damn," he said. "What was the point of burning it?"

"She *did* have to go to the hospital," Carl said after a minute or so. "Maybe that's enough."

"I wish. She's got nine lives like a cat."

"Boss ain't gonna be happy," Carl grumbled.

"Then maybe she damn well ought to work some on this," said Larry, a layer of taut anger in his voice.

"If she wasn't paying us so good, I'd walk away."

"Yeah," Larry answered. "Are you sure she's gonna give us that money? I don't trust her."

"She'll be one sorry fool if she don't pay up. We can deal with her."

Larry nodded. A look of satisfaction crossed his face. "Yeah, we can."

Midafternoon, Mitch took Grace home with him. She not only looked weary, she appeared to suffer quite some pain. Tomorrow would be better. Bound to be.

Right now she wasn't very far from a bad burn on the very tender palms of her hands.

"I want to go home," she said.

"We can talk about taking you home when those bandages come off." He saw her bristle, then relax. Damn, that woman really bridled when someone else tried to take charge.

When they started up the bumpy drive to his house, she remarked, "I'm supposed to change these bandages every day. No one told me how to do that."

"We'll manage."

"They sure gave me enough rolls of gauze and that gel." Then her head drooped onto her chest.

Mitch smiled faintly. She was more tired than she realized and he was damn glad to be taking her to his house. Lila would mother her despite any protests. His housekeeper could be a bulldozer when she wanted, a quality he didn't always appreciate. But it was what Grace needed now, whether she wanted to admit it or not.

He was willing to bet that somewhere inside that

plastic hospital bag were discharge instructions. He and Lila could ensure that Grace got everything she needed.

How had that woman ever thought she could go home by herself?

Because she could be mulish, pigheaded and so damn independent. All qualities he enjoyed in her. Usually.

Right then, he wasn't admiring them. He kept seeing the fire in his mind's eye, kept seeing her staggering out of that conflagration. He'd have hated it if those horses had died, but he'd have hated it even more if Grace had died.

An ache filled him at the mere thought. He understood why she went in there. Hell, he'd have done it himself. That was somehow different. His heart hurt every time he remembered.

There was no doubt in his mind that Grace would experience another wave of grief as she emerged from the suffering of the last few days. Grief over the loss of her property. Then she'd be afraid, because who would want to do that to her? Finally she'd get angry. Furious.

Rocky days lay ahead.

Maybe two of those pills at a time was too much, Grace thought as Mitch helped her wobble into the house. But oh, they helped the pain. Perhaps tomorrow she'd try to cut back to one. If she was brave enough.

The way she'd been hurting earlier, she doubted it. There were times when courage failed her, and maybe this time it should.

Inside, Lila appeared instantly. "Put Ms. Hall on that recliner nearest the living room door. Unless you'd rather go to bed, dear?"

"No, really…" She wasn't ready for bed. She'd had

enough bed in the hospital to last her for a while. "No bed."

Mitch laughed. "Tired of that, huh? Here we go."

He steadied her while she walked into his living room, then helped ease her into a chair and reclined it.

It had been a long time since she'd been in here, but she remembered the warmth of the decor. She didn't know who had chosen to cover the walls with horizontal knotty pinewood planks, and the floor with darker planks, but the room was inviting. Mitch had a couple of plaid recliners in dark green and burgundy, as well as a few other chairs upholstered in hunter green.

A huge fireplace dominated, surrounded in natural rock with a thick, rustic piece of wood serving as a mantel. The room had a very Western feel to it unlike the living room in her own house, which sported some very old wallpaper. Their homes spoke of very different tastes.

Both were welcoming.

Lila soon placed a hot cup of coffee beside her, and tossed a light knitted throw over her legs. "You'll get a bit cold if you're not moving around."

"I feel wrapped up like a baby," Grace said.

Lila smiled. "Good. Now you just rest a bit. I need to finish making dinner."

Grace wasn't sure what time she woke, but she knew one thing: her hands hurt as if they were burning all over again. She couldn't prevent the groan that escaped her.

She opened her eyes, longing to escape everything. Then Mitch appeared, bending over her. Without a word, he slipped his arm behind her shoulders and lifted her to a seated position.

"Hold this," he said quietly.

She looked down and saw an open bottle of water. She took it between her hands. It was wet and her mouth felt as if she'd been eating dust. She raised it quickly and drank deeply, ignoring the water that dripped down her chin. She must have drained half the bottle before she took a breath.

"Now, here," he said, holding her prescription bottle in front of her. "I know you can take these with some effort, but why don't you just let me pop them in your mouth?"

She opened her mouth to say she could do it, but immediately felt two pills on her tongue. Well, now she *had* to drink.

With the pills washed down, she said, "You're the devil after all."

He chuckled. "Guilty. You want me to raise the back of the chair?"

As she felt his arm slip away, she wished he'd continue to hold her. How long had it been since anyone had held her?

As soon as she met the back of the recliner, she knew the answer to his question. "Up, please."

He reached for the control switch on the end table beside her and raised her as smoothly and easily as if she was on a hospital bed.

How had she missed that earlier? Probably because she'd been so weary.

Mitch backed away and tugged one of the upright chairs over so he could sit facing her.

"Hurting?" he asked.

"A little," she allowed, then wondered why she was lying. He'd just put two pain pills in her mouth. He already knew the answer. "I hurt like hell. When I woke I wanted to run from my body."

"That's awful," he said. He leaned forward, took the water bottle from her and placed it on the end table. Then he put his elbows on his knees. "Just take a few to wake up and let those pills start working. Then we can discuss dinner."

Dinner? The last thing she felt like doing was eating. The pain from her hands seemed to be shooting up her arms, like a living monster. This hurt worse than when she was in the hospital. Then she realized she'd probably been on something stronger than what was in the prescription bottle.

"It shouldn't take longer than twenty minutes for the pills to start working," Mitch said. "God knows I've had them a few times myself."

Seeking distraction, Grace asked, "What for?"

"You really want the laundry list?" He sounded amused.

"I don't know much about your life before we met."

"True, I guess. I'm mostly forward-looking. Well, let me see. There was the time I got thrown by my mount, landed on some rocks and broke nearly half of the bones on my left side. I was twelve at the time, stuck in a bunch of casts, needing some surgery to put in pins."

She drew a breath. "That bad?"

"I was good at accidents around that age. One of the worst was when I fell from the barn loft and broke my wrist. Damn thing was at an angle no arm ought to be. To get it back in line to be set, they had to put this torture device on me, pulling all my fingers hard while I did some caterwauling." He shook his head. "That's on the top of my list for miserable experiences. Cracked ribs hurt pretty bad, too."

"It sounds terrible." She felt the first stirrings of relief from the medicine. Thank God. "Accidents, huh?"

He shrugged. "Let a young boy loose on a ranch, and he'll find some trouble. Fell into a pile of barbed wire once. Took my dad and two of his men close to an hour to cut me loose."

"How in the world did that happen?"

"I was running and tripped. I also wasn't being very cautious. Should have picked a better place to run."

"Like you'd have been thinking about that when you were so young."

"That's how the young get some sense," he answered. "From mistakes. My dad took it in stride. Mostly. The time I got thrown he wasn't completely sympathetic. A boy on a ranch ought to know how to keep his seat better. Doesn't matter if a snake terrified the horse."

"So you fell near a *snake*? And I suppose you were too hurt to move?" The idea was scary.

Another smile appeared. "My mare kinda took care of that. Wasn't much snake left after she trampled it good."

"So that's why the horse was bucking?"

"Yup. She saved both of us by killing it. Then she nuzzled me a time or two. My memory isn't completely clear. After that she took off hell for leather back home. Let my dad know I was in trouble, then brought him to me."

Grace thought about that as the pill begin to soften her pain. "I always suspected horses were smarter than we know."

"I couldn't agree more. She was a good old mare. And my dad was right about keeping my seat. It kinda stung when he said I didn't have as much sense as my horse."

Grace laughed. "That *would* sting."

"When you're twelve? Yeah. I had to admit Baby was getting skittish and I didn't pay attention, just kept guiding her into danger. More sense than me for sure."

"Horses will die for us," she remarked.

"They sure will. Run themselves to death if we demand it. Go straight into battle." He paused. "Feeling any better?"

"Think so. I'm getting a bit muzzy."

"How about some coffee? Lila always has a fresh pot. After, we can talk about what you feel like eating."

Coffee sounded good. It might even keep her from falling asleep. "Please."

She hoped she'd be able to hold it between her hands. It had worked earlier at the barn raising She'd even managed a spoon. Basically she was working with two hands formed into claws.

Much as she hated to admit it, she was very glad Mitch had brought her home with him. She couldn't imagine taking care of herself right now without help. She just hoped having her here wouldn't burden anyone.

Mitch returned in quick order with a brushed steel mug. "It's insulated, so be careful when you sip. The coffee's a little hotter than my tongue would like."

"No more burns for me, thank you very much."

She was able to hold the mug between both her hands and draw in the aroma. Rich and nutty. He was right about the heat, though. She could feel it as she carried the cup closer to her face.

"It won't cool as fast in that mug," he said. "You already know that. Whole reason I got a cupboard full of them."

"I have a few, too. But they have tops."

"So does that one, but I didn't want you to take a

swig before you knew what you were getting into." He pulled a top out of his breast pocket. "When you think it's cool enough, I'll put this on."

He was so considerate, Grace thought. Little seemed to escape him.

A few minutes later, she brought the mug up and tested it with her lip. "I think it's ready."

He took the cup and pressed the top on it. "There you go."

She accepted it and tasted the coffee, savoring it. Just what she needed.

"Now to dinner," he said. "Lila made a great one, but she always does. She was thinking of you, too. Not much that you can't eat with a spoon."

All this caring might overwhelm her. She said so.

"Like I care? Damn, woman, I'm just thrilled you're alive. Let me know when you're ready to eat."

A while later he said, "Lila went over to your house to get you some night things and a few fresh changes of clothes. She also said when you're ready she'll give you a sponge bath."

"Oh my God," Grace answered, her cheeks heating. "That's too—"

"Too much," he interrupted. "I know. Let me remind you she's taken care of a family and she volunteered. Besides, in a day or two you're going to start feeling like something that needs to be mucked out of a stall."

That actually made her laugh. "You're awful, Mitch."

"I work on it." He flashed another grin. "Much better than Lila telling me I have a God-given purpose. I don't see ranching that way. It's a job, like any other. I'm just luckier than most."

She shook her head. "You do a great job looking after your animals. That's not all luck."

"Maybe not, but I've got this big spread. My great-granddaddy left it behind. Dad and I always felt lucky. You gotta have the land and this is damn fine land."

She knew it was true. Her own place was blessed with enough water unlike so many around here. She and John had definitely been lucky to get it at auction for such a good price. Otherwise they'd never have had their flock, their life together on the land.

A wave of sorrow passed through her, then released her. She sipped more coffee and realized she wasn't getting as sleepy on the pills as before. Getting used to them?

Then she noticed she was getting hungry.

As if reading her mind, Mitch asked, "Getting hungry now?"

"Amazingly, yes."

He nodded. "Good. Lila would be upset if you didn't eat at least a little of her chefery. I can recommend the stone soup. Easy to eat with a spoon."

"Stone soup? Really?" There couldn't be stones in it.

"That's what she calls it. A bit of most of what she has in the fridge and the cupboards. Trust me, it's always an adventure and surprising how she can make all that taste good."

He frowned a little, evidently in thought. "There's some mashed potatoes. Some fruit salad that has pieces small enough to eat with a spoon. That salad is the best. She makes it from fresh fruit."

Grace was impressed with the splendid smorgasbord he offered her. "You choose," she said after a moment. "I can't decide. Everything sounds good, even stone soup."

He chuckled at that. "I know. Really? All right, I'll come back with the first course."

He paused in the doorway, looking back at her. "Like I said, she was thinking of you when she made dinner. Small pieces."

Grace was touched, if a little embarrassed that the woman had gone out of her way. This was the kind of thing she always tried to avoid.

Mitch returned with a deep bowl, not a soup plate, putting it on a TV table in front of her. Beside it he placed a napkin and spoon.

"Don't worry if you dribble a bit," he said. "Whenever I eat soup, I always swear there's a hole in my lip."

That relaxed her because she shared the feeling. Before she began to eat, she took the napkin and tucked it in to her collar as best she could.

"Good idea," Mitch remarked. "I've often talked about finding an adult-sized bib."

The soup was every bit as delicious as he'd promised. Grace had no idea what Lila had cobbled together, but it was the best soup she'd ever tasted.

Shortly after she finished, however, she fell asleep sitting up.

Her day was done.

Chapter 10

Over the next few days, Grace came to accept that she couldn't have gone home by herself. Lila took over her bandaging according to Grace's discharge instructions, patiently smearing on the gel. At last the day arrived that her fingers could all be bound separately. What a relief!

Lila would sit with her for a while, chatting about irrelevancies, then head back to her domain, the kitchen. Marvelous food came out of that kitchen, every kind of baked good, from croissants to pies and cobblers. Grace was sure she was going to plump up.

Mitch went out every day to look after his operation and to help finish her new barn. She still couldn't get over that. How had she come to have such good neighbors?

"It's simple," Mitch answered when she mentioned it. "You're part of the ranchers' family. All of us are."

Mitch had taken to eating his meals with her. As she had begun to back off her pain medication, she joined him in the kitchen, sometimes with Bill and sometimes with all three of the hired hands. Conversation was generally light, mostly talk about cattle. Grace listened eagerly, feeling she had stepped back into part of the life she had lost.

Then Bill said, "Grace, your new barn is finished. I hope you'll get to see it soon. It's so great that I'm thinking we ought to burn down ours."

"Don't you dare," Mitch said with a laugh.

Bill and the others laughed with him.

The roast beef was perfectly done, the mashed potatoes a scoop of heaven and the broccoli impeccably cooked. "You're a wizard, Lila," she offered sincerely.

"Just you wait until I really rev up. Bet these guys never expected to eat fancy cooking."

"This is pretty fancy," Bill remarked.

Grace watched Bill and Lila, thinking that Mitch might be right about the two of them. Something in the way they looked at each other. She dipped into the food on her plate again, savoring every mouthful and enjoying having nearly functional fingers again.

The mess on her hands, which she saw every time Lila changed her bandages, was bad but healing. She suspected that they were going to be tender for some time to come. That was down the road, however, and she was enjoying being able to hold a fork again, even if not the way she used to.

"Tell me about the barn, please," she asked when the conversation flagged. The four men were clearly on a wavelength together, an easy flow of talk between them. She enjoyed listening but was still curious.

"It's something to behold," Jeff said. "Don't see too

many new barns in these parts. Almost a shame it'll have to be painted."

Painted? Grace hadn't thought about that, and her stomach sank a bit. Paint for a building that big would be monstrously expensive.

"Or," Mitch interjected, "she could just let it age awhile. Maybe until the wood silvers a bit."

Jack laughed. Bill answered, "Boss, you know how long it takes for wood to do that?"

"I do. I also know how a freshly painted barn would look in these parts. Like a damn lighthouse."

Grace laughed, too. He was right about that. Her own barn, the one that had burned, had been all silvered with age but still usable. How many years ago had it been built? She had no idea.

Jeff spoke again. "Aw. Here I was thinking we could gussy it up with some bright red paint. White trim."

Jack looked at him. "You want to go all New England?"

"Hey," Jeff answered. "These days most new barns look like Quonset huts, all built out of steel. Which doesn't last as long, you ask me."

"Don't believe I did," Jack retorted.

Another round of laughter ringed the table.

"Well, I never did like rust all that much," Jack continued. "Whatever they make them barns out of, it still rusts eventually. Like those the ones you got to park all the heavy equipment and vehicles in."

"Then don't burn my wood barn down," Mitch said. "Otherwise you'll be patching metal more of the time."

Jack feigned a frown. "I stay on a horse better than a ladder."

More laughter. Grace thought about how easy it

would be to slip into this camaraderie and forget everything else. It wrapped around her like a warm blanket.

After dinner, Lila settled her back in the recliner with a hot cup of coffee and a piece of peach pie. Grace wished she could help the others with cleanup, but that was impossible right now.

Still, she apologized to Lila. "I'm sorry I can't help with the dishes."

Lila put her hands on her hips. "I got four healthy men out there taking care of it, and well they should, if they want me to keep cooking. Besides…"

Lila's face softened. "Honey, you ain't gonna be doing much with those hands for a while. Even after the bandages come off, they won't like hot water. And I *really* don't want my pots and pans washed in cold water. Like I need to tell you that."

Lila sailed away, probably to spend more time around Bill.

Grace looked at her hands. Lila was right. She'd had burns before, much smaller, but hot water was like holding a match to them. God, would she ever be able to stand on her own two feet again?

Time passed, although far too slowly for Grace. The days fell into a routine: breakfast in the kitchen, usually with Lila and Mitch, then Mitch setting out for a day of work. Before long, Grace would be settled in the living room with a cup of coffee, the TV remote and a book.

Despite what Mitch had said about watching TV so rarely he couldn't find the remote, there was a large flat-screen enthroned over the fireplace. Not that she'd ever seen Mitch turn it on, and she wasn't inclined to. Daytime TV rarely offered her anything she cared to watch. She knew because she'd tried it for a while after

John's death, seeking distraction. However, it hadn't provided any.

Her own channel selection had been limited, but Mitch had a satellite dish out back that looked big enough to track the stars.

The thought amused her. A remnant from years past, she supposed, that still worked.

Time dragged anyway. Holding a book fatigued her sore hands rapidly. She still took a pain pill from time to time but they no longer made her sleepy. God, why had she never appreciated how much hands did? How often they were needed even for the simplest things.

She had begun to take walks outside. Sitting around so much was weakening her, and stretching her muscles felt good. The sun kissed her skin with heat, the breeze tossed her hair around, but before long her eyes began to water. The sun was too bright. Damn, she needed a cap of some kind. Sunglasses. Blue eyes sucked when the sun was really bright. An eye doctor had told her once that they didn't block the light as well as darker eyes.

Before, she'd been mostly content with solitude. Now she found herself eagerly anticipating Mitch's appearance in the late afternoons. He'd shower, then come to keep her company.

The amazing thing was that he hadn't become bored with her. Instead he'd sit with her, telling her about his day, asking her about hers. She rarely had anything to offer, but he could make amusing stories out of the mundane matters of operating a cattle ranch. Or some story about what the sheep were up to.

Listening to Mitch, she wondered why she'd never noticed the sheep antics he reported. Maybe she hadn't been paying close enough attention.

"The spring lambs are developing a real sense of

adventure," he told her. "Into everything, according to Zeke and Rod. You'd think they were young goats."

"Really?" she asked. "I never noticed that."

"You aren't Zeke and Rod. They live with that flock. They've had to rescue youngsters who tried to leap barbed wire."

Grace sat up a little straighter. "That's hard to believe."

"Feeling their oats, I guess. Their wool is growing in and they get caught easier. Zeke said the ewes are forever trying to round them up, but this group is really adventurous. He says they aren't moving with the flock, the way sheep usually do. He and Rod are getting frustrated. I got the word again that they need a dog. Sure sounds like it. You can't run fast enough to keep up with that crowd."

"Amazing. I never guessed."

"Neither did I, and I've been watching over that group for a little more than a year now. I get them enjoying running around, burning off all that youthful energy. Kinda like puppies. But trying to jump fences?" Mitch shook his head in disbelief. "I wonder if a goat or two got in there during mating season. Although I have no idea where a goat could have come from."

"Me, neither. I always wanted goats, but we couldn't because they need special fencing so they can't get out. Plus the cost of supplements was just too high. Maybe we should have just put up the fence anyway."

Mitch flashed a grin. "I'm thinking they'll settle down. I hope they will. And I've still got to look into a herding dog or two. I talked to Ransom Laird and he has some puppies who are being trained by his older dogs, but it'll be a little while yet before they're ready."

Grace nodded. "Didn't you use to have some dogs?"

"I still do. Out on the range. Mainly they keep wolves and other predators away. Never trained them for sheep."

"Was there ever a wolf problem here?" She'd never heard anything about it.

"Not in my lifetime. Some ranchers closer to Yellowstone claim to see them once in a while. Frankly, wolves aren't overpopulating the place. More trouble from coyotes, especially with spring lambs."

"That was our experience, too." She hesitated, gnawing her lower lip. "Mitch?"

"Yeah?"

"I've been trying not to think about it, but why would somebody burn down my barn? Or maybe more important, who would want to? I honestly can't quite believe it was the industrial farming company. They must have better ways of taking over land."

He nodded slowly. "I can't get it off my mind, either. I also can't figure it. Unless some firebug just wanted a big blaze."

Grace didn't like that idea at all. The randomness of that disturbed her deeply. Maybe because she needed a reason for most everything. "Coming so soon after that ewe was shot only bothers me more."

"Me, too," he admitted.

Grace was glad he didn't dismiss her worries. Much as she'd been trying not to build a massive case of anxiety, the anxiety remained anyway.

She closed her eyes briefly, remembering that night, the impossibly high flames, the screaming horses. She shuddered. "I'm going to have some bad dreams for a while."

"Understandable." He'd brought the inevitable cup of coffee in with him, and reached for it now, taking a couple of swigs. "It feels like beating my head on an invisible brick wall. I want answers. Seems like I'm not going to get any soon."

"I hate that," she admitted.

"You ain't the only one." He paused. "I've got all my men keeping an eye out for anything suspicious. I'm not ready to move on as if this is nothing but chance."

"I don't think I can."

His gray eyes met hers. "Grace, understand that I'll do anything to protect you."

The words caused her breath to catch in her throat, followed by the burn of unshed tears. His concern wrapped around her, answering an ache she hadn't even realized was there.

She looked away, swallowing hard. His statement had opened something inside her. It had been a long time since she'd felt such honest concern. Maybe Mitch had been offering it all along and she hadn't been paying attention.

Why would she? Grief had consumed her. Her entire life had become one of fighting to save what she could of her dream, leaving no room for anything else. She'd been obstinate and blind in her determination to stand alone, feeling she owed it to John.

Words couldn't convey the unexpected, hungry need that roiled inside her. How much had she missed having someone give a damn about her feelings and her needs? These moments told her that while she was mostly introverted, she still needed something more in her life.

Mitch's kindness reached beyond an ordinary friendship. He was offering something a whole lot bigger.

"Thank you," she answered, her voice thick.

"Hey," he said quietly. "I didn't mean to make you sad."

"You didn't." She turned her face back to him. "You…just made me feel special."

He smiled slightly. "Good. Because you're one hell of special woman. Stubborn as hell, but still special."

That drew a choked laugh from her. "I was just thinking about my stubbornness."

"I hope we've gotten you a little past that. The new barn and all."

"And taking care of me here."

He feigned astonishment. "I value my skin. Lila would have taken a piece of my hide if I'd done any less."

He'd lightened the moment, for which she was grateful. She seemed to be losing her balance somehow. Falling off the tightrope of emotion she'd been walking for so long.

Maybe she ought to excuse herself. The barn, her injuries, her steady but slow recovery, the mess all this had made of her usual life… Plenty of reason to feel shaky emotionally.

It wasn't just that. Who would have guessed that emerging from long stasis could feel so painful? Far from feeling as if she were coming out of a long nightmare, she felt as if her protective layer was being stripped away. It hurt.

"Ah," Mitch sighed. A few moments later he rose. "More coffee? Mine's cold. Or something stronger?"

"Coffee, please." She wasn't sure how alcohol would mesh with the pain pill she'd taken two hours ago. Because her dang hands had started to seriously hurt again. As if the bandages were irritating them now.

She rested her head back against the chair while he went to the kitchen, trying to quash the feeling that he'd just offered her a gift she wanted badly to accept. All he'd said was that he'd do anything to protect her.

Simple words, a strong promise, leaving her exposed like a raw nerve ending. Worse, she now had to face the gaping holes she'd dug in her own life. Not just missing John, but burying herself alive.

Damn, she couldn't deal with this right now. No way. Bad enough that she was wondering who had hung this sword over her head and what might be coming her way.

Because deep inside, she didn't believe the barn was the end of it.

"You guys gotta do better," the boss told them over the phone they'd put on speaker. "I don't see any sign of the Hall woman hightailing it."

"She ain't home," Carl argued. "She's living with that Cantrell guy now, and she ain't showing any sign of going home."

"Damn Cantrell," the boss said. "Damn him to hell. Why is he getting involved?"

Neither Carl nor Larry had an answer for that.

The boss nearly snarled. "You gotta scare her more. Figure it out. But not too soon. Too soon and we blow it. Just remember, if she doesn't leave, you don't get paid the rest."

Both Larry and Carl were aware of the money that she'd dangled before them. A small down payment to be followed by an appreciable sum when their job was complete. But damn, this was taking an awful long time. Who'd have thought some damn woman could be this stupid. Or this stubborn.

It wasn't at all the way that Larry and Carl thought of gals.

* * *

As the evening deepened, Grace circled around once again to her fears. Or maybe concerns. She'd rather not think she was afraid.

"Someone had to have done it," she said yet again. The uneasiness wouldn't back off.

"The fire, you mean? Well, yeah."

She nearly sighed. "And the ewe. You know what I'm talking about. They could be linked."

"I know."

He didn't dismiss her worry and she was thankful. Over the years, being a woman, she'd been dismissed many times, especially when something bothered her. As if her feelings didn't count.

She spoke again. "I keep thinking of that industrial operation. I can't get it out of my head, even though I also can't quite believe it. Great way to get me to sell and leave you their only problem."

He nodded slowly. "I've been thinking about them, too. Doesn't make sense to me, but they keep popping up. Thing is, I've been too busy worrying about you lately to do what I should have."

Her heart quickened a bit. "What's that?"

"Call the sheriff and tell him I've got this suspicion. If anyone can find out if that company has left a trail of fires or anything else shady in their wake, the sheriff's office can."

"I hope so. I wouldn't know where to begin. You don't have to worry yourself over me."

He spoke firmly. "Someone has to."

Again that rending inside of her, opening like a door closed too long. Squeaky and creaky as it pulled away from its frame on unoiled hinges.

She cleared her throat. "Thanks for not thinking I'm being silly."

"Why in the hell would I do that? The ewe incident might have been one jerk being stupid beyond belief. But the barn? One plus one equals two. Or three, depending on how you count on your fingers."

That made her laugh again. "Thanks."

Mitch was enjoying having her in his house, and definitely enjoying how she was laughing more. The sound had been absent from her for so long. Her face lit up and she became more than pretty. She became beautiful. Sometimes he just wanted to feast his eyes on her but resisted the urge. He didn't want to make her uncomfortable.

Why would she suspect that he might find her silly for her worries? Even had he not agreed with her, he never would have thought that. There was nothing about Grace that anyone could call silly.

He wished he could heal her hands with a magic wand. It hurt him to see her bandaged like that and to know that when the bandages came off her hands would be painfully tender. It might be a while before she could do simple things, like hold something heavy, or endure her palms rubbing on anything. And forget hot water.

He focused instead on the courage that had led her into a burning barn to save the horses. Amazing woman.

Thinking about that night led him to say, "I've got some free time in the morning. Want to see Dolly and Daisy? They're out in the far paddock."

"I'd love to see them!"

He smiled. "Then we'll drive over to see your new barn. You can also decide if you want it painted."

She laughed again. "I take it no red?"

"Only if you want to become a local landmark."

Her grin widened. "I think I already am, given that there aren't too many newly constructed barns out there."

"Eighth wonder of the world. You'll be attracting tourists before you know it. Crowds will come from all over the county, rarely having seen a brand-new wood barn."

The idea clearly amused her.

"How are your hands feeling?" he asked.

She waved one at him. "Painful. I'm sure sick of the bandages."

"I can imagine. Consider them to be protective gloves."

She frowned a little. "I hate to think what it's going to be like when they get unwrapped for good. I've had burns before."

"Yeah. Well, since I don't have a magic wand, how about you stay here for a bit? You're not going to manage well on your own for a few weeks." Then he added, "I'm still astonished that you ran into that barn."

"I couldn't do anything else." Her expression turned sober. "Mitch, it would have been awful to let those horses burn. I couldn't do it. I'm sure you'd have done the same thing."

"Maybe. I've never had to. Probably a reason I'm not a fireman."

She shook her head. "Quit being so modest."

At least she didn't pursue that. He doubted he could have stood the embarrassment.

Needing to change the subject, he asked, "Wanna watch some TV?"

She dropped her somber mood and her face relaxed.

"Hey, aren't you the guy who said he didn't care for it? The guy who said he couldn't find the remote?"

He pointed to the table beside her. "I think Lila found it when she was cleaning."

"Does she find everything for you?"

"More than I'd like sometimes. Seriously, it was up on the mantel. I've got little use for it."

"You, the guy with the huge satellite dish out back."

He laughed. "Blame my dad. Man, he wanted those sports shows come the weekend. That thing is a dinosaur."

"Bet it picks up radio signals from distant galaxies."

"I've never checked, but maybe I should donate it to the Smithsonian."

"Or to some observatory," she teased.

God, it was good to see her spirits this high. Tread carefully, he warned himself. Don't say anything that might sadden her again.

He knew that she was always tipping toward grief. Always. That was another thing that made him wish for a magic wand. With John she had been happy most of the time. He could understand why John's death had gutted her. Eventually, though, everyone had to move on.

Grief would always be with her, but it didn't have to smother her. It didn't have to penetrate her every day and control her. But how did you make someone see that?

Only Grace could do that. When the time for her was right.

Later she dozed off. Clearly still recovering from her harrowing experience and her burns. He found a throw and gently draped it over her. His mother had crocheted that throw, one of the good memories about the brief time he'd had with her. She'd died from breast cancer when he was six, but he could still remember her sitting in her rocking chair and working that crochet needle all evening while talking to him and his dad.

He walked quietly to the kitchen to grab a beer, then came back to the living room to stand at the front window. It had never been covered with curtains because this far out, the likelihood of anyone traipsing here to peer in was minuscule.

Next, he grabbed a few of his journals and magazines from his office and settled in to read.

Oh, yeah, he thought. The dogs. A couple more months, Ransom Laird had said. By then autumn would be creeping in with winter hard on its tail. The sheep would be heading to their fold as the cold winds began to blow. The shepherds had a small house for protection and warmth as they continued their duties. And the dogs? He'd have to ask about that.

This sheep thing was still very new to him. He was grateful for a couple of guys from Portugal whose knowledge appeared to be bottomless. Best investment he could have made.

Mitch almost laughed at himself as he sipped his beer. Those guys allowed him to look confident whenever he was asked about the venture. But mainly they prevented him from doing something stupid that might harm the sheep.

Then there was Grace, whose pretty head probably held a wealth of knowledge about sheep. He should have asked her but didn't want to jar her into unhappy memories.

He turned to look over at her as she slept. He wouldn't mind that view for a long time to come. Then he forced his attention back to his reading material.

Chapter 11

In the morning, Grace was eager to take the drive Mitch had promised.

Well, of course, Mitch thought. She must be awfully tired of the inside of his house and walks around the outside of it. His front yard wasn't much of a yard, rather a scrubby patch that hadn't been good enough to graze.

Out back were the barely discernible remains of his mother's kitchen garden, once always brimming with vegetables throughout the growing season, followed later by endless days of canning and freezing. Now it had become a weed patch through which could be seen the vestiges of once-neat rows.

One of his favorite memories was of the end of the growing season when she'd say, "Get out back and eat some of them tomatoes, boy. Can't can 'em all."

Nothing, he believed, could quite measure up to a warm, sun-kissed tomato right off the vine. He ate himself sick. Then it was over, cold weather moving in again.

He recalled the year when she let him choose any vegetable he wanted to grow, and how astonished she'd been when he'd picked radishes.

What had sent him down this particular path of memory?

Over scrambled eggs and bacon, he watched Grace chat with Lila about inconsequential matters. He enjoyed her animation, her hands gesturing as she spoke. He hadn't seen her like this since his last visit before John died.

He wished the mood would last.

A short time later, she got into his pickup truck with him and they set out on their minor adventure. "We'll go see Dolly and Daisy when we get back."

"Okay."

He suspected she was about ready to bounce on her seat.

After twenty minutes or so, her barn emerged from behind the rolling land.

"Oh man," she said quietly as she took it in. "Oh man."

He unbuckled her seat belt, then leaned across her to open the door. As soon as she could slip out of the truck, she hurried toward the barn.

It was a beautiful construct, rising as high as her old barn, maybe higher. As soon as he caught up to her, he opened the huge door to let her in.

"Oh man," she said again. Six stalls, three on each side, stood ready for horses. At the back could be seen a work room and a tack room. Overhead, a loft for storage.

Grace spoke again. "Smell the wood. Oh, I love the smell of fresh lumber."

He did, too. He inhaled the scent and thought his neighbors were a pretty damn good bunch of people.

When she looked at Mitch again, there was no mistaking the sheen of tears in her eyes. "It's beautiful. How do I ever thank everyone, Mitch?"

"I believe they know without being told."

"I sure hope so. Maybe when my hands are better I can hold a barbecue."

"They'd like that. Everyone out here loves a good excuse for a shindig and a day away from work. You must remember that."

She whirled around with her arms extended. "It's more than beautiful, it's perfect." Then she laughed. "I need some horses in here. Well, maybe not for a while."

"And a decent pair of work gloves," he reminded her.

That drew another laugh from her. "They even put in some small windows."

"Well, ya gotta be able to see in here. At least when the sun is bright. You don't want to be burning lights all the time."

"I wish…" She fell silent.

He knew what she wished. That she could share this with John. Hadn't this woman been kicked around enough, at least for a while? He ached to make her life better, happier.

For now, she *was* happy. Thrilled even. And it hadn't taken a piece of fancy jewelry and a dozen roses to make her feel this way. No, a barn, and one that she really didn't have use for at present.

The glow in her face was lovely. He hoped it would remain a little longer.

She ran the length of the barn and back, as excited as a kid on Christmas. "I can't believe this."

"Believe it. Touch it if you have to."

She just shook her head, joy written all over her. "Let's go to the house," she suggested. "I need to make sure everything's okay."

"Lila's been over here every few days."

"I know, but I still need to look around."

That made sense to Mitch. It was her home, one she and John had shared for nearly a decade. The sights and smells would be familiar and welcoming.

They walked together over to her house, leaving behind the smell of fresh wood. There was still a spring to Grace's step, for which Mitch was grateful. At last something had truly cheered her up.

He followed her more slowly, wanting to give her time to feel at home again. Like most folks around here, she probably hadn't locked her door.

The he heard her cry, "Oh my God, oh my God."

Mitch hit a full run, reaching her door in seconds. Grace had collapsed on her floor, and his heart started skipping wildly. The front door was busted in.

Then he saw her living room and, through the open doorway, her kitchen.

Her house had been trashed.

Chapter 12

Mitch hurried to Grace, instantly worried that the fall might have harmed her. "You hurt anywhere?"

"No…" Her voice broke, barely audible as she gasped for air, and a huge tremor ripped through her.

Mitch picked her up, holding her close and hugging her tightly. Her body shook as she sobbed violently. She'd reached her breaking point. His mind skittered around uselessly, desperate for a way to help her.

"Why, Mitch? Why?"

He couldn't answer that. There was no answer he could give that wasn't a lie. She clung to him as best she could, but he had no intention of letting her go. Giving her comfort with his embrace was all he *could* do.

"Let's go outside," he suggested when her sobbing began to ease.

"I need to look," she said brokenly.

"We shouldn't touch anything. I'll call the cops. Please, Grace."

She let him keep an arm around her waist, to steady her. Her feet proved unstable and he wondered how much her hands were going to hurt after falling on them. Right then she was in too much shock to notice.

Anger burned in him once he had her settled in one of the chairs on her porch. Who the hell would do something like this? Remembering all the things that had happened to her, he decided it felt like a siege. But why?

Then he did the only thing he could. He pulled the satellite phone off his belt and called the sheriff.

Velma, the dispatcher, answered immediately.

Mitch spoke right away. "Someone trashed the inside of Grace Hall's house. It may have been a robbery."

"Fifteen or twenty minutes," Velma answered promptly, wasting no words. "Don't touch anything."

He squatted, placing a hand on Grace's shoulder, feeling the tremors that still rippled through her. Whatever was going on, it was snowballing, racing down a mountainside. He hoped like hell that there wasn't more to come.

Next, Grace would want to stay to clean up. He knew this woman. Ten years of friendship had taught him a lot about her. She'd emerge from this shock with her backbone stiff and angry determination driving her. She wasn't going to leave after this. No way. She'd want to protect her house. The ragged ends of a dream.

The thought of leaving her here alone was more than he could bear. She wasn't going to feel safe, maybe never again, unless they caught whoever had done this. Hell, he wasn't going to *believe* she was safe until this all got sorted out.

Anger simmered in him until it erupted into rage.

At this point he could have cheerfully killed the perp without a bit of guilt.

He had something more important to think about. He dropped to his knees beside her. Tears still rolled down her cheeks. His rage turned into a deep-seated ache for her, a compression of his chest so powerful it hurt.

"Don't leave me, Mitch."

"I won't." Not ever, but certainly not right now. He dared to squeeze her forearm gently. "I'm right here. I'll be here as long as you want me."

She nodded, closing her eyes as more tears fell. "What did I do wrong?"

Oh, God, he didn't want her to think that way, to blame herself. "Nothing," he said firmly. "Not one damn thing."

"I must have done something!" Her voice broke.

"How could you have done anything? You've locked yourself away for damn near two years. Anyone who had a grudge would have long since cooled down. I seriously doubt you and John could have upset anyone. You were both tied up most of the time with your sheep."

Ranchers of any kind rarely went to town except to get supplies or go to church. The rest of the time they kept their noses to the grindstone. John and Grace had been no different. Even back when they'd been able to afford a couple of hired hands, they didn't leave for long. There was too much work to be done. Always.

Grace calmed down, a little at a time, and finally fell still and silent, staring out over the open land toward the mountains. From here they looked closer than they really were, their purpled slopes looming over the county.

Mitch got off his knees and sat cross-legged beside her, waiting for whatever came next. Anger, now accompanied by fear for Grace, whipped at him. What would come next?

He knew Grace would be hit with a whirlwind of re-actions when the shock passed. Fear was going to lash her, the way it did him. But Grace wouldn't knuckle under to it. Not Grace. She'd try to turn her back on it, and nurture her anger the way she had her grief. She'd want to get whoever had done this, not allowing anything to halt her.

She would certainly see that the killing of the ewe couldn't have been isolated, nor the barn fire, not when compounded with the ransacking of her house. She would feel she was being targeted and he wouldn't be able to disagree.

She'd wonder why forever, and so would he. The damn cops better solve this one. He didn't want her to be shadowed by this, nor did he want her to run away, giving up everything she'd been hanging on to.

At last he heard sirens coming their way. Sirens seemed a little much given that no life was in danger and the back roads around here were pretty much empty most of the time. Still, they were coming as fast as they could.

Because most of them knew Grace, knew of her troubles and her solitariness out here. They wouldn't allow her to sit amid the shambles if they could arrive faster. The flashing blue and white lights turned into her driveway, sirens silenced. Three cars and a crime scene van. The perpetrators better not be hanging around anywhere nearby.

He rose, remarking uselessly, "They're here." The silence had grown too long and too deep. The rustling of the endless wind didn't fill it.

The vehicles pulled up fast. Guy Redwing was the

first to climb out, and from the second came Gage Dalton, the county sheriff. Mitch was surprised to see him. Gage didn't often answer calls anymore. Back in the day when he'd headed up crime scene investigations, he'd been out and about more, but since taking over as sheriff, he'd been buried in management and politics. Everything came down to politics sooner or later.

Several other officers arrived and began fanning out around the house, probably seeking evidence. But Gage and Guy came up the steps to the porch.

"Grab me a chair, please," Gage said without addressing anyone in particular.

Guy quickly dragged a wooden chair over and Gage sat. "Not the way it used to be," Gage remarked. "That damn car is a torture device."

Used to be? Mitch wondered. Gage had been so seriously injured by a bomb during his DEA days that Mitch doubted he'd had a single pain-free day since.

"Ms. Hall," Gage said. "You okay?" His scarred face reflected intense concern. "You weren't here?"

Grace shook her head. "I'm okay." Then she asked, "What's okay?"

Gage gave her one of his patented crooked smiles. "Not much right now. So you weren't here?"

Grace looked up at Mitch.

He answered for her, since she seemed to want him to. "We'd come over to take a look at her new barn. She's been staying with me because of her injuries in that fire."

Gage nodded. "Believe me, I heard about that. Fire inspector said it was arson. We have people working on the case."

"I know you do," Mitch agreed. "Anyway, we thought

a trip out to see the barn might make for a brighter day. It did until Grace went inside her house."

"Ransacked?"

"If there's anything in there that wasn't tossed, I'd like to see it."

Mitch sensed a shudder running through Grace, and he reached up to touch her arm. "We'll get through this, Grace."

She nodded jerkily, but another big tear ran down her face.

"Do I need to get medics out here?" Gage asked. "Shock."

"No...no," Grace said. "No. I'll be...okay, whatever that is."

Mitch could tell that she was floundering, trying to fit all this into a permanently changed worldview. This had to be earth-shattering. Well, he wasn't doing too well with it himself. The enormity of all this felt beyond human ken.

Who the hell? And why the hell? They both needed answers, and if the techs didn't find any clues, there wouldn't be any answers. How did they deal with that?

Four crime scene techs, wearing white Tyvek suits and booties, their hands gloved in blue, entered the house. Grace turned her head and watched them without expression.

"I hope they find something," Mitch said.

"Me, too," Grace answered.

Mitch looked at her, sensing she was edging out of shock, reconnecting with all this in a different way. She was coming back. He hoped that was a good thing.

Gage leaned back in his chair, wincing. "Doesn't this all beat hell? The ewe, the barn and now this. Damn it, Grace, if someone wants this place, why destroy it? Why not make an offer on it?"

Which reminded Mitch. "Earlier in the spring we had an industrial operation out here who wanted to buy both our places."

Gage stared at him. "You have any information about them?"

"I think I've still got the leaflet they left with me."

The sheriff nodded thoughtfully. "I want to see it. You both have some of the finest land in this county. I'm not surprised someone would want to buy it. But this?"

"It does seem like a long shot."

"Maybe. You get me that information, Mitch, and we'll find out everything we can about them. I'm going to know what the boss uses to wipe his nose."

"When can I go back inside?" Grace asked, out of the blue.

Gage replied. "Not for a few hours, I'm afraid. When the techs are done, we'll need you to go in and tell us if you notice anything major missing. If not, you can add items later. Knowing what was taken can help with the investigation."

She nodded slowly, and a sigh escaped her that sounded pent up for a long time.

Mitch walked to the far end of the porch and used his phone again. "Lila? Grace's place was trashed. We'll be over here for a while with the sheriff."

He listened to Lila's exclamations of horror, then asked, "Can you bring over sandwiches and coffee? It's looking to be a long day."

"Absolutely. How many?"

He looked around, counting. "Including Grace and me, we've got nine altogether. Maybe more coming."

"Give me an hour. I'll get Bill to help."

Then he disconnected, hanging his phone on his belt. Life was sure going to hell in a handbasket.

Grace didn't know what to do. The first shock was passing, and she needed action of some kind. Sitting around doing nothing had never been her forte. Not even during the endless two years since John had died. She probably had one of the cleanest houses on the planet, outside of a hospital. Make-work, mostly, that kept her moving.

She was itching to get inside and clean up the mess. She'd definitely need help. Some heavy stuff, like her furniture, had been upended.

She looked at Gage again. "It was more than a robbery," she told him.

He nodded. "Why do you think that?"

"Because it looks like a tornado whipped through there."

"That's unusual," Gage agreed. "But we'll have to wait and see. Drugs might cause someone to go to that extreme."

"Really?"

"Yep. Trust me, I know recreational drugs inside and out. What's more, they don't affect everyone the same way. I've seen rages that are terrifying, and not necessarily directed."

The idea that some junkie had done this was easier to swallow than the other ideas that started to circulate in her mind. She couldn't imagine that anyone *wanted* to attack her this way, but with this break-in following the barn being burned…well, the fear was inescapable.

She ransacked her mind, trying to think who might want to harm her, and came up empty. None of this made sense. None of it.

And while Mitch had again mentioned the people who wanted to buy her land, that seemed outlandish. A big company had a lot to lose from doing something like that. A whole lot.

The drug addict idea felt better to her, but then why both the barn and the house?

She'd stopped crying and shaking, but her insides still roiled. The way the house was trashed, her one overwhelming sense was that it had been vicious. Even more than the barn.

Her barn had practically been tinder, old as it was. It had been empty a long time and might have appeared attractive to a firebug. But the house? It made no sense at all.

She couldn't stop linking them, nor apparently could Mitch. He'd even suggested the ewe had been part of it, too. Like a warning of worse to come.

She shuddered and tried to drag her mind away from her worst speculations. If she was going to get through the next days and weeks, she couldn't afford to harbor such ideas. She needed to deal, not sit around worrying.

Time seemed to be moving through sludge, holding her captive. She wanted those techs to be done so she could get in there and assess the damage for herself. When she thought of all the keepsakes from her marriage, the photos of John, her stomach turned over and she felt she might vomit.

Those were the only important things in that house. They'd better still be there and be okay.

Lila pulled up in a truck like Mitch's and hopped out. She'd brought Bill with her, and after a wave, she and Bill started setting up a folding table and bringing out large plastic containers.

"Coffee?" Mitch asked her. "I'm sure Lila brought enough for an army."

She looked up at him and tried to manage a smile. "Thanks. But I'll just go over and see if I can help Lila with anything. I sure don't want to sit here and brood."

As if she hadn't done enough of that. She shook herself, rose to her feet and hurried over.

Lila greeted her with a hug. "Poor honey," she said. "Poor, poor girl. Somebody needs to meet the business end of my long meat fork."

"I wish," Grace answered. "What can I do to help?"

Lila pretended to size her up. "With those hands? I don't want my sandwiches spilling." Then Lila gave her a big smile. "You just sit here, sweetie. You can keep me and Mitch company. Looks like those guys are going to take forever."

It sure seemed like it, Grace thought. Maybe with the mess in there, their job needed to take longer.

Mitch trotted down from the porch with a couple of folding chairs. He urged Grace into one. "Let me get you that coffee, then Lila can start ordering me around."

"I'd never do that, boss," she said, a twinkle in her eye. "I don't need to anyway. That's what I have Bill for."

Bill feigned a sigh. "Yeah, she's training me good."

Lila gave him a look then told Mitch to sit down, too. "You keep Grace company."

"Yes, ma'am."

Lila handed them both coffees, then lickety-split put out sandwiches and paper plates for everyone. "I hope," she said as she finished layering the sandwiches on several big plates, "that those guys can eat, too. Else we're going to be eating sandwiches for a lot of meals this week."

* * *

"Damn, it looks like a party down there," Carl grumped to Larry.

"Didn't look so good earlier. That woman was scared, I tell you."

"Maybe so," Carl muttered. He looked through his binoculars again. "She *did* call the police."

"Well, yeah," Larry answered. "Like she was going to walk in there and ignore it. Which we didn't want her to do, did we?"

"Hell no. So okay, maybe all that food is just neighborly."

"Most like." Larry peered through his own binoculars. "Them sandwiches look good. Wish I had me some."

"Fresh bread, too, I bet." Carl's mood wasn't improving. He got heartburn every time he thought of their boss. Her demands were beginning to chap his hide. Nothing was enough to make her happy. Or at least to satisfy her. *Witch.*

"I hope we didn't leave nothin' behind," Larry remarked, giving Carl another dose of heartburn.

"You better not," Carl retorted angrily. "We talked about it before. Gloves, hats... What could be there?"

"Nothin'." Larry hated these moods of Carl's. When they got going, Carl just got darker and angrier until they blew past. Lately they'd been almost constant.

"I hope she's satisfied now," Carl grumbled. "Damn, what more can we do? Shoot the Hall woman?"

"Murder's out," Larry reminded him.

"I *know* it's out. But what more is there?"

"Not murder," Larry said. "Not that."

"Hell's bells."

Now they both stared glumly at the scene below. It

did look like a party. And when had the woman, who was almost always alone, got herself so many friends?

Everything just kept getting more and more complicated.

The instant the techs cleared out, after they and the deputies nearly cleaned out the food, Grace was allowed into the house. Gage Dalton had gone back to the office, but Guy Redwing and Sarah Ironheart remained behind to accompany her as she sought any missing items.

As if she could see any, given the mess in the house. She headed straight to the bedroom where she kept photos of her wedding to John, as well as photos of him, in frames on her dresser.

She gasped with horror as she saw the photos had been tossed around. Lifting a couple of them with her bandaged hands, she felt huge relief as she discovered that while the glass was broken, the pictures remained unharmed. She could deal with that. New frames and they would be ready to place again.

Her dresser, a piece of very heavy and very old furniture, had been left untouched, except for a few drawers that were open, her underthings and a couple of sweaters hanging out. That worried her less than the one drawer at the bottom.

She knelt, needing to open it, but her hands wouldn't allow her. Then Mitch was beside her, brushing her scrabbling hands away.

"Let me," he said. With one easy move, he pulled it open and she nearly collapsed again. Huge tears rolled helplessly down her cheeks. The mementos were all there, from her short bridal veil to the plastic-wrapped ornament from the top of their wedding cake and John's ring. Even the bouquet of red silk roses looked back at her.

She found the diamond studs that John had given her for their first anniversary. She'd never understood how he'd afforded them. She'd never asked.

The important thing was that all the reminders of her time with John she'd saved over the years hadn't been touched.

"It's all here," she whispered. "Thank God."

She spent several minutes staring into the drawer, so glad the looters had left this alone. Nothing else really mattered.

Then she had to face the rest of the damage. Together with Mitch and the two deputies, she walked through the entire house, reaching a scary conclusion.

"If anything is missing, I can't tell."

Sarah and Guy exchanged looks.

"Weird," Guy said. "Well, if you notice anything later, give us a call."

She promised to do that, then was alone with Mitch and the destruction of the rest of her life.

"How am I going to clean all this up?" She asked the question of herself, but Mitch answered.

"You're not. You've got help. And wouldn't this be a good time to rearrange that living room?"

She looked at him, conscious of a brief sting of annoyance, then remembered their earlier conversation. "You're right," she answered, feeling her shoulders stiffen. "A good time. I don't think I ever again want to see this place as it was."

Late afternoon had arrived. Mitch spoke. "Lunch was hours ago. I think if we don't get back to my place soon, Lila might get upset for ruining another of her excellent meals."

She was ready to close the door on all this. Before Mitch could secure the broken door behind her, something she rarely did, Betty Pollard drove up.

"Oh, God, not now," she muttered.

"I thought she was your friend."

She looked at Mitch as Betty strode toward them.

"She is, but I'm not up to being lectured about how I need to get rid of this place. I understand her concern, I should appreciate it more than I do, but I'm tired of it."

"I'm starting to agree with her," Mitch said.

Grace felt almost betrayed, but she bit her tongue as Betty reached them.

"Let me guess," Grace said before anything else. "You heard it on your police scanner."

"Of course I did. I would have been here sooner except I was out with Dan. Priorities, you know." She flashed a smile, then passed Grace before she could protest, and entered the house.

"Oh man," Betty said. "Oh man."

Grace had to agree, but she wanted to escape. She'd already spent enough time in there, studying the wreckage.

Betty emerged quickly, saying, "I don't want to look. How can you stand it, Grace?"

"I don't have a choice."

"Guess you don't." Betty closed the door firmly behind her. "God." She reached out and hugged Grace. "I can't believe it."

"I'm having some trouble with it, too."

Betty evidently wanted to remain, but Grace had reached her limit. No polite chitchat, not now. She felt all roiled inside and couldn't have stood any inanities.

"I'm just going to say one thing," Betty said firmly.

"I know. I should get out. I told you I don't want to hear that anymore."

Betty looked a little offended. "I almost didn't come to the hospital after the barn burned down because I thought you didn't want to see me again. But this is beyond enough."

"Meaning?"

"The ewe. The barn. And now this. If you don't feel hunted out here, then you should."

Betty reached out to hug her once more, murmuring, "Stay safe."

After a farewell to Grace and Mitch, she left with a wave.

"That was frosty," Mitch remarked.

"On my part. I suppose I should feel guilty."

Mitch looked at her. "For what? You're entitled to your feelings, and I can understand why you don't want to be bothered right now. Anyway, let's go home. If you want to yell at me, do it there. Lila will probably join in."

"What would she yell at you for?"

"Being late to dinner. Although in fairness I gotta say that Lila doesn't yell at me. She can give me looks, though, to put me in my place."

While Mitch honestly agreed with Betty—it did feel as if Grace were being hunted somehow—he understood why Grace didn't want to hear it. Especially now. As she came out of her shock and horror, she was going to defend her life choices, especially the one about keeping her home and her memories there.

Betty's common sense didn't stand a chance against that.

He could have sighed but refrained. Grace might hear him, even over the growling and squeaking of his old pickup. He didn't want to have to explain that he agreed with Betty.

Grace had always been a bit difficult to deal with, especially since John's passing. Stubborn, opinionated about some things, and totally refusing to let go of any part of her grief.

Stubbornness had probably gotten her through a lot, but now here she was, being obstinate at exactly the wrong time. The only thing that consoled him was that she couldn't return to that house until her hands were well enough for her to take care of herself.

He had no doubt she'd race right back as soon as she thought she could manage. But he wasn't going to let her go alone. Not now. Not after all this hell that had been visited on her.

Back home, Lila greeted them with delicious aromas and a smile. "Go wash up, boss. But not you, girl. You get yourself right into the kitchen and get your saliva running. I want to see you eat a big meal."

Grace spoke quietly. "I don't feel very hungry."

"Of course you don't. But you get in there and smell yourself into hunger. Nobody can resist my food for long."

"I'm sure of that," Grace said. She looked at Mitch.

"Go on," he said. "I can find my own way to the bathroom sink."

"I hope so. You've only been living here your entire life."

Teasing. A very good sign. Maybe she'd emerge from this grimness faster than he'd thought possible.

But of course she would. Grace was remarkably resilient, except for one thing.

John.

Chapter 13

Three days later, Grace stood in her house, directing the arrangement of her living room. Bill and Jack were there to help, a good thing considering the weight of some of those pieces.

Rearranging the room was harder than she had expected, but Mitch nudged her along, suggesting different placements. Left to her own devices, Grace might have put everything back in the original arrangement.

But Mitch was right. She needed to claim this room for herself.

"I should clean the rug," she remarked as the room fell into order.

"Are you sure that rug would survive it? Wasn't it already here?"

"Yeah." It had been one of the economies she and John had practiced, using most of what had been left in the house. With a tax sale, nobody came in to clean the house out.

It had sure served them well.

She smiled. It felt good to smile again. The anticipation of change had lifted her spirits some. "I never asked, but did you know the previous owner? I never even knew who he was because the deed came from the county."

"Not well. Crusty as I recall and I don't think I ever knew his name. Not the friendliest of guys, which probably explains why no one tried to help him out of his tax problems. Or maybe no one knew about them. I don't remember that I ever did."

"Shame that he lost it. That would kill me." She sighed. "Well, it turned out to be a blessing for me and John. Hardly seems fair, though."

"What's fair about life? The man didn't pay his taxes for at least five years. The county let him run longer than most would, I suspect. I thought about buying it myself."

She turned toward him. "Why didn't you? You could have bid more than we did."

"Because I saw your face at that auction. Bright and hopeful. Couldn't take it from you."

Her heart jumped. "Oh, Mitch..."

He shrugged. "Not a big deal. I got you two for neighbors, then I got your land anyway."

That made her almost laugh. "You're awful!"

"Never denied it. Hey, Bill?"

"Yeah, boss."

"Put that ugly old chair in that corner."

"Ugly!" Grace couldn't resist, although she'd often thought so herself. Horsehair, too, which was impossible to sit on with bare legs. Over the years it had been mostly useless.

Mitch eyed her. "I'd send it to the junkyard, myself. Or to a charity. Someone else might be desperate enough to buy it."

"Desperate?" Grace had to laugh at that one.

"That's what it would take. Lot of new upholstery, too. Maybe a charity would be too picky to want it."

Now the laughter rose all the way from her belly. Troubles seemed to slip into the background. Man, he was good for her.

"You want it here?" Jack asked, grinning himself. "Reckon we could take it out to the truck right now."

Mitch laughed. "Don't steal the lady's antique."

"Antique?" This was too much. "It can't possibly be that old."

"My guess is a hundred years. Not that that feels like much, the old century being so close."

He had a point there. Suddenly, this furniture re-arrangement became an adventure. Like a fresh wind blowing through.

Grace drew a deep breath, then nearly choked on the musty smell that had risen from that long-unused chair.

"Oh, take it out," she begged. "I can smell it, and it's not good."

"Happy to oblige, ma'am," Bill answered, tipping an invisible hat. "Some things just aren't meant to be. Where to, boss?"

"Our burn pile, or some charity. You guys decide."

"Burn," Bill and Jack said simultaneously.

Bill added, "The smell must be in the cushions. Ain't nobody gonna want that in their house."

Mitch's hired hands grunted as they carried the chair out into the sunshine.

Bill groused, "Might make good target practice."

"Beer?" Grace asked when they returned. Both Bill

and Jack were sweaty. "You'll have to get it yourselves." She waved her bandaged hands.

"I think I can manage that," Jack assured her. "Mitch?"

"Yeah, that sounds good. Worked up a bit of a sweat myself, overseeing all this."

Another joke. Grace had watched him work as hard as the other two. Mitch was no slacker.

She was also glad that Mitch had brought over a couple of six-packs when she and he had come over this morning. She could act the gracious part of all this when she couldn't help.

But it was just acting. A whole lot of her life seemed to be acting. Damn, she needed to get out of the hole of self-pity.

Quit pretending, she told herself. Things were *not* okay and might never be again. *So cope.*

"Now we gotta refix things," Bill said. "Nothing balances."

"That's a point," Mitch agreed as he popped the top on his longneck. "But is balance important?"

"It is to me," Bill replied. "The lady decides."

Three pairs of eyes settled on her.

"I need to think about it. Maybe I'll have a beer, too, while I study it."

Mitch brought her a beer and opened it for her. "Take your time," he suggested. "We might get into another longneck before we're ready to get on with this."

The two hired hands went outside to sit on the front steps and argue about how they were going to get the "dinosaur" onto the truck bed.

"Wanna sit outside?" Mitch asked her.

Given the smell that still permeated the room, and the dust that had been stirred up by all the moving, she definitely did. Amazing what accumulated when you didn't move furniture for a while. As for that old chair, she'd never been able to move it at all.

She and Mitch settled into the wooden rockers on one side of the porch. John had been so pleased with himself for building them during long winter nights.

"Beautiful day," Mitch remarked.

Indeed it was. Bright sun combined with the steady wind into perfection. Rocking gently helped soothe her, carrying her away from the mess inside her house and what it might mean.

"I'm so grateful to you guys," she said.

"Hell," Mitch said. "None of us could have done this alone."

"Especially that dinosaur."

Bill and Jack had come over to join them with their own beers. The "dinosaur" still sat on the ground behind the pickup truck. "Let me guess," Bill said, leaning back against the porch post. "You never got rid of that chair because it weighs a ton."

Grace had to laugh, although at the moment she didn't especially feel like it. "You're right," she admitted. "Besides, it filled a bare space."

That brought laughter her way.

Mitch smiled with his eyes. "A bare space, huh. So you arranged the whole room around it?"

"I guess so. As time went by, we added a little here and there, but we were too busy most of the time to be thinking about decorating."

Busy indeed. Once they'd started the flock, there weren't enough hours in the day. They had a good time together, though. She doubted they would have made it if there'd been nothing but work.

She'd tried so hard to keep that flock, but she was

glad Mitch had taken over. It was definitely too much for one person as the flock had grown larger. Two hired men had been required along with John, who'd told her to take it easier.

Because they'd hoped to have a child, and he believed that her working so hard might be hindering that. Then he had died, and shortly after she'd had to let the two hired men go because she couldn't afford to pay them.

At first, doing everything herself had occupied her enough that grief had remained in the background. Then she'd had to face the reality that she could not go it alone.

She had to deal with the fact that John would never return. Grief was one hell of a roller coaster, but she seemed to have left the anger behind. And the bargaining. Nothing she could do, say or promise would bring her husband back.

She sighed, dragging herself into the present moment. Retracing those steps wouldn't help anything. It certainly wouldn't help her move forward in a world without John.

It was a wonder Mitch hadn't washed his hands of her long ago. Steadfast, he'd become a rock for her. When she had let him.

Like now, helping her to clean up this mess. A lot of detritus from the break-in was gone, but there were still plenty of things to put right. Like the living room.

Oddly, as she watched it take new shape, a kind of relief started to ease through her. Maybe she should have asked for Mitch's help sooner. Keeping most of the house like a museum wasn't changing a thing. It certainly wasn't making anything better.

She looked down at her hands, still bandaged, although not as thickly. She was supposed to be flexing them now to avoid stiffening. Tomorrow she'd visit the doctor again and find out just how much more she could do. When she could get rid of these bandages. Just their mere presence had become seriously annoying. Thank goodness for Lila, because Grace sure as the dickens couldn't have cared for herself the last few weeks.

She even suspected that she still wouldn't be able to do much once the bandages were gone. Through the layers, she could feel tenderness.

Meanwhile she was beginning to feel as if she had a target on her back. She hadn't mentioned that fear to Mitch because she didn't want to appear silly, but this had just been too much. A fire and now this?

She couldn't help but feel stalked.

As she scanned the world beyond her porch, she wondered if she was being watched right now. A shiver passed through her even though the day was warm.

Who then?

She guessed she had to wait for the sheriff's findings to be sure, and she and Mitch *had* felt there was a link between the events. But they hadn't discussed how this was making her feel. Or him, for that matter. She'd shied away from talking about it. Conspiracy theories had never been her thing. She had always resisted them.

But this?

Bill and Jack had finished their beers and now started discussing how to move the chair onto the pickup.

"It's not that heavy," Bill insisted. "Maybe three hundred pounds and it'll be split between us. We're strong enough to do that."

Mitch set his bottle on the porch beside his chair and went down to them. "I'll help. Then nobody will break a back."

"Thanks," Bill said. "I was thinking about making

a ramp but dragging this damn thing will be as hard as lifting it, maybe more."

"I absolutely agree," Mitch said. "We just gotta be careful to balance it or somebody's gonna take it on the chin. Find a spot to grab, guys."

"I'll count to three when we're ready," said Jack.

"Just one thing," Mitch said. "Everyone counts to three, but no one ever says whether to lift *on* three or just after the number is said."

The two other men exchanged looks.

"Good point," Bill said. "Okay, right on three, the number being the lift when it's spoken."

On the porch, Grace had to smile. She'd never thought about that. Count on Mitch not to miss a detail.

All three squatted down, feeling around as they sought purchase on the wood frame.

"It's gonna want to tip," Mitch said. "Toward the truck, so you guys lift your ends a little higher than me."

Which was going to put more weight on Mitch, Grace thought, but didn't say anything. Mitch knew what he was doing.

Two minutes later they had the chair loaded. Bill and Jack said they'd take care of tying it down, so Mitch came back to sit with Grace.

"No major injuries," Mitch remarked.

"And that's why I never moved it. Is your back okay?"

"It is. Now that chair will go to its FRP."

She raised her brows. "Its what?"

"Final resting place." He gave her a crooked grin. "Maybe you don't have the problem, but I've noticed that when you set something down it almost never moves again."

"I like that." In fact, it tickled her.

"At least the guys won't have any trouble getting it off there. A couple of good shoves and it'll tumble away."

The afternoon was waning as the two cowboys drove away. A little coolness had entered the breeze, feeling good. The wind caught wisps of her hair and she had to shove them away from her face. Despite her uneasiness earlier, she began to relax. It was so beautiful here with the western mountains changing color throughout the day and she hadn't been noticing for a while.

But she needed to bring the subject up. "Mitch?"

He turned toward her. "Yeah?"

"I'm feeling watched."

She saw him sit bolt upright, his face creasing with concern. "Since when?"

"Today. Just today. Well, maybe a few times before the barn burned."

"Hell."

"I can't imagine where anyone would be hiding."

He could. There were a few copses of trees out there. And then there was the side of the mountain, not too far out of reach for a good pair of binoculars. "Why didn't you mention it before?"

"Because it sounds crazy. Totally off the wall. This is the middle of nowhere, and it'd be hard to hide around here."

He hesitated, then said, "Let's go home. Dinner will be ready soon, and we can talk about this later. And trust me, you're not crazy."

She'd begun to wonder. She'd cut herself off from everything since John's death. She'd allowed Mitch to show up from time to time, and she'd made friends with Betty.

But still, without much to wind her mind around

other than grief, she wondered if her mental wheels had come off the rails.

Time would tell.

No, Mitch thought as they drove back to his place, it wouldn't be impossible for someone to watch without being seen. Especially if no one was looking for it.

Watched? He hadn't thought of that part. No one would actually have to watch Grace to do these things. The barn had burned while she was there. She'd been home so rarely since her release from the hospital, anyone could have done this at almost any time.

Except for Lila's visits to pick up clothes or other items Grace wanted and her checks on the house.

Someone would have to watch to figure out Lila's schedule, to know for sure when the house would be empty. A truck sitting out front didn't mean much, especially since he'd put Grace's pickup in the new barn to protect it. It could have been *her* truck out there.

Regardless, someone had to watch to be sure when Grace's house was empty.

Someone who needed enough time to get into the house and trash the place thoroughly.

"Nothing was taken," he said aloud as they drove up his drive.

"Nothing I can tell."

Which made this even weirder. "We'll check again tomorrow to make sure nothing else is missing."

"I have a doctor's appointment at three."

"We can do both. Besides, there's more cleanup I can help with."

Jack and Bill had ridden out to check on the herd, and Lila said they didn't plan to be back for a couple of days.

Mitch wasn't surprised. The cattle had been needing attention and they always needed to be watched for problems. Jeff couldn't do it all single-handedly, although he'd sure as hell try.

All three of his hands were good men and he was lucky to have them.

Speaking of which, it was getting on time to check on his shepherds and take them the staples they'd need, including a little extra that Lila always baked for them. Plus the hot meal he'd carry in the pails.

Since Grace had come into his care, he'd been letting matters slide a bit too much. Especially his bookkeeping. The longer he let that go, the more of a headache it became.

As Grace made her way to the living room after dinner, he stepped outside into the long twilight of summer. Scanning the view, he wondered if someone was really hiding out there.

Grace had felt watched, and that sense was often true. Not often, but too often to be ignored. Well, there were groupings of trees all over the land since he and Grace had enough water. Easy to hide in one of them.

Or on the side of the mountain as he'd thought earlier. One really good pair of binoculars would make that possible.

But how could anyone ramble around too much without being noticed? The folks around here made a tight-knit group. A stranger would be noticed, maybe remarked on. Well, more than maybe after that barn fire. No one had caught attention.

Weirder and weirder.

Night crept slowly in, starting to reveal some of the brighter stars. He kind of missed the days when he'd slept out there with his bedroll, his horse and the cattle. The sounds they made had been his lullaby.

He shook his head, deciding he might take a look around Grace's place the day after tomorrow. But first the doctor. He hoped she'd get the news she could stop bandaging.

Not that that would help her discomfort.

Hell, he thought. Just hell.

He was a man who liked to be in control as much as possible. Life didn't always allow that, but right then he felt totally helpless. Helpless to solve this problem. Helpless to make Grace safer. Helpless to make her feel better.

Tired of his rambling thoughts, he went inside to join Grace. At least this evening he could make her comfortable and make her safe.

He should have guessed what was coming, but he knew Grace well enough that he shouldn't have been surprised.

"I'm going home," she announced as they drove from the doctor toward his place. Her hands, freshly unbandaged, still looked red and sore. Those blisters had been really bad.

She was ready to take up the reins of her life, and he had no way to stop her except by argument. When had a disagreement ever stalled her? Never, of course.

Stubborn. Cussedly stubborn.

"When?" he asked after a minute or so.

"I'd like to go tonight."

"Grace…"

"I know," she answered. "I know. Okay, tomorrow but no later."

"Of course not."

"Mitch, I can't leave the place unattended any longer. Look what happened because I wasn't there."

True, but it was also a signpost she was choosing to ignore. It could get worse.

The idea clamped his stomach into a knot.

How to handle this? He wondered why she'd let him do anything at all. There'd been very little she'd allowed him to do since John had died.

He stifled a sigh and kept driving. He had to figure out a way to stop her. But he doubted he could.

Grace had gone from frightened to furious. If someone was attacking her for any reason, he was going to meet the business end of her shotgun. She knew how to use it and wasn't afraid to.

Especially not now. Shock after shock had knocked her back on her heels, but no more. It was time to stand up for herself against this shadowy threat. Time to reclaim her life and protect her ranch.

No one was going to get away with doing this to her.

She sensed Mitch's disapproval and wasn't surprised. He'd spent the last two years trying unobtrusively to look after her. He'd be wanting to make her safe right now.

Except he couldn't do that. No one else could make her safe. She was absolutely certain that if he could find a way to stop this and protect her, he would.

There were no answers to this conundrum. What could he do? Camp on her porch? He had important duties on his own ranch and couldn't afford to let matters go. She knew he'd been doing a lot of that while she stayed under his roof.

Enough. Short of abandoning her ranch to more mischief, she had to stand up for herself.

In a way, the idea pleased her. She didn't like being

weak, and this threat was weakening her because she wasn't facing it squarely and standing guard.

"Can I borrow a horse?" she asked.

"Oh, for Pete's sake."

"No, then. I can understand why after the barn."

"Damn it, Grace you saved those horses and risked your life doing it. It's not that I'd be afraid for a horse."

"Then what?" she demanded,

"I'd be afraid for you."

That silenced her.

Mitch knew what she was going to do. She was going to get on that horse and start riding around, looking for any evidence of a campsite or a campfire on her property. Looking for traces of the perp.

She'd be out there all alone, a perfect target for a serious mishap. The idea that he'd convinced her to carry a sat phone didn't make him feel any better.

Worse, if he'd ever found a way to divert her when she was set on something, he didn't know it. Even John hadn't been able to. As far as Mitch knew, John had only been successful when it came to the goats she wanted. And knowing Grace, John had been obliged to sit down and show her the numbers.

Not just the cost of a fence, either. But the reality that there wasn't enough forage for goats, who didn't graze the same greens as sheep. Which meant nutritional supplements and additional food.

Want them or not, they could become very expensive out here if you had more than a few. As near as he could tell, goats bred, too. Then what?

He might have laughed about it all if Grace hadn't decided to do something that he considered remarkably foolhardy in these circumstances. But he could also understand her desire to protect what was hers and put any threat to bed.

He'd have felt the same himself. Except he had hired hands to stand with him. She had no one but him.

Oh, crap. He could see the storm coming.

Chapter 14

Two mornings later, Mitch took Grace over to her house and helped clean up some of the last of the detritus because he didn't want her overworking those hands.

He also didn't lend her a horse.

"You simply can't go riding with your hands in that condition. No way."

He wouldn't budge, either. Part of the truth was he didn't want her riding alone when there might well be someone out there watching her, possibly with worse intentions that just messing up her property.

He needed to go to town for some feed, but she didn't want to accompany him. Of course not. She was determined not to leave her property unprotected.

He got that. Totally. But however strong and brave she might be, she was still *alone*.

He dealt with that by asking one of his men to keep a distant eye on her.

And whether she liked it or not, he was coming back with his own shotgun to stand guard with her. He'd have skipped going for the feed except he'd let that go too long while spending more time with her.

The devil and the deep blue sea, he thought. That famous rock and a hard place. Scylla and Charybdis. The problem was so common to life that there were any number of references to it.

He was not a happy man as he headed out. He didn't want Grace mad at him, and he didn't want her alone. He couldn't completely fail to take care of his cattle, however.

He could have asked one of his men to run for the feed, but he was getting uneasy about his animals. Whatever was after Grace might extend to *his* herds. Especially if this turned out to be that operation that wanted his land, as well. A brief gallop by one of his men over to check on her would be okay, but he didn't want to reduce the watch on his cattle for too long.

Hell. He hurried into town as fast as he could. The feed store was ready for him and loaded his truck bed quickly.

Another reason for the trips to town was to grab something at Maude's diner. It always gave Lila a break from making him lunch and dinner and he thought she appreciated it.

Grace wouldn't be able to cook right now. She might be able to manage a peanut butter sandwich, but no more.

That decided him. He dropped into Maude's and placed a very large takeout order. He could cook for both himself and Grace, but she'd probably get edgy as twilight deepened, and he didn't want her standing out on her porch.

Hell, he thought for the second time. Maybe he needed to get a horse over to Grace's for himself. Maybe if *he* rode around, he could ease her mind on that score.

Or, he might just make her mad.

He sighed. You couldn't deal with a prickly pear cactus without getting stung by spines. Grace would just have to get over it.

Maude quickly delivered him a couple bags full of his order as if she sensed his urgency.

Then he had another thought. He couldn't drop the feed off at his own place. Not without leaving Grace alone for longer. Another cuss word escaped him. He gave in to need.

So he called Bill. "I've got the feed, but I need to stay with Grace. Can one of you bring me a horse and get the feed?"

Of course they could. He thought once again how lucky he was in those three men.

When he reached Grace's, he carried the bags inside to discover she'd managed to make coffee. She'd also found it necessary to bandage her palms again.

"Hurting?" he asked as he put the bags on the counter.

"A little," she admitted. "Not quite ready to have things brush against my hands."

"Hardly surprising. You know they'll be tender for a while. Well, I brought us some food. No cooking for you. Whenever we're finished eating this, *I* can cook. Believe it or not, I know how, and while it'll be simple fare, it won't require an outdoor grill."

That made her laugh, and his heart lifted a bit.

"Jack of all trades?" she teased.

"Cooking on the range and, for a while before Lila, cooking for myself. If it's easy I can do it."

"I feel so useless."

He looked at her. "Don't. You've been injured. You didn't cause any of this. Anyway, I like being of use myself, so live with it."

He paused, hating to bring the gloom to her again. "I need to go out and get my shotgun."

Her small smile vanished. He detested that, but he'd be of no earthly good to her if he wasn't prepared to defend her homestead alongside her.

He might try, but there was no way he could turn this into a fun campout. Sooner or later the darkness would have descended anyway.

"Thanks," she said, her voice small.

This seemed to be his cussing day. While he went out to his truck to get his shotgun and a box of ammo, plus the pistol he always carried to put a sick or injured animal out of its misery, he muttered a few choice words.

He had to hope that he could really help Grace, that he could put someone behind bars so that she could breathe easy again. All he needed was some concrete evidence to pass to the sheriff. Although it would make him feel a whole lot better to hold the guy at gunpoint for a while before the sheriff arrived.

Inside he found Grace seated at the table with a cup of coffee. She didn't look even remotely happy anymore.

He'd done that by reminding her of this god-awful situation. Well, that made him feel about two inches tall.

He put his shotgun in a corner, and his locked pistol case on the counter.

"Guess what I brought to eat?" he asked, trying to cheer her a little.

She looked at him.

"I went to Maude's. I must have made her happy

since I ordered at least two meals worth of most items, plus some big pieces of strudel."

That perked her interest. "Strudel? That's a beast to make. I'm surprised she bothered."

"Maude's always a surprise, except when she's slamming dishes on the table."

That brought back her smile. "Too true. The clattering you hear in any diner doesn't reach the decibels in Maude's."

"I'm amazed she has a whole dish left, honestly."

Still smiling. Thank God. They'd get through this mess somehow. "Are you getting hungry?"

She didn't have to think about it. "Famished."

"Good. Maude would be appalled if we didn't eat while it's mostly fresh."

"Just don't tell her if we don't."

"She'll never know," Mitch pointed out. "Unless you want to tattle on me."

Twilight began to creep over the land, flattening the shadows, making the land darker even as the sky remained blue overhead. One of the beauties of the mountains. They swallowed the sun before they stole all the light.

Grace decided to sit on her porch with her own shotgun cradled across her lap. Mitch joined her soon with fresh mugs of coffee.

"To keep us awake," he said as he passed her one.

For all she resented not being able to take care of all this herself, she was terribly glad of Mitch's company. It struck her again that she'd been keeping him at a distance for a long time.

Why? Because he was a supremely attractive man? Because noticing that might be a betrayal of John? All she could be certain of was that she was drawn to Mitch and it didn't feel like a major crime.

As if it ever had been. Even when she was married. She'd seen John notice other women, a very male thing to do. Well, she was a female and she was noticing Mitch. The sight of his backside in jeans was enough to make her heart skip a beat. The narrowness of his hips reminded her of his masculinity. Almost constantly.

Mostly, just then, she was glad he was here. The coming night didn't quite seem so scary.

Anyway, it wasn't the night that scared her. It was what it might conceal.

"It's probably too soon to expect anything more to happen," he remarked. "There were a few weeks after the ewe, and between the barn and the home invasion. Moving slowly. A rapid blast wouldn't give enough time for the threat to sink in."

She nodded, basically agreeing. But not certain by any means. She supposed he wasn't, either, or he wouldn't be here.

"You're just trying to make me feel better, Mitch."

"Probably," he admitted.

"But you called it a threat."

"Hard to see it any other way now."

The evening breeze was shifting direction a bit, bringing a colder breath to the land, washing the air, cleaning it for another day.

Grace drew in the familiar scent of sagebrush. She loved the aroma. Nature had a beauty all its own, even out here where many might find the vast expanses dull and the dry summer colors boring.

The land rolled gently, trees grew everywhere they could find enough water. There were wildflowers in the spring, delicate beautiful blossoms. Sometimes as winter approached, she even caught the smell from the evergreens on the mountains. If you were quiet enough, you could see deer who'd jumped the fence and grazed.

It was a beauty many couldn't appreciate, but she certainly did.

A sigh escaped her.

"What?" he asked.

"I was just thinking how much I love it out here. I'm not going to give it up, Mitch."

"Me, neither."

After a bit she remarked, "You had Bill bring you a horse."

"Clearly. But not for you. Your hands…"

"I know about my hands," she said querulously, then wished she had softened her tone. "I got a whole introduction to what I can't do today. After you left, I tried to clean up some more. No go. At least I could make that coffee."

"Small victories. Take them when you can. Look, those hands you're angry about are a badge of honor."

Her head swiveled toward him. "What do you mean?"

"You burned them risking yourself to save two horses. That was brave. Take your badge or medal or whatever you want to call it, because you deserve it. You could have saved your hands by letting those horses die. You didn't."

She couldn't very well argue with that. "Well, I couldn't have let them burn. Period. So I didn't really do anything special."

"Most people are too afraid of fire to go into a burning building. Welcome to the reality and courage of one Grace Hall."

"You think so?" Inside her, an icy knot began to

warm for the first time since John's death. Courage?
She hadn't been showing much over the last two years.

"I know so," he replied firmly.

As the last light began to fail, he reached over and
took her hand. It was a careful, gentle touch that caused
her no discomfort.

Well, except for the leaping of her heart and the almost forgotten tingle that ran through her. Within herself she could feel creaky doors opening wider, letting
in fresh air, sweeping away dust and even the fog that
had shrouded her.

A new day was beginning.

If she could just tunnel through this mountain of
trouble.

She looked at Mitch again, seeing his face in shadow,
and wished she knew how to close that last bit of distance between them.

It wouldn't be easy, not after that way she'd built her
self-protective wall between them. Keeping them at the
level of friends and colleagues.

If she wanted to go that way—and she wasn't yet
certain she dared to take the risk—she might have to
make the move herself, knocking the barrier over.

But still there were the other things, the ugly things
that seemed to be pursuing her. Her needs versus her
wants. Dangers of two different kinds that couldn't possibly mesh just now.

While she tried to deal with it all, warning flags
were spinning around her head like disembodied de-
mons. It might be wiser to solve the big problems before adding the possibility of another to the list. What
if he wasn't interested? What if he just saw her as a
friend, or as a sister?

Oh, God, could she take the humiliation?

But she couldn't deny he was waking her from her long slumber in the depths of despair. Pulling her up from the mire that had been in danger of becoming comfortable.

She drew a deep breath of the cooling air that cleansed her physically. Maybe she was cleansing herself inside, too?

"We ought to go in," Mitch remarked. "Unless you want me to go get you a jacket."

That was Mitch. Caring. Always caring.

"Let's go in," she decided. Because as night crept in, with all its mysterious shadows, a threat felt as if it were sneaking closer.

She couldn't imagine what it might be, but knew it existed.

This was not over.

Chapter 15

The upstairs of this two-story farmhouse was empty. Grace and John had used it for storing a few things, but otherwise it had been extra, unneeded space. Bedrooms they had once thought would eventually be filled with children. If they'd had children, they'd have moved their bedroom up there, too. Plenty of room.

But there was a room downstairs that was adequate for them, and they'd used it as their bedroom. A much smaller room had been given over to a tiny office of sorts, now filled with papers and loose-leaf binders and boxes, all holding the inevitable documents for running any kind of business. Over the years the stacks had grown, and since John's death had been mostly untouched.

As a business, Grace was practically nonexistent. She recorded the sale of the sheep to Mitch, diligently recorded the payments he made on the land he leased from her, recorded a rare expense that fell to her.

Then she always closed the door on it all. Leaving it in the dust.

Grace and John had had little in the way of savings, only socking away what they could for emergencies. So far, she had managed to survive on the proceeds of his life insurance. That wouldn't last forever, but it had gotten her through. Sooner or later she was going to have to face economic reality. Mitch's intervention had merely postponed it.

The unwanted thoughts wafted through her head in the morning when she rose. Mitch had spent the night in the living room, sleeping on a recliner. John's recliner. It somehow felt right.

He was already up and dressed, standing in the kitchen. He wore his shotgun chaps over his jeans, topped by a chambray shirt with snaps. The sleeves were rolled up. On his feet were cowboy boots, not work boots.

"Coffee's ready," he remarked. "As if you couldn't smell it coming down the hall. I recommend a piece of Maude's blueberry buckle for breakfast."

"That sounds great." She hadn't even showered yet, and was still wearing an old terry cloth robe over her nightshirt. Feeling suddenly embarrassed, she pushed her hair back and hoped it didn't look too much like a rat's nest. Heck, why had she stumbled out here before taking her shower, cold as it would have to be because of her hands?

He placed a mug of coffee on the table and motioned her to a chair. "Sit, milady, and sip."

A surprised laugh escaped her as she slid into the chair.

He turned back to the counter to open a container and pulled a couple of plates out of the cupboard.

Which gave her a nice view of the worn seat of his jeans that cradled him oh so perfectly.

She blinked, shocked by the turn of her thoughts. *Really, Grace?* Fearful he might read her mind, she yanked her attention elsewhere.

"Boots and chaps?" she asked as he brought squares of the blueberry buckle to the table. "I haven't seen you wear chaps often."

"That's because, lately, I haven't been riding into brushy areas." He sat, facing her.

"Are you planning to?"

He shrugged one shoulder, as if trying to minimize. "I thought I'd ride around and look for trampled brush, spots under the trees, things like that."

Anxiety swooped in like a hawk. She had to swallow hard and drink some coffee. "I should do that with you."

He cocked a brow at her. "Really."

It wasn't a question and she flushed. "Mitch…"

"I get it," he interrupted. "You want to do something, anything. You don't want me taking over. I know how independent you are."

She opened her mouth to answer, but he forestalled her.

"Well, I've got a job for you, if you're willing."

She quelled an instinctive burst of resentment. This was her homestead, *her* problem, and she ought to be managing it. But the instant the irritation flared, it subsided. There was a difference, she reminded herself, between being stubborn and being reasonable. She certainly wasn't capable of doing what he was proposing he do. Her damn hands.

"What do you need?" she asked after another sip of coffee and a stab at the cake with a fork.

"Guard the place. Just sit out front with your shotgun. The sight of that ought to help any miscreants decide to go elsewhere."

Half an hour later, outside the barn, Grace watched Mitch mount a palomino named Joy. Leather creaked, a sound she had long loved. She handed him his shotgun and he slipped it into the saddle holster. Just like a cowboy of old, he wore a gun belt, his pistol safely sheathed. He crammed his battered Stetson with its stampede string onto his head.

Not a show cowboy, but a working one.

Iconic image, she thought, as he touched the finger of a gloved hand to the brim of his hat then rode out with the jingle of harness. She'd never become immune to that sight or those sounds over the years.

Grace spared a sigh, then returned to the house. She filled a tall insulated mug with coffee, then returned to her porch with her shotgun. The single barrel held six shots. No hasty reloading required.

The ceaseless wind blew, stirred to wakefulness by the rising warmth of the summer day. The humidity was so low that she considered rubbing moisturizer into her face, but let it go. Now that she was alone, the shadows that haunted her seemed to be rising even in the sunlight.

Almost too much to comprehend, she thought.

She was alone now, as she had been since John's death. But this time the loneliness was enhanced. Mitch's absence presented her with a whole new emptiness.

A few hours later, she spied a vehicle turn into her driveway. Distant though it was, she quickly recognized Betty's car.

She and Betty had been friends for a while now.

Betty was one of the very few people she'd allowed into her life since John's passing, and in the past, Betty's visits had always been welcome, pleasurable.

Lately she'd found her friend annoying. Why? She couldn't really say. Even Betty's repeated suggestions that she needed to move couldn't be all of it. It wasn't as if Betty had done more than suggest, and even Mitch had said he kind of agreed.

But Mitch didn't bring it up, and certainly not repeatedly.

No, Mitch just kept coming around to look after her. Man, she was a mixed-up mess. Both Betty and Mitch were trying to protect her, and she sprouted sharp quills any time they tried.

The look at herself was uncomfortable. It wasn't as if she were the only solitary widow in the world. She certainly didn't need to get her back up every time someone cared for her.

As Betty climbed out of her car and approached, Grace summoned a smile and a wave. "Howdy, stranger," she called.

Betty waved back and grinned. "It's been a while. I'm still not sure I'm welcome."

"Of course you are. It's just been rough lately."

"So I hear."

Grace leaned forward, ready to put her gun aside. "Coffee, blueberry buckle?"

Betty waved a hand. "I know my way around your kitchen. I'll get it myself. What about you?"

Ten minutes later, they both sat in wood rockers, coffee on the wooden end table between them. Betty had helped herself to blueberry buckle on a small plate.

"Catch me up, as in why you're sitting there with a shotgun," Betty said, then lifted a forkful of cake to her mouth. "Tell me nothing else has happened. Lately I've been feeling like every time I turn up, it's the worst time imaginable. You're entitled to a break."

Grace balanced the shotgun across her lap and surrounded the mug of fresh coffee with both hands. "You'd think. But no, nothing else has happened except Mitch's men got rid of that horrid, heavy chair from the living room. They were calling it the dinosaur."

Betty laughed. "Great description."

"I hate to admit how long I've loathed that thing. It's as if it was rooted to the house and would never move."

Oddly, she thought she saw a faint shadow pass over Betty's face.

"That it did," Betty said after a couple of seconds. "Why didn't you and John ever get rid of it?"

"Too heavy. Neither of us thought it was important enough to struggle with. Boy, did it smell when the guys moved it."

"Age does that," Betty remarked. "But I'm not here about the furniture. I'm here about you. Had enough yet?"

Grace felt herself bristling again and tried to stamp down on it. "Meaning?"

"Just what I said. God, Grace, it's been one thing after another. You're sitting there holding your shotgun, for heaven's sake. This goes way past what some might call karma. Besides, you've never done a bad thing in your life."

That drew a quiet laugh from Grace. "Everyone has, Betty. I'm not ready for sainthood."

Betty grinned. "Well, I can't say I can argue with you. I've been so bad lately. And I'm loving it."

"Tell, tell. I need something good to think about."

"I figured you might. Well, the boyfriend. He happened."

"You told me."

"But not that he moved in with me."

Grace drew a surprised breath. "Really? *Really?*"

Betty nodded with a satisfied smile. "Really. We're not talking marriage or anything, but it's starting to look long-term." She sighed happily. "I was beginning to think this would never happen to me, Grace. Usually one of us figures out that it's not working, pretty quickly. Usually me, since I'm so picky."

Grace tilted her head a bit. "Picky is important in relationships. You know that."

Betty leaned toward her. "No kidding. Worse to become picky after it's too late. Anyway, I figure I'll give him a workout. Does he do dishes? Laundry? Can he mop a floor? Because I swear I'm not going to turn into Suzy Homemaker for any man."

"Good for you."

"I mean, look at you," Betty said, waving a hand toward her. "You got married and started working on a ranch. Raising sheep. Pitching hay or whatever. I suspect all the cooking and household chores didn't fall on only your shoulders."

"No, they didn't. John and I were shoulder to shoulder with everything. He was also tall, so that gave him some added use."

Betty laughed loudly. "He was a stepladder?"

"One of his amazing talents."

This was the way it had been before, the easy camaraderie that the two of them had often shared. Grace relaxed.

After a bit, Betty spoke again. She eyed Grace. "Have I stepped into the Wild West?"

Grace's gaze snapped to her. "Meaning?"

"Girl, you're sitting there with a shotgun across your lap. Old West for sure. You didn't really explain."

"Or modern West," Grace answered, feeling her mouth twist a bit.

"You're on guard, then?"

"Wouldn't you be?" It looked so peaceful out there that even Grace had trouble believing that so much bad had happened lately.

"Well, you look ready for anything. Did you find much missing after the break-in?"

Grace shook her head. "That makes it even weirder. Like someone got all they wanted by tossing the place. A mess, but anything that matters is still there."

"Strange." Betty frowned and leaned back, rocking gently.

Grace tensed in expectation of Betty's usual insistence that she needed to dump the ranch. It didn't come this time.

Betty spoke again eventually. "At least you've got those guys to look after the sheep for you."

"Yes." Grace said no more, mindful of Mitch's desire that no one know of their arrangement. "They do a good job."

"I'm glad. But why Portuguese?"

"They're famous for their shepherding. Breeders all over the country hire them. Maybe because it's impossible to find anyone else willing to actually live with a flock."

Betty pursed her lips. "No kidding. For a while most cowboys were coming from south of the border. People who didn't mind working for a pittance and living on the range. Not so much anymore."

"Things change with the times and there are few enough cowboys who need to herd on horseback."

Betty giggled. "It's all about ATVs now."

They chatted a while longer about Dan, about romance, about the summer that was coming to a slow but steady close.

When Betty left, Grace still smiled. At least one part of her life had recovered some order.

But she still felt incredibly alone and wondered how long Mitch would be gone.

Mitch scoured every place he thought it might be possible for someone to watch Grace's activities, where someone might find a decent launching place from which to attack her property.

He'd wondered if someone could be observing from the western mountains, but maybe they could camp up there, then come down here when it was time to act.

He didn't like it. None of this. Not only the attacks themselves, but the shadowy person and purpose behind it. Uneasiness was becoming his constant companion, as he was sure it had for Grace.

He barely wanted to think about anything else, and was leaning heavily on Bill, Jack and Jeff to handle most of his ranch. Then there were the shepherds, Zeke and Rod.

They were farther out, too far away to be at a good watching point, but the two of them were out here most of the time. They might have caught wind of something.

He widened his circle until he heard the sheep and finally saw them over a rise. And there were Zeke and Rod, not far from their charges.

He rode up, and they both stood immediately. They'd been sitting around a small propane stove, brewing some coffee, and instantly offered him some. He de-clined.

"You guys doing okay?" he asked.

They smiled. "Yes," Zeke answered. "The dog?"

Mitch laughed. "I'm working on it. A couple of pup-pies, later this summer, trained by their mommas and papas, if that's okay."

"Best kind," Rod said approvingly.

"Great. Listen, I wanted to ask you if you've seen anyone out here. Maybe near Grace Hall's place? Or camping?"

The men exchanged looks. Then Zeke said, "I would tell them to go away. This *your* land. No camping."

"That's good. Just keep a sharp eye out. Bad things are happening."

"The fire," Rod said. "Very bad."

"Very bad indeed. You men need anything?"

As he rode away, the westering sun told him it was time to head on back, with or without information. Grace would begin to wonder and he didn't like leav-ing her alone for so long.

Grace was relieved to see Mitch's silhouette ap-proaching, but alongside relief came a huge dollop of excitement. She let it come, allowing herself to take pleasure in the joy she felt.

About time she permitted even a small amount of happiness to enter her life. Well past due.

He waved as he approached, heading straight for the barn. Carrying her shotgun, she followed him, not wanting to wait until he finished tending to Joy's needs.

He was removing the palomino's saddle as she en-tered the darker space inside. Her eyes needed a few seconds to adapt to the change, but then she saw him clearly.

Still iconic, she thought wryly as she approached.

"How'd your day go?" he asked as he settled the saddle on a long-unused leather-padded sawhorse. His saddlebags already hung there. He pushed the Stetson off his head and allowed it to dangle on his back by the stampede string.

"It was good," she answered. "Betty came by for a visit and for once she left the elephant alone in the room."

He laughed. "The elephant being wanting you to move away from here?"

"I'm not aware of any other one. Maybe she left it alone because she's so happy in her new relationship. The guy evidently moved in with her."

"Big step," he remarked. The saddle blanket joined the saddle, the halter settled on a hook at eye-height, reins draped back around it. Then he reached for the roll of farrier tools that occupied one of the saddlebags.

"I wish I could help," Grace admitted wistfully.

"That day'll come."

She perched on a stool to watch as he began to clean and, as necessary, rasp Joy's hooves. The real question trembled on her lips, but she was afraid to ask it. Either answer wasn't going to please her.

Regardless, it was a pleasure to watch him as he bent and lifted each hoof, cleaning and caring for that horse as kindly as he would a baby. Each time he rose, he patted the side of the palomino's neck.

The best place to show affection for a horse. John had taught her that. "You know how they show caring?" he'd asked, pointing. "They kind of wrap their heads over each other. I read that's not only affection, but soothing. Calming."

The horses sure seemed to like it when she did it that way. Of course, they didn't seem to mind a pat to the flank, either.

"Well," Mitch said when he'd finished with the hooves and reached for the curry brush. The horse looked as if she were in heaven. "Wish I had something useful to report. I might have missed it, but I couldn't see any places where someone had been hanging out. I checked with Zeke and Rod, and they haven't noticed anything, either. They'll keep an eye out."

Grace had known that news either way wouldn't be cheerful but felt deflated anyway. She'd rather have had some kind of starting point.

"What now?" she asked.

"Tomorrow I'm hoping to check out the far side of the road. I'll call Burt Stiller tonight and make sure it's okay to poke around."

She nodded. "That's a good idea."

"Oh, I'm just brimming over with ideas. No call from the sheriff?"

"Nada."

"Hell." He remained silent as he finished currying Joy. Then he led her into a stall and loaded her up with hay and a mixture of feed. A huge bucket of water followed. "Those guys didn't overlook a thing when they built this barn."

"It's beautiful, all right. Still takes my breath away."

He smiled as he stripped off his gloves. "Can a man get some coffee and leftovers?"

Mitch made one more circuit of the house and barn before joining Grace inside. She'd made fresh coffee and brought out the remains of his trip to Maude's. Plenty enough for more than two people. The microwave went to work.

Mitch still wore his chaps and grimaced when they creaked as he sat. "Time for another oiling. So Betty provided a high spot in your day?"

"She did."

But there was another elephant in the room, and Mitch knew they were avoiding it. There didn't seem to be much they could say, however. No new information. Just another night ahead of watching the stars. Of standing guard. The frustration just then was powerful. He wasn't a man who could live comfortably without answers, and lacking answers to something this dangerous nearly maddened him.

Grace looked better, however. Maybe she'd needed a day of sitting in the fresh air and chatting with a friend. She sure didn't need to be sitting around here worrying nonstop.

Her color was higher, her movements more comfortable. And unless he missed his bet, she'd put a little of those missing pounds back on. Her face had softened, although he didn't want to get into measuring her head to foot. That struck him as both rude and dangerous.

Not that he could entirely avoid it. Grace was attracting him more with each passing day, and there was no good reason to ignore it as he had when John still lived. Not anymore.

Not that he'd pounce on her or press her in any way. She deserved more respect than that. Still…

He almost smiled at himself. The rock and the hard place again. He might as well resign himself to living there at least for a while and ignoring her charms. She had plenty of them.

Their ad hoc supper was a perfect finish to the day. Then they moved outside to keep an eye on the place. An insulated bottle of coffee sat on the table between them along with a small plate of the remaining blueberry buckle.

The strong breeze swept across the darkening land, bringing a variety of scents, from the pines up on the mountains to the distant smell of cattle and grass.

Grace spoke. "You'll be bringing in the hay again?"

"In a couple of weeks. The alfalfa and clover aren't ready yet. The heads on the hay are a ways from ripening, so we're safe for now."

Familiar, easy front-porch conversation. Anything but the elephant. It was such a beautiful, peaceful evening it would have felt criminal to invite the ugliness in again.

But it waited anyway, just a little to the side, but not gone.

He was sure that she was wondering how long they were going to have to keep this up. He certainly was. They couldn't even be positive that anything more was going to happen.

What *had* happened couldn't be brushed off. Too much to think it was some rowdy kids getting their thrills.

He smothered a sigh, not wanting her to hear it. She must have felt it, though.

"Mitch, you can't camp here every night. You've got important things to do. Heck, you even have a life you need to look after."

The words hit him oddly, making him realize that Grace had become a big part of his life. The distance he'd tried to keep in response to her obvious wishes, in response to his own desire not to thrust himself where he wasn't wanted, was gone.

"Are you throwing me out?" he asked lightly, though the question wasn't light at all. He nearly held his breath waiting for her answer.

"No!" She sounded shocked. "Not at all. Lord, Mitch, you've been my salvation through all of this."

Well, he didn't want to be her salvation. Or anyone else's for that matter. "Just being neighborly." A bald-faced lie.

"Yeah," she said quietly. "You've said."

Neighbors always helped one another, standing shoulder to shoulder as necessary. It was the way. He wouldn't have dreamed doing anything else.

Depending on the threat, there simply wasn't time to wait for the authorities to arrive if anything happened again. Yeah, he was standing guard, and that was how it was going to be.

The night remained quiet, peaceful. The stars wheeled overhead as they had for millions of years. A waning gibbous moon was setting in the west.

A thought struck him. "How's this all fit in with the phases of the moon?"

"What?" She sounded startled.

"Maybe nothing. Maybe a touch of my lunacy. Just wondering if these events have been tied in any way to the phases of the moon."

"Lunacy?" she asked dubiously.

"Not what I mean, not sure I even believe in it, other than that most animals get more active as the moon brightens. No, I was just wondering if these guys are waiting for moonless nights. Nights when it would be harder to see them."

"I hadn't thought of that."

"I half wish I hadn't. It sounds crazy in a world brightened by flashlights."

She rocked steadily, clearly thinking about it. "I was home the night of the barn fire. Flashlights might have given them away if I'd looked out a window. So the moon would have had to be bright that night, wouldn't it?"

"Like I said, crazy thought."

"I'm not sure it is. The moon is waning right now. It would have been bright when they broke into my house, assuming they did it at night."

"True. I was just spitballing, because for a fact they needed light to do either thing. So clearly they wouldn't be waiting for new moon."

She laughed and he joined her.

"Crackbrained thought," he admitted.

"Not really."

"Okay then, backward. I'm thinking of all this happening in the darkness, but you're right. There's some bright light at night."

None of this was really useful, however. Just spitballing, as he'd said.

"We're getting tired," she remarked. "Too much running around like hamsters in a wheel over this. I guess you want answers as much as I do."

"Believe it." Mostly he wanted to be certain of her safety.

A while later, he walked the perimeter again, checking the barn, checking around the house, checking a little farther out. Peaceful. Probably too soon for the next action.

When he returned to the porch, he said, "You go in and get some sleep."

"That's not fair to you!"

"Fair enough. We'll split the night if you want. And I can holler for you if anything happens."

It took a few minutes, but she finally agreed. "Just make sure you wake me for my watch."

He watched her go inside, then settled in the chair once again.

He'd wake her all right. Mainly because he didn't want her to become furious with him. But not as early as she probably expected.

Watch the coddling, he warned himself. She'd hate it.

Once inside, Grace unwrapped her hands and indulged in a shower. Yes, the warm water hurt the tender skin, but she couldn't stand feeling dirty. Anyway, the light bandaging had gotten to the point where she could bind her hands herself if necessary. Not as neatly as Lila would have, but neatly enough.

She was reluctant to get into bed wearing only a nightgown, though. What if she needed to run outside, or run across the ground? She settled on a pair of pajamas as a compromise and found her thickly soled slippers that had loop and hook closures. That would have to do for quick response.

When she climbed into bed, however, sleep escaped her. So many thoughts swirled in her head. Unanswered questions about what was going on.

Thoughts of Mitch. Many thoughts of Mitch that seemed to counterbalance all her worries, at least for a short time.

He was steadily becoming a part of her life, taking up space in her mind. Not necessarily a bad thing, since it gave her some relief from fear, but another discomfort to plague her.

Desire for him was slowly growing, and even as she

lay in her bed, she squirmed a bit from the direction her mind kept taking.

How could she not wonder how it would feel to kiss him, to feel his hard body against hers? How it would feel to run her hands over his skin, and how it would feel if he ran his hands over hers? What culmination would be like.

Even in the dark she blushed. As her face heated, she pulled her hands from beneath the covers and pressed them to her cheeks. The gauze prevented them from doing much to cool her face. The heat did seem to drive downward, spiraling ever closer to her center, making her *need* to feel a man's weight on her.

It had been so long and, strangely enough, she didn't feel at all guilty. During the last few weeks her grief over John had steadily eased. It would never leave, but she had begun to doubt it would rule her life.

She knew John would have wanted this because she would have wanted the same for him. To move on and build a new life, preferably a happy one. She never would have wanted to deprive him of that.

All these troubles seemed to have kicked her into gear, pushing her out of neutral, out of stasis.

That was a good thing, right?

While she might daydream about Mitch, she had no right to expect him to feel the same. He was already doing too much for her, entirely too much.

She couldn't stand alone. She knew it. Whatever was going on, there was no way she could face this solo. That annoyed her and scared her. Problems too big to handle on her own. She hadn't had them before, not really.

Except with the sheep. She'd been forced to face reality there, as well. One person couldn't do it on any useful scale. She'd had a choice: sell them or pare the flock down until they were essentially pets. Neither solution would have helped her keep the ranch.

She was grateful to Mitch for the way he had stepped in. He'd made it clear he wanted the sheep, all without her mentioning her increasing troubles, but as part of the deal he'd insisted she lease him most of her pasture and would sell him her hay crop.

"How am I supposed to graze the animals without the land?" he'd asked her.

Good question. The answer, she thought, was good business for them both.

Now he was stepping in again, this time with no apparent motive except to protect her. His concern warmed her but also worried her. She didn't want to become dependent.

She didn't want him to step back once again, either. Like it or not, she was growing dependent on his company.

That could be a very bad thing.

Eventually sleep snuck up on her and carried her into some surprisingly pleasant dreams. The nightmares didn't reach her.

Chapter 16

Mitch waited to wake Grace until the first very early gray light began to wash out the stars. He hadn't had the least trouble staying awake and he hated to rouse her.

He also figured her wrath wasn't worth letting her sleep. He went to her bedroom door and called her gently, not wanting to frighten her.

"Huh?" she asked drowsily.

"Your turn on watch. I'll go make you some coffee and rustle up some food."

If she woke up, good. If she went back to sleep, not his problem. Hah!

He needed some breakfast, too, and looking in her fridge he found eggs and some shredded cheese. A promising start. He opened the breadbox beside the stove and discovered English muffins. Good accompaniment. Plenty of butter in the fridge. Hidden in her pantry was an unopened jar of raspberry preserves.

He could already taste the food to come.

He turned his head as he heard her behind him.

"I can cook," she said.

"I know you can."

"You must be tired. And you let me sleep too late."

"Late is a matter of perception, I can sleep just as well during the morning, and look, lady, I *can* cook. So just sit yourself down and enjoy the service."

Hell, she didn't look fully awake yet. Mitch suspected she hadn't slept very long.

The coffeepot finished brewing just as he was cracking eggs into a bowl. "Scrambled okay?"

She nodded, her chin on her hand. "Thanks." Her eyelids kept drooping, which amused him. Yeah, she was awake. Barely.

He poured her a big mug of caffeine to help, then set about toasting bread and whipping the eggs with a dash of milk and a lot of cheese. "I am such a skilled cook that I'll take your breath away. Well, not really. I warn you, I couldn't begin to hold a candle to Lila."

That drew a weary chuckle from her. "I don't think anyone could."

"I think it helps that she loves cooking. Me, I'm a survivalist when it comes to that."

"I think I've pretty much become one, too. Feed me before I faint."

He laughed. "I read you."

Across the road, in the foothills of the huge mountains where pines towered and a few cottonwoods succeeded, Carl and Larry lazed in the warming day, awaiting their next assignment—if one was needed.

"I'm going to town," Carl announced abruptly.

"You sure you should?"

"Look, I'm sick of eating out of cans. I want me some decent food. A burger and some fries. A milkshake. You sure as hell can't make a milkshake over a camp stove."

Larry didn't put up a fuss over that. "Milkshake sounds good," he admitted. "Beer's getting cold enough in that stream, but you're right about anything colder. Hell, I'd just be glad of the taste, even melted."

"You see? I'm gonna get us something decent."

Larry rolled over and looked at Carl. "What about the boss?"

"She ain't asked us to do one damn thing except at night. I'll be back before then. You can take a message…if she ain't done with us."

In her small apartment in Conard City, Betty Pollard brushed her hair. Dan was a figment, an imaginary boyfriend to throw a concealing cloak of normalcy over her real plan for Grace.

All these years later, Betty still grew furious at the chain of events that had ripped that ranch from her father. So what if he hadn't paid his property taxes? Did that mean a man should lose everything?

She ignored the other debts that had mounted, debts she didn't know about until it was too late. Most ranchers and farmers ran an open line of credit to deal with major expenses. Her dad had eventually stopped paying those, too.

The foreclosure had come from taxes and that lien was filed first. Since the county wasn't trying to make a profit, and the lenders had accepted the newer equipment for collateral and not the land, the auction had been for peanuts. Peanuts! That whole damn place was worth a hell of a lot more.

But Betty had only been a high schooler. She'd

learned about the taxes but hadn't been able to do anything because she didn't have any money. She'd told her dad to sell off a parcel, but he refused.

"It'll get better, honey. It always does."

It had in prior years. But this time he'd let it go too long, and the county foreclosed well before Betty expected it. As soon as the lenders had heard about the foreclosure, they'd moved in to take anything of value.

Then her father had died, with nothing left to live for, and Grace and John had bought the homestead for a song.

Betty didn't have a personal grudge against the Halls, but she wanted her childhood home again. She wanted it with an enduring ache and unrequited fury.

Thanks to a legacy from a nearly forgotten aunt, she now had the money to pay a fair price for the ranch. A decent price. She wasn't trying to rip anyone off.

Without John, it seemed crazy for Grace to hang on to the land and the house. It was fair for her to be reluctant about selling, but managing the ranch was entirely too much for one person alone. Hell, as near as Betty could tell, Grace was having trouble keeping up. Of course, she had those two shepherds but Betty sensed an opportunity.

Betty sighed and poured herself a double shot of bourbon. She tried to contain her anger, but since John's death her self-control had grown increasingly difficult.

While she didn't want Grace to see that anger, it simmered in her anyway. She had finally gotten to the point of trying to scare Grace away.

Nothing that would actually hurt Grace. She didn't want to do that. She felt terrible about Grace's burns but she hadn't known there were horses out there, and apparently neither had the men she had hired for this job.

But if Grace didn't fear that she was being targeted, then she was stupider than Betty would have believed.

So why wasn't she hightailing it to town? Away from the repeated threats?

Betty finished off her bourbon and poured another. It was too soon to demand that Larry and Carl do something else to scare Grace.

Give it time to sink in, Betty decided. Let the threat linger longer.

Then she would tell those two idiots to get going and warn them again about not hurting Grace. Hell, she was paying them enough with a bonus at the end. And they were despicable enough to do it. The whole barn-burning, while it had seemed like a good idea when those guys proposed it, still made her sick to her stomach. What was she paying those men for? They should have known there were horses in that barn.

But the break-in should have been enough to drive the point home to Grace. Especially when nothing had been taken but an old computer and TV.

"Hell," she said, this time aloud. Then several times she repeated the word emphatically.

It made her feel only a bit better.

Mitch slept until nearly noon, which was fine by him. He expected the worst of the danger would come at night, that the mornings were free of the threat. The earlier events had given him reason to think so.

He sat up, closing the recliner, ignoring the stiffness that came from not being able to move much in his sleep. Well, it was better than bedding down on rocky ground.

He could hear Grace on the porch, so he took the opportunity to shower and change. He'd brought extra clothes with him, enough for a few days, and the change was welcome.

By now he must have the same stench as a barn animal. His chaps still hung over the back of a chair, needing that oiling he couldn't give them just yet. They'd do okay for a while.

And now he'd do okay smelling more like shampoo and soap. Only thing he regretted was that he must be smelling like a field of lavender.

Funny he hadn't noticed that aroma when it lingered around Grace. But maybe it had been part of her all this time, like her wide smile, her pleasantly curved figure, her light and enchanting voice.

Oh, boy. He was getting it bad.

Then he realized he also smelled bread. He sniffed with pleasure, then stepped outside to find Grace, her shotgun nearby, leaning against a stanchion and surveying the property toward the county road.

"Do I smell bread?" he asked.

She pivoted and smiled. "Gotta do something during this stakeout."

"But bread? That's a lot of work, especially with your hands."

She raised her arms. "More like a workout for the upper body. It felt good. As for my hands, we've come to an agreement. They're going to hurt regardless. Anyway, four more loaves coming up since the remaining ones are getting stale."

"Four?"

"If I was going to do one, I might as well do more. Same mess. The kneading part is great exercise. Cleaning flour off the whole damn kitchen, not so much."

A grin emerged, stretching his face. "You're a messy cook?"

"More like a messy baker. I might do drop biscuits later."

"I love biscuits."

"Who doesn't?" Grace resumed her watch. "Nothing. I even walked around the house and the barn to see if I could catch sight of anything at all."

His heart skipped. "Grace—"

"I know. Skip it, Mitch. I went alone because I've been doing it for years. If someone wants to take a potshot at me, then this whole thing wasn't going to end well anyway."

He could see that stiffening in her backbone. Not a good time to press her. The obstinate Grace was out in full force.

"I'll make us some coffee. Want some?"

She nodded. "Thanks. I guess it's almost time for lunch."

"I'll take care of that. I have this delusional idea that I can be good for something."

At least that drew a laugh from her. "Good for a whole lot, Mitch. Like staying here when I need some help."

"Such a sacrifice," he joked. No sacrifice at all. He had people he could rely on for his ranch. She had no one else.

Besides, he was seeing parts of her that he hadn't seen since John. He liked them.

Mitch had rustled up sandwiches made with cold cuts, lettuce and mayonnaise. He brought them along with coffee out to Grace.

"Thank you," Grace said as she accepted a paper plate. She looked at the thickness of the sandwich and asked, "Did you use up all my cold cuts?"

"Yup. I like 'em hearty. Don't worry about it. Lila will replace them and more. Just enjoy."

Enjoy enough for two people, she thought, surveying the size of the sandwich. Gamely she bit into it and decided his choice had been a good one. "Delicious," she said.

"I'm sure the bread would have been better if it was yours."

She glanced over her shoulder. "Believe it. It must be close to done with the final rise, so I need to check on it after lunch."

"Making bread is a mystery to me."

"It was to me, too, until I made my first loaf."

A songbird seemed have taken up residence on the porch roof and provided a happy accompaniment to the meal.

The world still sounded cheerful, Grace thought as she listened to the bird. And the food and coffee still tasted good. She needed to hang on to those things, to remember the beauty nature offered. The beauty of having a friend make her a stupendous lunch.

She was seeing Mitch so much differently now, more than a friend and neighbor. As a man. Her first real inkling was when she had watched him mount his horse to set out on a hunt for the transgressors. Now she felt it even more.

A man. An attractive, weather-hardened, work-hardened man. A stand-up guy. If he had any real failings, she hadn't encountered them. Or at least none that bothered her enough for them to rise to her awareness.

The bird continued to tweet happily as the sky overhead darkened. The wind shifted a little, bringing new scents to the world.

"Rain soon," she remarked.

"Smells like it. I hope it doesn't blow over. I saw some dry patches in the pasture when I was out yesterday."

Amusement struck her. Such a prosaic and ordinary conversation between two ranchers. As if the weather and the state of a pasture were all that mattered. As if the threat of danger didn't lie in every shadow.

A comfortable rhythm, however, dredging up memories of many conversations over the years, with John and neighbors. In ordinary times, such thoughts were essential. They usually led to conversations about livestock, feed, pasturage, crops, the most important thing in most lives around her. Common ground indeed.

It still felt odd to be having such a conversation in these circumstances. Both of them sitting there with shotguns ready to blast away. Both of them scanning the countryside for any sign of threat.

A jarring counterpoint.

As soon as she finished her sandwich, she rose to go check on her bread. Almost ready for the oven, she decided. The rising could be slow or fast depending on ambient temperature. Today, inside, there was a coolness that probably lingered from the night before and she wouldn't have expected the dough to rise so fast.

She turned on the oven, set a timer, then headed back to the porch with the coffeepot. "Top you off?"

"Sure. Thanks." He held out his mug.

She topped her own mug, then placed the pot on the table between them. "This," she said as she sat again, "feels too much like an ordinary summer day."

"It is," he said.

"Oh, yeah."

His gray eyes twinkled as they settled on her. "Well,

apart from that. Let's enjoy it. In a bit, I'll walk around, maybe ride out again to look for problems."

"Did you get Burt Stiller?" she asked.

"I got his voice mail. He's probably out on the range."

"Yeah." The idea deflated her a little. Mitch would go out to cover the same territory he'd covered yesterday and learn exactly nothing.

The timer inside beeped and she returned to the kitchen to put the loaves in the oven. Four, side by side, just like she used to bake when...

She cut that thought off. She couldn't let every damn thing carry her back to the past. Today was a new day, one that carried its own set of problems. Time to deal with here and now.

She set a timer for the bread, then went outside again in time to see a pickup coming up her drive. "Who's that?"

"I guess we'll find out." Mitch stood with the shotgun cradled in his arms. A warning to whoever.

No warning needed. Out of the car stepped Jenny Wright, a ranch wife Grace had once known but hadn't seen again until the barn raising. A lot of things had disappeared after John, mostly her own fault.

"Hey," Jenny called with a cheerful wave. "Thought it was time to be a good neighbor, so I brought you my famous chicken and green bean casserole. The beans are from my kitchen garden and while you'll taste the white wine, it won't make you drunk." She grinned almost ear to ear, then leaned back inside her car to bring out a very large casserole dish. She carried it up to the porch. "At least enough for several meals, even with a hungry cowboy around."

"Thank you so much!" Grace was touched. How had she pushed people like this away?

"I'd give you a hug of greeting, but I'd like to set this down somewhere it won't draw flies and other critters."

Mitch spoke. "You ladies go on inside. I'll stay out here."

Inside, Jenny placed the casserole on the counter. "Mmm, I smell baking bread. Got ambitious this morning?"

"I did," Grace agreed. "Stay awhile and I'd be happy to send you home with a loaf."

Jenny shook her head. "I'd love it, but I have to get back. I left three boys with an overwhelmed husband who would rather be herding cattle."

Grace laughed. "Three now?" She seemed to remember Jennie had been pregnant way back, but hadn't thought about it.

"Yup, and they're all hell on wheels. The youngest, Timmy, is way too young to ride yet, except on a pony, so the older boys can't go ramming about on their horses because Daddy can't take 'em out. Because of Timmy. Hell, they say the youngest child is always spoiled, but Timmy will never get the chance thanks to his older brothers."

"Tough on him?"

"Oh yeah. They also don't much like it when he keeps them from doing stuff because he's so young. Not that we let that happen too often, but you wouldn't believe it because of the way they complain."

"Oh, I can believe it."

Jenny raised a brow. "That's right, you taught elementary school. Lots of experience."

"Enough to know that many boys are more active and adventurous than most girls their ages. I've often wondered if that was social."

"I'll let you know if I ever get my daughter." Then

Jenny frowned. "Grace? I heard about your break-in. Are you getting scared? I would. First the barn and then this?"

"I'm not scared, at least not yet," Grace said with determination. "I'm angry, though, angrier than hell. Scared might come in the middle of the night if this keeps up."

Jenny nodded thoughtfully. "It seems like an awful lot. At least you have Mitch here. I wouldn't want to be alone just now."

"I'm grateful I don't have to be," Grace admitted, although it felt a little like weakness to lean on someone else. It had been different with John. They'd leaned on each other. Mitch didn't seem to need anyone to lean on.

Jenny stayed long enough for Grace to make another pot of coffee, then they joined Mitch on the porch. Jenny sat where Mitch had been perched and looked up at him as he leaned against the porch railing.

"What do you think is going on here?" Jenny asked Mitch.

"Damned if I know."

"But you don't think it's over," she said, pointing to his shotgun.

"Don't dare to. Not yet. All of this is moving closer to Grace."

Grace drew a sharp breath. She hadn't thought of it that way. That she might be targeted, yes. But that the threat was moving toward her, like a shark circling in the water? The idea went past property crimes, and for the first time a nearly overwhelming fear filled her. She also felt a little stupid for not thinking of this in such a way, not when it was as plain as the nose on her face.

"Do you really believe that?" Grace asked Mitch.

"Like I said, I don't dare to assume it's over. We both already knew that, though."

Yes, they had. The threat hadn't disappeared for her personally, not yet. It had been against her property, all of it. She had been convinced that it was all directed against scaring her, not against hurting her physically. But she hadn't noticed the fact that it was indeed moving closer to her. All the way down the driveway, then the barn, then the house.

Jenny finished her coffee just as the bread finished baking. It was too hot to send a loaf with her, so Grace said, "Another time?"

"Any time you get another yen to do all that work, call me. I'll be over as soon as it cools."

Smiling, giving another friendly wave, Jenny departed. Grace watched her car pull away, and the darkening day seemed to grow darker.

The air delivered the strong smell of rain and the faint scent of ozone. The storm was coming.

"I need to get out and ride around again," Mitch said.

"Are you sure you should? Lightning."

"I haven't seen any, nor heard any rumble of thunder. I promise I'll take shelter under a tree if I see or hear any."

Grace gaped at him. "You wouldn't!"

Mitch laughed. "Gotta go. As many times as I've been through it, I still hate getting drenched."

Feeling even lonelier, she watched him ride away. At least he had an oiled leather duster for protection.

She pulled the bread out of the oven and dumped each loaf onto a cooling rack, then set them upright. Pretty darn good, she decided as she looked at them.

She hadn't forgotten how. Then she went back out to keep watch.

Gusts of wind blew rain every which way, driving Grace indoors. The day had darkened until it seeped through the world like approaching night. Inside was even darker, and she didn't want to open curtains, advertising to any watcher where she was in the house.

Which sounded paranoid, but that was where events had taken her.

In times past, she had always enjoyed storms like this. Unless she and John had been out with the sheep, the graying, wind-and-rain-lashed days had felt cozy. Time for a cup of hot chocolate, lots of laughter, and lovemaking.

That part of her stirred awake again. She wondered if she should be disturbed or feel disloyal. No. She knew as sure as she was walking around her house that John wouldn't have wanted that. He'd been a generous man and, while his death had been totally unexpected, she knew him well enough to believe he would not have wanted her to spend the rest of her days in lonely grief. In emptiness.

Inevitably, her thoughts turned to Mitch and the desires that had begun to take on life. She had no idea if he might be feeling the same toward her. No idea at all.

But maybe he sensed he might be transgressing. Hardly surprising considering the distance she had placed between them.

She started the casserole heating for supper, the entire dish. It would be more than the two of them could eat, but she had no idea how hungry Mitch would be after riding in this rain. Rain was always cold. Almost icy.

When the squall line finally passed—it had sure

taken a sluggish path over the house—the wind settled to more usual levels and stopped driving the downpour in every direction. Excuse enough to return Grace and her shotgun to the porch.

It would have been an opportune time, with the dark sky and flat light, for someone to have approached.

As she was emerging from her cocoon, she saw Mitch ride up to the barn. A wave of relief filled her. Knowing Mitch would take care of his horse before anything else, she went inside to heat water for instant cocoa. With a bit of cream, it tasted almost like the real thing.

Finally she heard Mitch's boots on the porch. She ran to open the door and saw him dripping despite his duster.

"Did you go swimming?" she asked lightly.

"I thought I might need skin diving gear. Listen, I want to strip out here, so if you wouldn't mind bringing me the bag I left on the mud porch so I have dry clothes, I'd appreciate it."

She hurried to get the bag for him, along with a towel. "Dry off, too."

He flashed a grin. "Now get inside unless you want to see me as naked as the day I was born."

She wouldn't have minded that at all. In fact, she quickened between her legs. But he deserved his privacy, so she went back to the kitchen to wait. She could imagine the sight well enough anyway, and a sigh escaped her.

While she waited, the phone rang. Guy Redwing was on the other end.

"We researched that big cattle operator who tried to buy your operation earlier this year."

"And?"

"Their business practices appear to be aboveboard. No complaints anywhere from property owners. In fact, no complaints or disputes about their contracts, either. Whatever hijinks they might be up to are buried within the corporation itself."

Grace's stomach sank. She had hoped for information the sheriff could work on. "I wish I could say that's good news."

Guy sounded sympathetic. "I hear you, Grace. We'll keep looking. You know that. We want to solve this problem as much as you do."

The nice part of living in an underpopulated area was the attentiveness of police. She was sure they wouldn't drop this because they couldn't immediately find good information.

Although how they would, she couldn't begin to imagine.

Mitch entered the kitchen barefoot but otherwise covered in dry clothing, a khaki safari shirt with faded jeans.

"I'm going to let my stuff hang out front to finish dripping, then I'll beg for the use of your laundry."

She smiled. "What would you do if I said no? Of course you can use them."

She turned to the boiling water on the stove, switched off the gas flame, waiting for it to cool just enough so she wouldn't singe the dry milk in the mix. "Cocoa?"

"Sounds great."

She heard the chair slide away from the table as he sat. She didn't turn around immediately because she was having just a bit of trouble breathing and she didn't want to devour him with her eyes.

Dang, where had this come from? It was rising in her like a powerful tide. She needed to resist it for Mitch's sake. What if she embarrassed him? A good friendship might die.

At last she felt comfortable enough to sit with him. She avoided his gaze for a few minutes longer, though.

"This is good," Mitch told her after he'd sipped. "A package mix made this?"

"Cream helped make it richer."

"I'm sold."

What a mundane conversation. "Guy Redwing called. Nothing about the company that approached us seems problematic."

He sighed. "I should have been smarter than to hope it would be that easy."

Now she *did* look at him. "Then what?"

"I don't know. I'm running out of suspicions, not that I had many to go on at the start."

A grim prospect indeed. Where did all of this go from here?

Nothing seemed promising.

Mitch insisted on cleaning up the cups and pan. When he turned around he found Grace right behind him.

He saw the heat and longing in her gaze and was almost afraid to believe it. Good God, was it possible? And why *him*?

No, it wasn't possible. He didn't dare risk the fragility of whatever was growing between them. Too quickly, too soon.

Then she leaned into him, wrapping her arms around his waist.

"Don't hate me," she whispered. "Just hold me."

Hate her? That could never happen. Without a word, he surrounded her shoulders and held her close. He would have held her even closer except he didn't want it to feel like a squeeze.

But his body, damn his body, was reacting to her in the most obvious way possible. Her face rested against his shoulder, a trusting gesture, and he half expected her to break into tears.

She didn't, though. She turned her face up to his and said one simple word. "Please."

Chapter 17

Mitch's head nearly exploded in response to this unexpected development. He could feel her shaking like a leaf against him and couldn't mistake how much courage that one word had required of her.

All he could do was tighten his hold. "You sure?"

"Yes," she murmured.

Grace might be using him to make her first step back to a fuller life, just a stepping-stone, but he didn't care, not at this moment in time, with her leaning into him. Regardless, he couldn't reject her, no matter how gently, and leave her feeling unwanted.

Well, he didn't want to reject her. Not at all. Barely formed desires had erupted inside him and he wasn't going to walk away. If persuasion of some kind was needed afterward, then, damn it, he'd worry about it then.

He doubted her steadiness, so he lifted her in his

arms to carry her back to her bedroom. She was too light, too much like a bird in his arms. Fragile.

He was almost afraid he might hurt her. He was equally uncertain of himself. It had been a while, and he feared he might be rusty.

Sitting her on the edge of her bed, he knelt and gazed into her blue eyes. They appeared almost smoky just then.

He had to know before he laid a finger on her. "Grace. You can say no. Now or later."

She gave a jerky nod but did nothing to send him on his way.

His own hands shook a bit as he reached for the top button on her simple checked shirt. He wished they were snaps but opening the buttons one at a time gave her another opportunity to back off. She didn't. Instead while he released the buttons, she lifted her hands to his shoulders. Inviting him.

He was leaping off a cliff with no idea what lay below.

His worries soon slipped away as he revealed the beauty hiding beneath her shirt. Her full breasts were encased in a lacy confection that surprised him. She was always dressed in work clothes, and he hadn't expected to find she had a secret liking for special undergarments.

His mouth dried a bit as he pushed the shirt from her shoulders and reached behind her to release the clasp of her bra. More beauty filled his gaze, large pink nipples rising from the smooth skin of her breasts. So enticing.

He murmured her name, overwhelmed by the desire that pounded through him. How long had he wanted her? It was a question that needed no answer, even as the longing began to be answered. All that mattered was that he wanted her now, and that she seemed to feel the same.

He brushed his thumbs over the peaks of her breasts and wished his hands were smoother, as she surely deserved. Glancing up at her face, he saw her eyes closed, her entire face growing softer than he'd ever seen her look.

Her breath came faster, too, another lure that wrapped around him like a spell. Ensorcelled, he could be stopped by nothing now, except a protest from her. But she didn't protest, merely leaned back on her hands, welcoming and inviting.

Too much. He rose and began stripping away the clothes that he'd donned such a short time ago. Her eyelids fluttered open and she smiled sleepily as she watched.

Heaven had just entered the room along with rising musky scents.

Grace watched him strip, her heart jumping and accelerating until she was sure the last air had been sucked from the room.

He was gorgeous, she thought hazily. More gorgeous than her imaginings. Hard muscle from work created a captivating body, so masculine and perfect in every way. A few scars nicked him here and there, but they only added to his desirability.

He was ready for her. So ready.

She throbbed achingly at her center and could hardly wait for his weight to cover her. She needed nothing further to make her eager, and resented the delay.

But there was more. He knelt again, leaning forward to take her nipples into his mouth, sucking so strongly that the pleasure dived through her, coalescing in her core.

His fingers reached for the snap of her jeans, and she didn't appreciate the last impediments that needed to be removed. He pulled her jeans down until they rode her calves, then pulled her boots off in swift, easy movements. So strong!

At last her jeans were gone, and only a wisp of panties stood in their way. Once again, he pulled back to look at her.

"Damn, you're beautiful," he muttered. Then he reached for her delicate panties that matched her bra.

The moment she was naked, she basked in his hungry eyes, in his faint smile. Then he moved between her legs, teasing her breast with his tongue, reaching out to stroke her petals with gentle fingers.

The last of the world was lost in an explosion of magic so powerful it hurt.

Need. She became a needy vessel, impatient for him.

"Mitch," she groaned.

With a slow, steady movement he slipped inside her, carrying her ever upward to the stars. She fell back, giving herself completely over to his ministrations, so thrilled by the feel of him deep inside her that she came close to losing her mind in pleasure.

He pumped into her, caressing her sensitive nub with his finger, driving her upward to heights that felt new to her, fresh, as if she had never visited them before.

"Grace…"

Her name reached into her, filling places she'd hardly been aware of.

Need. She was needy and rose ever higher until she trembled on the peak and tipped over, a climax so strong it nearly hurt.

* * *

Mitch felt the exact moment of her culmination, and drove one more time, hard, so hard he could barely stand it. Then he followed her into the slow fall on the far side.

He fell forward, his face resting on her midriff, satisfied as he was sure he'd never been satisfied before.

Then, at last, some strength poured into his muscles. Just enough.

He rose, lifting her until she was under the comforter on her bed. Moments later he fell beside her and took her into his arms, hugging her tightly.

He felt blessed.

Minutes passed. Maybe hours. At the moment, time no longer mattered to Mitch. When Grace stirred, he asked huskily, "You okay?"

"Better than," she whispered in response. "Far better."

Happiness flooded him. Joy. When had he last felt as high as a kite? He couldn't remember. Life so seldom left room for it.

"Me, too," he answered. "Me, too."

She snuggled closer, offering him a trust that made his throat tighten.

"Grace," he murmured again.

Her fingers touched his lips. "Shh. Let perfection be."

Perfection? The word crashed through him like thunder. Then he realized she was right. Perfection. She shared the feeling with him. He couldn't have asked for more.

Eventually, because eventually always came, they rose and dressed. Hands touched lightly, a few kisses were exchanged but reality had begun to creep into the room once more.

There might be a threat out there, and neither of them could ignore the possibility for long.

Mitch went outside again to check around the house and barn. Reluctantly, Grace watched him go but knew he was right. They had to keep an eye out. Rain still fell, but lighter now. Even the leaden gray of the sky had changed to a lighter color, announcing it had dumped most of its watery burden.

She touched her loaves of bread, surprised to realize they had cooled. Had they made love for that long?

She blushed faintly, guessing they must have. It had seemed to be over too soon, but time had faded in Mitch's arms.

It had been beautiful. Whatever happened between them now, she decided she didn't care. The past hours had been so fantastic she wouldn't have missed them for anything.

Regardless of what she told herself, there was a nugget inside her that hoped for more than the friendship they had shared. Much more.

Another tumble in the hay? She almost giggled aloud. Oh, she had it bad. She needed to brace herself, though. As she'd long since discovered, life rarely turned out the way one hoped.

Mitch walked around in the gentle rain, hoping it would cool him down a bit. Damn, he wanted that woman again, and he wasn't at all sure she'd welcome another advance.

Maybe she'd just been overcome by stress. Maybe

she had reached out for comfort and not for him in particular.

Maybe she regretted the sex they'd just shared.

One thing he knew for certain: he didn't regret it. He hadn't lived a celibate life but he knew when sex was special. This had been, beyond his wildest dreams.

Facing yearnings he'd been denying for a very long time, he accepted that he was drawn to Grace for reasons that had nothing to do with sex. Something deeper had rooted inside him, and he might need a tiller to pull it out.

Leaving a gaping hole behind, with no way to fill it in.

"Now what do I do?" he asked himself as he continued his patrol. The rain didn't give him an answer.

But a surprising roll of thunder did. He looked up at the sky and saw it blackening again. Cripes, one squall hadn't been enough? Two in a row?

Climate chaos, he thought. God knew he'd been seeing enough of its effects on his ranch. You couldn't wander around as much land as he owned without noting steady changes. You could try to remain blind until lifelong observation told you that you had your head in the sand.

Or this might just be an isolated incident. He wanted to hope so.

He hurried his survey but contented himself that no threat hovered yet. How long did they have to wait for the next one? Because he believed there would be a next one.

He wished he could imagine why Grace was being targeted this way. It would have at least given him a direction to pursue.

At last he headed back to the house and entered,

hoping Grace might give him a slab of that fresh bread. Preferably with a thick coating of butter.

She greeted him with a smile, but he didn't miss the faint touch of heightened color. Was she embarrassed? Uneasy?

Not knowing what else to do, ignoring his slightly dampened state—even the duster hadn't been able to keep him completely dry—he walked to her and gave her a tight hug.

"Missed you," he admitted. And it hadn't even been that long.

"Missed you, too." She sighed and returned his hug.

They separated, as if neither was sure how to continue.

"It's still raining," he remarked. "That's no big deal, but there's another squall moving in."

"Really? That's odd."

"The sky is mad at us, I guess. Now, how do I beg for a big piece of that fresh bread?"

She laughed, sounding easier. "You sit at the table and wait for me to cut it. How hungry are you?"

"Well, I could probably eat half a loaf, but I'll be polite."

"Polite is eating up all my bread. If you stop after one slice it definitely won't be polite."

His turn to laugh. He was feeling better by the minute.

She must have taken him seriously, because she *did* cut him a couple of thick slices and passed him the butter dish along with the butter knife.

"Have at it," she said. "And tell me what you think. It's been ages since I made bread."

He spread the butter thickly, then bit into the soft

bread with its crunchy crust. "To die for," he announced, even though he hated that phrase.

"I detest breads where you can't taste or smell the yeast."

He hadn't thought about that. All he knew was that he liked it a lot.

She sat facing him with her own, thinner, slice of bread. "So nothing outside?"

"Nothing I could detect. It's a miserable day out there, and about to get worse. Colder, too, I expect."

"Good. I hope the bad guy is out there and is freezing and wet."

A surprised laugh escaped him. "I never dreamed you could wish ill on anyone."

"Well, I can, and this guy deserves it. Maybe he'll even get hypothermic."

Mitch grinned. "Remind me never to get on your bad side."

Then she surprised him again, saying softly, "I don't think you could, Mitch."

"I'm no saint," he protested.

"Neither am I. As you just saw."

She finished her bread and rose. "Want more?"

"A couple of slices just like these."

She cut them for him, then began to wrap the loaves in plastic. They went into a large breadbox. "Jenny's casserole for dinner?"

"Sounds great."

"Save some room. She brought enough for an army."

Then she pulled back the curtain at the kitchen window for a minute. "I'm scared Mitch. Someone is out there and I don't even know what he wants."

"Maybe to scare you," he said slowly, repeating a concern they had shared.

"But why?"

He wished he could answer. They *both* wanted that answer.

Carl held the satellite phone away from his ear as the boss shouted at him. Larry could hear it, too.

"What is it with you two," she yelled. "I'm paying you to do one simple thing!"

She was going nuts, Carl decided. Losing her marbles. What was eating her? They'd done some pretty bad and dangerous things for her, now they was getting screamed at?

"We can't *make* that Hall woman do a damn thing," he retorted, his own voice rising as anger triumphed over his perplexity. "You want her out of there, *you* go do something."

"Like hell. You're getting money for this. You'd better think of something soon."

"Not too soon, you said. Give her time to think about it, let it eat at her, you said. Well, you get your freaking butt out there and *you* do something."

Silence greeted his words.

"I thought so," Carl spat. "You keep wanting us to risk jail or death, then you can just put up with this. Alls I want to know is do you want us to speed up or wait like you said."

More silence answered him.

Carl continued his rant. "You ain't got no idea what's going on. That woman's got a guy with her and they's patrolling the place with shotguns as if they was military."

Then her voice returned to the earpiece. It sounded steely as all hell, throwing some icy water over his indignation.

"Just remember, you don't get your money until this job is completed. And I don't mean halfway." Then she disconnected.

Carl listened to a different kind of silence before he closed his end of the call.

"Man, that was some yellin'," Larry said after listening to a godforsaken and lonely bird calling another of its kind.

"She ain't happy," Carl said needlessly.

Larry lost interest in the singing when the bird flew away. Damn thing needed to find a mate for hisself. Good luck. Not that Larry had had much luck with finding a woman, and it kinda soured his view of romance. Or sex. Whatever. He didn't know the difference and he didn't care.

"What now?" he asked.

"We follow our orders for a bit. Wait and see. Then we's gonna worsen it."

"How?" asked Larry, who'd about given up trying to think of something new to do.

Carl didn't answer for a minute. "Somebody gonna die," he said. "We tried it her way too damn long."

Grace and Mitch felt safe. Briefly. The time between incidents had been long and neither of them expected one immediately.

Maybe, thought Mitch, their patrolling with guns could hold the threat at bay. For a while. He didn't expect their guns to be a permanent magic charm, and he couldn't help wondering how long he and Grace could keep this up.

As long as necessary, he decided. If he had to go back to his own operation for a short while, one of his men could come and stand watch.

Because he was damned if he was going to leave Grace alone.

She joined him on the front porch with a carafe of fresh coffee. When she sat, she picked up her shotgun.

The sky remained leaden, still pregnant with rain. It would be surprising if the clouds dumped again because the rain shadow of the mountains generally caused rain to fall farther east. Summers here were usually dry. Well, drier than this one was turning into.

Grace spoke. "You don't think they'd kill anyone, do you?"

The fear was uppermost in his mind, too, although he was reluctant to voice it. But now she had.

"I don't know." Never lie to Grace. His guiding star.

"I don't know either, obviously. I shouldn't even have asked."

"Why not? It's impossible not to wonder at this point. Worry is buzzing inside both our heads like angry bees."

She nodded, shooting him the smallest smile at his comparison. "I wish the sheriff had found something about that company. A word might have been enough to make them back off."

Now they were staring into a black hole with no idea if there was a bottom. Not an easy place to exist.

"We're doing all we can," he reminded her.

"You must need to get back to your life."

He almost said she had become the most important thing in his life, but after the time they'd shared in her bed, he suspected she might scamper away like a frightened rabbit. He had little doubt that the specter of John would swim to the forefront of her mind, making her feel disloyal. Lucky man, John, to have known Grace's love.

"Not yet," he told her. "Not yet." He said no more, giving her room to escape if she needed it.

Nothing permanent. Maybe her reference to him getting back to his own life had been her first attempt to push him away. God, he hoped not. The attraction to her that he'd buried during her marriage to John, that he'd buried in the face of her widowhood, had sprung to full life. She was beautiful, to his eye anyway, but she was even more admirable in so many ways.

Stubborn, yes, but tough and loyal and so lost over the last two years. He wanted to put the sparkle back in her eye for longer than a brief spell. He wanted to put it there most of the time.

He nearly sighed as he realized he'd wandered away from their purpose, the most important purpose. Keeping Grace safe.

Rising, he announced that he was going to take another walk around.

"No coffee first?"

"When I get back. That carafe will keep it hot enough." Then, gun in hand, he stepped off the porch and began to walk his mental perimeter, not only looking for a man, but looking also for anything out of place.

Soon he'd need to ride out again, even though his men were keeping an eye out for any indication that a stranger had been there, camping on his ranch.

He still hadn't heard from Burt Stiller about riding around his land. Stiller wouldn't mind, but it wouldn't be neighborly to just go ahead. And Stiller must be out somewhere on his own ranch, a big spread that sometimes needed a lot of attention. As they all did.

Chapter 18

The next week passed without any threatening events. Grace began to suggest that it might be over.

Mitch didn't accept that. The barn-burning and the break-in had been designed to terrify her. Directed at her. Why else would someone do those things if they didn't want her shaking in her boots? And clearly she wasn't shaking.

She'd become as immovable as a post sunk six feet in the ground. Which was good for *her*, he supposed, but it wasn't good for *him*. If she'd wavered at all, he'd have swept her off to his house, left her in Lila's competent charge and waited with a whole lot less fear for her until the next thing happened.

It would be a helluva lot harder to frighten Grace in his house. Too many people around, and Lila was a deadeye marksman.

Not something anyone would expect from a housekeeper.

Of course, the other side to that was that the threat might indeed move to his place. Not that he was worried if it did—he could deal with whatever—but he doubted it would. He could imagine no upside to coming after him. Besides, if there was a target in this madness, it certainly wasn't him. But it would sure trouble Grace and convince her to return to her own land to protect *him*.

Inwardly he fumed about the entire mess. Without a direction to pursue, there could be no useful action.

Then there was the immovable steel that was Grace. She hadn't shown any desire to repeat their memorable hours in her bed.

John, he thought. Or maybe he just wasn't a good enough partner to make her want another round—despite what she'd said.

Aw, hell. He couldn't remember ever having felt so many rats scrambling around in his brain. This way or that way? Hah! Damn fool.

Peace of any kind had escaped him.

As he watched Grace rocking on her front porch, shotgun across her lap, he wondered if he just needed to approach her himself. Maybe she interpreted his reluctance to mean he didn't want to have sex with her again.

How was he supposed to know? And as the days dragged by, making them both edgier about the possibility of more trouble, he felt less inclination to distract either of them with time in the sack. He knew from their one time together that a bomb could have exploded beneath the bed and he wouldn't have noticed it. Lost to the world with her in his arms.

He stopped pacing around the house and settled beside her on the porch. The inevitable carafe of coffee sat there with two mugs. He didn't think he'd drunk as much coffee in his entire life as he'd swallowed in the last few weeks.

But it jazzed him enough to keep him from fatigue, which he supposed was Grace's idea. So he poured another cup.

"You should go home," Grace said again. "You must be sick of being here."

Far from it, he thought. Given his choice, he'd tear the fences down between her land and his and move into her house with her. No way to say that, though.

"I'm fine," he answered. "Damn well fine."

She looked at him and he was relieved to see her smile. If she could still do that, she'd be okay.

"That sounded like you're aren't, Mitch."

"Believe what I do. I'm here. My choice. I'm just furious about the situation. You should be wanting me here, not needing me. Anyway, I sure as hell don't want to be anywhere else."

How could he not be sure? The witch had cast her spell and he had no desire to dispel it. The description amused him.

"You're sure your guys are handling everything well enough?"

"I trust them or I'd fire them. Hell, they're probably managing so well that I'll feel useless when I get back. My secret fear, that the ranch doesn't really need me."

She laughed quietly, then startled him enough to almost lock his breath in his throat. "Mitch, what you said—do you want to be needed or need to be wanted?"

His neck suddenly stiffened. He had a bit of trouble turning his head to look at her. "Both," he said finally. "Who doesn't?" Brushing it off when he felt it was truly important.

She nodded and returned her gaze to the wide-open

spaces, beyond which mountains loomed. "Once I had both."

He nearly stopped breathing. Here it came again. John. Not that he could blame her, but he nevertheless sent some silent words heavenward. *Let her go, man. You loved her. Love her enough to let go.*

A selfish thought on his part. All about him.

Then she surprised him again. "John wouldn't have wanted me to grieve for so long like this. I know I wouldn't have wanted him to."

"Meaning?"

Her voice grew soft, wistful. "Before all this I'd just started letting go of the past."

"Then this."

She nodded. "The thing is, I was just beginning to think about the future. Just thinking that maybe I could have one. Then this."

"And now?" He was emotionally on the edge of his seat, expecting her to say that the grief had risen again.

"This? This makes me so angry there aren't words. Someone is trying to steal my future."

Slam. Like a body blow. He hadn't thought of that. "You can still have a future," he insisted.

"Not if I'm sitting on my porch all the time with a gun in my lap. This has to end. Maybe it already has."

He poured some coffee and sipped the hot brew. He needed to think carefully before he blundered into the wrong words. He chose a quiet response, rather than an impassioned one.

"We can't afford to think that way, Grace. Give us another six months."

"That's an awfully long time to be on guard with a gun."

"Try the military."

Thank God she laughed again. "Good point."

At least he'd pulled her into a less despairing mood. He just had to hope it would last.

During the night, three gunshots sounded on the air. Mitch bolted upright from the porch chair. They'd come from a long way, carrying better on the cold air, but they were still an ominous sign.

He heard clattering feet behind him and turned. Grace emerged from the front door clad in pajamas, armed. "What was that?"

"I don't know. It came from a distance."

"God!"

He was already pulling the sat phone off his belt. After a very long minute or two, he heard Bill's voice. "You hear that?"

"I sure did. Jack and Jeff are riding over that way from the cattle pastures and I'm about to follow as soon as I get saddled up. It may take a while, hard to tell where the sounds came from. I'm thinking the sheep. Again."

"Damn. I'm going to ride that way, too."

"Not necessary, boss. You keep an eye on Grace. In case. Lila says she's getting a rifle and will keep an eye out here."

"Let me know."

"Like I'd keep it secret. Relax, man, we got three guys to check it out."

He disconnected. "See, I'm useless. My guys are heading out to look into the shots."

"Mitch, you can go if you want."

He faced her. "I'm not leaving you alone. Most especially not after gunshots." Bill had been right. He'd have been more useless out there than he was here.

"But…"

"No buts. Well, except one. If you want to keep watch with me, I wouldn't mind it."

Grace hesitated. "Shouldn't you be over there watching your own house?"

"Bill tells me Lila is getting a rifle. I wouldn't want to be at the wrong end of it."

Yup. They didn't need him. But the thought didn't sour him. He was grateful to those men, and to Lila. He had a family of his own, built of four people who'd earned not only his trust, but his strong affection, as well. Now he was going to worry about them, too.

"They mean a lot to me," he remarked even as he was debating whether to patrol around the house and barn. The moon was practically gone now, providing lots of cover. Now he knew. This criminal worked in total darkness. Night vision goggles?

Hell's bell.

"Your men and Lila seem almost like a family," Grace remarked.

"They are. I was just thinking that."

"So now you have someone else to worry about."

"You're very intuitive," he replied.

He saw her shake her head, even though there was no light but starshine.

"Nothing intuitive about it. I lived with all of you for weeks. I saw it. I also envied it."

That touched him and made him ache for her. She was feeling the loneliness. And here he'd thought her impervious.

"I'm going to make my rounds," he told her.

"I'll go get us some coffee—are you getting sick of it yet?—and something to eat. Anyone comes in that kitchen and he'll be dead."

He waited long enough to see her disappear inside, to see the kitchen light come on, then started his march again around the buildings. He didn't expect to find anything, but it was possible those gunshots had been a distraction. He couldn't risk it.

As Mitch had promised—had it only been a week ago?—Lila had brought over a generous load of supplies.

"I know how much that man eats," Lila had said. "He'll run through all this in no time at all. I'll bring more next week."

Lila had also brought two of her pies and a coffee cake. Evidently, Mitch had something of a sweet tooth.

The coffee cake sounded best to her, so she opened the airtight container and put it on a serving plate. There was enough sugar there to keep them both alert for hours.

The coffee didn't take that long to brew, and soon she was carrying the carafe outside. Another trip and she had the cake on the table along with a couple of small plates.

When Mitch at last returned, she was ready.

"Nothing," he said. It was becoming a refrain to their days.

"Damn," she answered. "Well, eat."

He sliced into the cake and slipped a wedge onto one of the plates. "I wish to God one of my guys would call."

"They probably haven't found anything yet. There's a lot of open land out there."

She understood his uneasiness, though. Livestock and shepherds. Plenty to shoot at out there. She just hoped it hadn't been directed at the shepherds. Bad enough to kill more sheep, but men? A shudder ran through her.

She was also sure this hadn't been directed against Mitch. Nobody knew he owned those sheep but he'd been specific about that and she sure hadn't told anyone.

"Mitch?"

"Yeah?"

"Why didn't you want me to tell anyone that the sheep now belong to you?"

"Because I sure as hell didn't want anyone thinking I'd taken advantage of you."

"But you didn't! I was going to have to sell them anyway."

"No one knows that. You didn't tell anyone. I also know how hard you fought against selling them."

She had, she acknowledged. Perhaps ridiculously so. Part of a dream she could never hope to maintain. She'd been relieved when Mitch made his offer. The sheep wouldn't leave—they'd remain on her land. They wouldn't go to slaughter but would continue to produce wool for years to come.

She understood the realities of raising livestock. Mitch couldn't hope to keep that many steers without sending them off every fall. The only alternative would have been dairy farming and in this dry country that would have been a bad bet.

Nor did she believe he was doing anything wrong. People ate meat. They'd been eating it for thousands of years and there was only one way to get it.

But the sheep…ah, that was different, and she liked that fact. So did Mitch, from everything he'd said.

"Thanks for taking my flock."

"No thanks necessary. I ought to be paying you royalties on all that wool."

She would have chuckled except something dark

was waiting out there and it wasn't the night. Something ugly.

It was impossible not to notice that ugliness was stalking her. Ugliness beyond her imaginings. No rhyme or reason to it. It just was.

They had to stop it somehow.

Two hours later, Bill called Mitch. "The shepherds have been shot. One of them managed to return fire. They're both alive. We bandaged them as best we could, but you should be seeing the helicopters coming soon."

"You get someone over here," Mitch said sharply. "I'm going to the hospital."

"Take Grace with you," Bill said. "I'll be responsible for her property but not her life."

"What?" Grace asked as soon as disconnected.

"The shepherds, Bill said. The rescue choppers are on their way. You're coming with me to the hospital. Bill is going to watch your property."

He tried to forestall an argument with her, but he wasn't sure it would have been necessary. Grace's values weren't in the least warped. She clearly thought the shepherds were more important.

"I feel responsible," she said as they climbed in her truck.

"Now how the hell can you blame yourself? You didn't pull that trigger. You didn't make that decision. Stuff a sock in it."

At least he'd made her smile faintly.

But *he* couldn't smile. He was beginning to wonder if he'd ever genuinely smile again.

A few years ago, local people had built a helipad and a wide cement path to the ER doors. They'd wanted to help, to end the necessity of carrying people from the outlying airport, which took time. Possibly precious time.

A blue sign stood near it, telling the world, Built and Donated by the People of Conard County.

Memorial Community Hospital had grown a bit over the intervening years, but it was still small. Given that it served relatively few people, many scattered over huge distances, the county was lucky they hadn't lost it.

But the hospital had resisted buyout efforts by large companies that wanted to make a profit from health care, mainly because the taxpayers continued to support it.

The two medevac choppers had already landed, so Grace and Mitch hurried through the emergency doors.

Mary, the nurse, greeted them. When she heard why they were there, she said, "I'm sorry, you can't see them."

"But how are they doing?" Mitch demanded. "Will they be okay?"

"How are you related?" Mary asked.

Grace stiffened, hearing in those words a refusal arising from patient privacy. That was why she'd had to give Mitch permission, unlike a regular visitor. She could only imagine how much more annoyed Mitch must be than she.

"They work for me," Mitch said, his voice growing edgy. "Whatever relatives they have are in Portugal."

Mary raised a brow. "In that case… They're going to be okay. The men who found them gave them some excellent emergency aid, and they got here in time. Both will need surgery. If you want to wait, it might be a few hours."

"I'll wait," Mitch answered. "And send the bills to me."

Mary shook her head. "You aren't legally responsible and we don't charge patients who can't pay."

As she walked away, Mitch gave a low growl. Grace reached out to touch his arm. "They're going to be okay."

"And I'll pay the damn bills."

She followed him into a nearby waiting room, convinced he wanted to do the only thing he could by taking care of the bills. He must not only be worried but totally frustrated that he'd been able to do nothing at all.

Angry that the shootings had happened on his watch. Furious that while he'd been protecting Grace two men had been shot, probably by the same criminals.

Grace was upset, too. If someone wanted to scare her for some reason, they'd just kicked up the level of her fear. Was everyone else merely an obstacle to what they wanted?

What if they went for Mitch? That was her greatest fear. She didn't care nearly as much for herself, but whatever was going on, innocent people shouldn't be targeted because someone was after her.

The whole situation sickened her and her stomach kept rolling over.

For a long time, Mitch kept tapping his fingers on his thighs, probably to release some of his tension. Eventually he stopped and simply leaned forward with his elbows propped on his legs.

He remained silent. Grace didn't much feel like talking, either. No words they could say would help. Hell, she thought, there weren't any words for this horror.

Two men shot. Shepherds. All those guys were doing was taking wonderful care of a large flock of sheep.

Mitch spoke eventually. "Where are your parents now? I don't think you ever mentioned."

"They're both dead." Her heart squeezed even though it had been ten years. "They were on a vacation and died in a mudslide in Oregon."

She couldn't say any more than that without reawakening the horror she'd felt when she'd heard *how* they died. She'd had nightmares for months, and days where she couldn't think of anything else. She still missed them, and always would, but she couldn't afford to think about *how* they'd died. Nor did she want to explain her reaction to anyone.

"That's awful," he said. "Not natural. That's so much worse than the usual."

Amazingly, he had intuited part of her reaction. The other part was imagining them being suffocated by mud. All she answered was "Yeah."

Two sheriff's deputies, Guy Redwing and Connie Parish, showed up to take their statements. Not that they had much to say. Mitch sent them along to talk to his men. "The three of them found the shepherds. All I know is they were both shot."

Connie leaned toward Grace before departing. "We're going to get to the bottom of this."

Grace wished she believed it. So far no one knew anything about who might be behind all this mayhem.

The waiting resumed. Though it was only three hours, it felt like eternity. Then the nurse appeared with news.

"They're in recovery," she announced with a smile. "Maybe another hour or so and you can see them, but they're both going to be just fine."

Grace sensed pressure escape Mitch, like a balloon

that had been overfilled. Relief came over her. Despite what Mitch said, she still felt responsible.

"Thank God," he murmured. "Thank God."

Instinctively, Grace reached for his arm and squeezed gently. He moved and clasped her hand in his.

"This is almost beyond belief," he said. "I'm going to catch whoever is responsible and they won't like the consequences."

Grace didn't doubt it.

Several hours later, Mitch drove them home through the deepening night. He stopped for about fifteen minutes at Maude's diner to get breakfast for the two of them, and for Bill, as well. Since they hadn't known when they'd be getting back, Mitch suspected that Lila wouldn't have brought over an emergency meal.

Both shepherds had spoken briefly with him, but as usual they didn't say much. They never said much. He thought that was because of their limited knowledge of English.

There had been anxiety in their eyes, however. Obviously there was. They'd been shot. He suspected some of that fear grew out of apprehension that they'd been attacked because they were immigrants. Too much of that type of violence going around these days.

But he couldn't reassure them. Not about that.

He hoped they wouldn't quit when they got back on their feet, but he wouldn't blame them if they did. He wished he could make them safe. Make them *feel* safe, but that might never happen again.

After all these hours, there was one thing he still needed to know. "You okay, Grace?"

"Sure. I'm not lying in a hospital bed with a nasty hole in my body."

Well, that was one way to look at it.

Damn it all to hell. He had to find some way to put an end to this. There had to be a way.

Even though he hadn't expected it, he wasn't surprised to arrive at Grace's house to find Lila basically in residence and cooking up a storm. She greeted him with a hug and looked at the bags he was carrying.

"Put them on the counter," she ordered. "I'm not gonna let Maude's food go to waste." She turned to hug Grace. "You okay, girl?"

"I'm okay." Grace's smile was thin.

"Like hell you are," Lila said. "You and the boss set your butts down at the table. Coffee's fresh. I bet you didn't drink much at the hospital. I know what that stuff tastes like."

Mitch chuckled. "You got that right."

"Of course I did," Lila answered with a sniff.

"Where's Bill?"

"He's out riding what he calls a patrol." She waved to the corner. "Don't worry about me. There's my long gun and I know how to use Grace's shotgun. I just wish the bastard had showed up."

"I wish he had, too," Grace told her as Lila put two mugs of coffee on the table.

"I'd have fixed his wagon, all right. Then I'd have nailed his hide to the barn wall."

Mitch almost spewed coffee, then he laughed. "My God, Lila, you're something else."

"Been working on it for forty years. Think I've done pretty well, too." She started buzzing around the kitchen. "So, boss, you want Maude's food or mine?"

"Yours beats anything this side of heaven."

"Well, Maude's pretty good, too. I can heat this up tomorrow."

Mitch watched her put Maude's food in the fridge, then go about heaping two plates with eggs and home fries.

"Eat up," Lila said. "I'll eat mine whenever Bill gets back."

Grace looked at Lila as she delivered the plates full of food. "Are you and Bill an item?" It was really none of her business but she had to ask.

Lila sniffed again. "You ask Bill that question. He's never said so to me."

Mitch spoke. "Then maybe I should kick his behind."

Lila roared with laughter. "I'd like to see that."

Later, long after a new night began in, Grace and Mitch sat out on the front porch. Inside, Lila and Bill shared a meal of turkey slices and gravy over Grace's bread. She had served Grace and Mitch the same meal a little earlier.

"I think I'm about to pop," Grace volunteered. "I ate way too much."

"That happens with Lila's cooking."

"So how do you keep from gaining weight?"

"With difficulty." He shook his head. "And some nights I go for very long walks."

She laughed quietly.

He missed those walks, he realized. And he would have liked to take them with Grace. "Grace?"

"Yes?"

"Are you regretting those hours we spent in your bed?"

He heard her swiftly indrawn breath. "No! I thought you were."

Boy, had he read the situation all wrong. "I didn't regret them at all. I thought you did. Hell."

She gave the most relaxed laugh he'd heard from her in a while. "Think of all those hours wasted since then. Not that we could have felt that relaxed very often."

The specter of the two shepherds rose before him. "No. I think I got too lax, though."

"How?" she asked. "How? Who would have ever thought…?"

She didn't finish the question. She didn't need to. The question he was asking himself, however, had no easy answer. They'd known Grace was being targeted. Why hadn't he thought that men believed to be her shepherds might have been targeted, as well?

He felt like a damned fool.

Carl and Larry were gloating. They'd been told not to murder anyone, but the boss hadn't said they couldn't shoot someone. The night felt fine to them, and they toasted it with a couple of beers, feeling terribly smart.

After this, that Hall woman would run for the hills.

When the boss called later, they expected to receive a heaping helping of praise. Instead they got her wrath.

"Damn it, I told you not to kill anyone."

Carl answered. "We didn't. We just shot 'em. They're still alive."

"You asinine idiots. That's *attempted* murder!" She was shouting again, loud enough for Larry to hear.

The two men exchanged looks. "We didn't kill nobody," Carl argued.

"Maybe not, but this is exactly what I told you not to do! I ought to fire you stupid fools!"

Carl clenched his jaw, fury enveloping him, then said, "You better not. We got a pretty story to tell the cops."

Silence greeted him, then an empty connection.

Larry spoke. "You got her, Carl."

"By the short and curlies," Carl said.

"Uh, don't that mean a man?"

"She's got short and curlies, too."

Larry lay back with his third beer. Yeah, he guessed she did. He savored the image.

Betty Pollard was even angrier than Carl and Larry. Their threat of telling the police had struck her with her first fear since she'd started this operation.

Walking around with a glass of scotch, she drank faster than she should have, the wheels spinning in her brain. They wouldn't tell the police, she assured herself. They'd only make things bad for themselves.

But given the dubious intelligence of those two, they might forget this was a damn conspiracy and they were as deep in it as she was.

Charges began to flicker through her thoughts. Conspiracy, certainly. Accomplice, maybe. Attempted murder? Well, she had specifically told them not to do such a thing, so they couldn't charge her for that. Maybe.

For the first time since she'd set this all in motion, it occurred to her that she never should have thought she'd skate through this undetected. From the moment she had hired those goons, she'd opened the possibility they might squeal. But she couldn't do it herself.

She blamed Grace for not getting out of Dodge. If Grace had just fled, the way she should have, most of this never would have happened. So yeah, it was Grace's fault. *All* her fault.

That didn't comfort Betty because *she* had been involved in the wrongdoing, not Grace. That was going to be a bright line if her scheme came before a judge.

Damn. Maybe she should abandon this all right now.

Pay off those guys and get rid of them before they could start talking. That might be the best way.

Yes, it would. Because she'd explicitly told them, as part of this deal, that they had to vanish with the tidy little sum she still owed them. They'd clear the county and leave her safe.

And she'd have to start all over again, trying to move Grace.

"Hell," she swore savagely at her empty apartment. "Hell."

Another two fingers of scotch went down easily. She continued ruminating because there had to be a way to fix this. To let Grace know this wouldn't end as long as she remained on that property.

Maybe she could give those stupid men an order to do one more thing. Betty would have fled by this point, so why wouldn't Grace?

Shooting those shepherds hadn't been a direct attack on Grace. Maybe she didn't realize it had been a warning to her.

So Betty would wait a little longer to see how this developed. If Grace still wasn't frightened enough to leave, then another incident would be required.

She'd leave it up to those fools. But this time she'd make it clear that no one was to be shot. Apparently the first warning hadn't penetrated. Next time she'd make it crystal clear.

Maybe that would get through to these dimwits.

Chapter 19

A week later, Zeke and Rod had settled into Mitch's bunkhouse. Neither was in the best shape. Zeke still sported a sling from being shot in the shoulder. Thank God, it had missed the artery. And Rod hobbled around on crutches, his thigh having been hit. Both men had been seriously injured enough to require blood transfusions, and they still appeared wan. They also tired easily.

As Mitch had expected, all of Lila's mothering instincts came to the fore. She seemed to be in her element between looking after Grace and caring for the two shepherds.

How she managed it all, Mitch had no idea. He was grateful, however, for every single thing she did.

Bill came over once to stand watch while Mitch went to visit his shepherds. Grace refused to be budged. If she'd needed a last straw to pile on her stubbornness, the shooting was it. That woman had a spine of steel.

Admirable but frustrating, too. She needed a break from being constantly on guard, but she wouldn't take it.

When Bill arrived, he talked about Zeke and Rod. "They may not be getting around too well, but they've given the three of us volumes of information about watching the damn sheep. Guess they're worried."

"I kinda thought they might be." Mitch smiled.

"Oh, and one other thing. They were asking about a dog."

"I've been waiting on two herding dogs from Ransom Laird, but maybe a couple of guard dogs would help sooner. If they'd had them, it's possible that creep wouldn't have gotten close enough to shoot."

"Good idea." Bill turned to look toward the mountains. "Oh, yeah, I saw Burt Stiller in town yesterday. He'd been out of pocket on a trip to see his wife's parents. He said go ahead and ride his range. You want one of us to do that?"

Mitch tilted his head. "How are the three of you supposed to handle all this? You're looking after all the livestock, you've added the sheep to your load, and now you want to go riding the Stiller place to look for signs of a watcher."

Bill answered wryly. "It'd give one of us a break."

Mitch laughed. "I hadn't thought about that. But I'll do it tomorrow, Bill. I need something to sink my teeth into or a throat to wrap my hands around. As long as I'm back in the afternoon, Grace should be fine."

"Nah," said Bill. "I'll be over here with her." He raised a brow. "But you knew that already, didn't you, boss?"

Mitch smiled. "I had a hope, that's all."

* * *

Nothing ever went according to plan. Carl and Larry hatched their own plan, and they didn't want any bull from *their* boss.

"Screw the waiting," Larry said. "She's nuts. If she din't make us wait so often this coulda been all over."

Carl thought about it. "You're right. Faster mighta got rid of that Hall woman sooner."

"You betcha," Larry answered. "Damn screwed-up plan. Ain't no way the boss figgered this right."

"No way," Carl agreed. "She been making me madder 'n' a wet hen. Right now, I don't freakin' care if we get the rest of the money."

Larry didn't like that idea. "No way. She's gonna pay us, man. Or we talk. Just send a letter to the sheriff or something, then get the hell out of here."

Carl nodded. "Okay, then. I don't wanna tell anybody what *we* done."

Larry scratched his chin. "Wish I'd never hooked up with her."

"It's a lot of money."

Larry shook his head. "And that's why we're in this mess, ain't we?"

Carl frowned deeply. "She got us by the short and curlies, too. We gotta take care of this, get paid and skedaddle. Or maybe if the heat's on, we just skedaddle anyway. But I did like shooting them Port-a-gees."

"Yeah," Larry agreed. "Did my heart good. Them furriners, stealing our jobs. I don't care that we shot 'em."

"I wish we'da killed 'em."

Larry made a sound of agreement.

"So think," Carl demanded. "Figger out how we do it and soon."

* * *

Mitch took the first watch again. The duty was beginning to feel useless. Maybe they were scaring the perp away. Their visible presence, always armed, might be acting like a flashing warning beacon on a road at night.

Or maybe it was over, never to be explained. Given that they had no idea of the purpose behind this, they were stuck with fear of more.

He hadn't been kidding Bill when he'd said he wanted to get his hands around someone's neck. At this point he couldn't even swear he wouldn't kill the guy.

He was feeling far too murderous for his soul's good.

Chapter 20

Mitch rode back to Grace's late the next afternoon, shotgun and rifle in their holsters in case he needed something more precise than a shotgun. The sun painted the wisps of cloud in the sky with a reddish alpenglow. A truly beautiful evening, and he gave it some moments of appreciation.

He felt decently satisfied. He'd discovered three places where someone had camped among the trees on Stiller's land, three places from which Grace's property was visible. Whoever it had been, they'd moved on, leaving nothing behind but a few beer bottles buried in the duff. He'd already called the cops, giving them the GPS locations he'd noted on his sat phone. He hoped they could find some prints on those bottles.

But now he had to relieve Bill and take care of Grace. He enjoyed taking care of Grace, and just wished the circumstances were happier. As it was, he had to be content with his discoveries.

When he reached the foot of Grace's driveway, he felt an internal shudder. The impression of wrongness over-powered him. He couldn't put a finger on it—maybe eyes watching?—but it caused him to touch Joy's sides with his heels.

Joy needed no other encouragement. She took off at a full gallop along the gravel road, crossing the mile to Grace's house rapidly. Not rapidly enough for him, but Joy went all out, lathering before they reached the house. She seemed to feel his worry and probably wouldn't have stopped if he had tried to rein her in.

Where was Grace? She should have been on the porch, especially upon hearing the swift pounding of Joy's hooves.

Joy skittered to a stop just before the front porch, sliding and spewing gravel into the air.

"Grace?" Mitch bellowed her name. "Bill!"

Nothing answered him.

His heart pounded as hard as Joy's did. Swinging his leg over the saddle, he dropped to the ground with a jolt, shotgun in hand. Releasing the reins, he left it to Joy to cool herself down. She wandered around the yard, then headed for the trough near the barn. She knew what to do for herself.

Not that he had time to think about that. He hadn't been shot at yet, so he didn't care about the racket he made running up the steps, across the porch and into the house.

"Grace! Bill!"

Nothing. No answer. He could scarcely breathe as his heart pounded, as terror filled him with renewed strength.

Then he heard a hammering from the back of the house. Racing toward it, he found Bill bound and

gagged with duct tape, sitting in a corner of the room.
Bill's eyes pleaded with him as his booted feet banged
the floor once more.

Mitch crossed the floor in two strides and ripped the
tape from Bill's mouth. Bill barely reacted. "Two men,"
he said. "They took Grace."

"Where?"

Bill shook his head. "No car. I'd have heard a car.
Cut me loose. We can track them."

Mitch yanked the ever-present bowie knife from the
sheath on his belt. With quick swipes he cut the tape
binding Bill's hands and feet.

Bill struggled upward, clearly stiff. "Twenty minutes. Let's go." Then he grabbed Grace's rifle, which
stood near the front door, checked the load. "Ready."

Mitch hardly waited. "Joy practically killed herself
getting me here."

"S'okay. Got two mounts in the barn, unless they
were taken."

Mitch didn't even ask why Bill had two horses here.
Explanations could wait. They ran to the barn to quickly
saddle Daisy and Joy. Both horses were a bit restive,
but quickly calmed to receive saddles and harnesses.

"Jeff brought us two horses this afternoon," Bill
said as he swung the saddle up onto Daisy. "Ms. Hall
was hell-bent on riding around the property, so I got
the horses. We locked up. Damn. We rode a bit, then
brought the horses in here. How the hell were we to
guess two guys were waiting inside? We didn't see no
one while we were riding."

"Don't blame yourself." Mitch tightened Joy's cinch,
patted her neck. The he slipped his shotgun into one
saddle holster and his rifle into the other. He mounted.
Bill wasn't far behind.

"They had to have left some sign," Mitch said as they rode out of the barn, more to reassure himself. "Especially if they didn't take her in a truck."

"Surely something," Bill agreed.

"Call the sheriff. I already found three campsites on Stiller's land, and they might be headed that way. We need the cops over here."

While Bill made the call, Mitch turned Joy in a tight circle, looking for any sign of how the men had taken Grace away.

Then he saw it: crushed grass, unmown this summer, deep enough that the passage of the two men and Grace might have paved a road. Bill followed.

"Twenty minutes," he repeated. "Not far."

"Unless," Mitch said, "they got her into a truck farther away. Grace wouldn't have made it easy on them."

Bill snorted. "That woman is a force of nature."

Then they fell silent, intent on the ground ahead of them. Even from the height of Joy's back, Mitch saw signs that Grace had dug in her heels. Fighting every step of the way.

God, he hoped they hadn't hurt her.

Grace was more furious than frightened. She struggled against the arms that dragged her backward, ignoring it when their grip hurt. At every opportunity, she dug in the heels of her boots, making them move slower.

She worried about Bill, left behind and bound. She worried about Mitch arriving at her house to find this mess. She noted the red glow fading from the sky, promising darkness that would make all this easier on her captors by concealing them.

The duct tape held her mouth in a tight grip, but that

didn't stop her from forcing her tongue between her lips and trying to loosen it.

Adrenaline poured through her system, but it couldn't make her strong enough to break free. All she could do was make this as difficult as possible for her abductors.

She had no idea what these men intended to do to her, but this was a far cry from burning her barn or ransacking her house. Did they intend to kill her?

She realized she no longer cared. She could no longer tolerate living in constant fear, standing on constant watch. Her life had become that of a soldier standing unending sentry duty in a dangerous zone.

She was more worried about Mitch. Her panic led her to diverting her thoughts down ridiculous paths. At least her death would set him free to return to his own life instead of letting everything go in order to watch over her. It was too much to ask of him.

He deserved to go home, to take care of his own affairs. Sure, he'd grieve, but nowhere near the endless sorrow she'd felt for John. Nor should he. She was merely a friend he'd cared for. Because she was a duty he believed he owed to a neighbor.

Their lovemaking hadn't changed a thing. It didn't matter that she'd been longing to repeat it. That was selfish.

She struggled harder against the kidnappers, wishing she'd changed out of her cowboy boots on the porch so she could have dug her heels in deeper.

Mitch, she thought, *go home. Let the police deal with this. Risk no more for me. I'm not that important.*

But that didn't keep her from fighting. It was not in her nature to give up, despite how it had appeared during the years she'd grieved for John. She hadn't given up her heartache, and she wouldn't give up her life without a struggle. Then they dropped her to the ground.

Mitch followed an entirely different line of thought. He might as well die if he couldn't find Grace alive. She'd become the center of his existence, more important than his livestock, than his entire ranch.

He *had* to save her.

"There," he said suddenly to Bill. Drag marks mashed grass and showed deep score marks in the underlying ground.

"Yup," Bill answered, turning his mount to follow Mitch.

Mitch pulled out his rifle, ready. Bill followed suit.

"Twenty minutes," Bill said again.

"She can't be too far from here." Hope spurred Mitch to a faster pace. Dolly agreed with him.

Concern for the horses on the rough ground gave way to urgency. Neither mount stumbled as night blanketed the world.

Please, God. Please. He had no idea if he spoke aloud, but he knew all too clearly what he feared finding. He hadn't heard a gun report, but that didn't mean a damn thing. Knives. A garrote.

Suddenly, even in the night's darkness, he saw her. Crumpled on the ground. Dead? Alive?

He slid from Joy, rifle at ready. Bill stood guard from horseback.

Then he fell to his knees. "Grace? Grace."

She stirred and his prayer of gratitude rose to the heavens as he began to strip tape from her.

"Mitch." The first word from her mouth. "Get them. Leave me. Get them. *Please.*"

"You…"

"I'm okay. *Go!*"

He mounted Joy so fast that she sidled. "I'm going," he said to Bill. "Stay with her. Protect her."

"You got it."

Mitch holstered his rifle and pulled out his shotgun. Now he wanted the widest spray possible. He was going to take those sons of bitches down. He wanted them lying on the ground, bleeding from every pellet of birdshot he could pump into them.

Rage could have blinded him, but he refused to let it.

Then he saw them, black shadows running through deep grasses that impeded them. He never hesitated as he sighted them and pulled the trigger.

Both fell screaming to the ground.

Mitch's satisfaction knew no bounds. Astride Joy, he kept the shotgun pointed at them.

"Don't try anything. I got five more shells in this."

They didn't move except to writhe.

The sheriff's men arrived at remarkable speed on their four-wheel-drive SUVs. Two cops took over the scene. Two more loaded the wounded men in the bed of their vehicles to carry them to approaching ambulances.

Mitch lifted Grace into the passenger seat of one of them, even as she protested that she was fine.

"I'll be riding alongside," Mitch promised. "Right here. Now, dammit, quit being so stubborn."

At last she subsided.

Back at Grace's house, as the two men were loaded into ambulances, a surprising sight greeted them. Betty Pollard, on the porch, her hands cuffed behind her.

Grace froze, staring at her friend. "Betty?"

"I came to confess to you. It's all my fault," the

woman said, tears running down her face. "I told them not to hurt anyone, most especially you."

"What?" Disbelief nearly made Grace deaf.

Betty poured out her plan to frighten Grace off the ranch, her reason for doing so. "But they weren't supposed to *hurt* you!"

That didn't seem to make any difference to the deputies who hauled her off and shoved her into a car. All Grace could do was watch, then turn to Mitch. "Did that make sense?"

"Unfortunately, yes. Now let the EMTs look you over."

"I'm fine." But no one was listening to her. They took her inside and began treating scrapes.

"All we can do about the bruises is let them heal," one said. "But you're going to be sore, very sore. We're giving you some muscle relaxants or you won't sleep tonight."

Grace felt too revved up to care. It was going to be a long time before she slept again.

Mitch changed all that. He carried her to her bed and gently removed her remaining clothes, then covered her with the blanket. It was easy to relax into his arms as he lay beside her, despite all her bruises. She needed him close.

For a long time he said nothing, hoping she would drift into sleep. She didn't and he could understand it. She'd had more than one shock tonight.

"Bill is okay?"

"Okay enough to ride with me to find you."

"Good. You came out of the night like an avenging angel."

He laughed quietly. "I felt like one. All I had was a gun when I wanted a flaming sword."

"The gun did well enough." She sighed, then groaned faintly as she wiggled closer. His arms tightened gently.

"I could get you some ice for those bruises," he suggested.

"Probably too late now. I was thinking when I was out there how much I've messed up your life."

That was more than Mitch could bear. "You know what I was thinking when I hunted for you?"

"What?"

"That you've become the center of my life. That you've become all that really matters to me."

She drew a swift breath. "Mitch...no."

"Grace, yes. I was thinking that I couldn't live without you. Grace, I love you. I realize you're not ready..."

"Oh, shut up," she answered, startling him.

"Huh?"

"If you start backing off what you just said, I may shove you out of my bed. Damn it, Mitch, are you going to keep me from loving you, too?"

Shock slowly gave way to a deep-seated warmth that filled him from head to toe. "Love as in marriage?" he asked tentatively.

"Of course," she replied promptly.

His heart soared. "Kids?"

"I always wanted them. I always wanted to see my kids riding ponies and laughing. You?"

"You bet," he murmured, then kissed her deeply. The heat that rose in him was entirely inappropriate given how sore she was, but he let it grow anyway.

"How soon?" she asked.

Damn, that was Grace. "How big a shindig do you want?"

"Just get Reverend Canton over here. How much more do I need?"

"Ah, man, Grace. Do you really think you could keep the neighbors away?"

She laughed then. "Tell them to bring their own barbecue."

It was his turn to laugh. "I love you, Grace Hall. Heart and soul."

She snuggled a tiny bit closer. "Don't ever let me go, Mitch."

"Never," he promised. "Never."

* * * * *

WE HOPE YOU ENJOYED
THIS BOOK FROM

⟨H⟩ HARLEQUIN

ROMANTIC SUSPENSE

Danger. Passion. Drama.

These heart-racing page-turners will keep you guessing to the very end. Experience the thrill of unexpected plot twists and irresistible chemistry.

4 NEW BOOKS AVAILABLE EVERY MONTH!

Marcus watched as she got to her feet. He was grateful to see that she was steady.

"Can we have a minute?" Marcus asked Blade.

"Yeah. Hang on to her good arm," his friend replied. Then he walked away, taking Dawson with him.

"What?" she asked, offering him a sweet smile.

"I'm going to find who did this. I promise you. And you're going to be okay. Jamie Weathers is the best emergency physician this side of the Colorado River. Hell, this side of the Missouri River. He'll fix you up. But don't leave the hospital until you hear from me. You understand?"

"I got it," she said. "I'm going to be fine. It's all going to be fine. I barely had twenty bucks in my bag. He didn't even get my phone. I had that in my back pocket. Nor my keys. Those were in my hand. So he basically got nothing except the cash and my driver's license."

Things didn't matter. "You want me to let Brian and Morgan know?"

"Oh, God, no. Please don't do that." She looked panicked. "Morgan can't have stress right now. I'm grateful that her room is on the other side of the building. Otherwise, she could be watching this spectacle."

They would want to know. But it was her decision. And she was in pain. "Okay," he said, giving in easily.

"Thank you," she said.

"Go get fixed up. I'll talk to you soon."

She nodded.

"And, Erin…" he added.

"Yeah."

"I'm really glad that you're okay."

Don't miss
Trouble in Blue *by Beverly Long,*
available March 2022 wherever
Harlequin Romantic Suspense
books and ebooks are sold.

Harlequin.com

Get 4 FREE REWARDS!

We'll send you 2 FREE Books plus 2 FREE Mystery Gifts.

Harlequin Romantic Suspense books are heart-racing page-turners with unexpected plot twists and irresistible chemistry that will keep you guessing to the very end.

FREE Value Over $20
